OUTLAWS

Josh Michaels

The Brabant Press
www.brabantpress.com

Publisher's Cataloging-in-Publication data
Michaels, Josh.
Outlaws / Josh Michaels.
p. cm.
ISBN 978-0-9890993-0-1 (pbk.)
ISBN 978-0-9890993-1-8 (ebook)
1. Incest—Fiction. 2. Sex (Psychology)—Fiction. 3. Mozart, Wolfgang Amadeus, 1756-1791—Fiction. 4. Florida—Fiction. 5. Venice (Italy)—Fiction. 6. Mozart, Wolfgang Amadeus, 1756-1791. Zauberflol͡te.—Fiction. 7. Universities and colleges—Fiction. 8. Death and dying—Fiction. I. Title.
PZ4.M6214 Ou 2013
[Fic] --dc23   2013935689

cover illustration credits:
"Stars " by Maxfield Parrish © Copyright 2013 National Museum of American Illustration™, Newport RI; photo courtesy of Archives of the American Illustrators Gallery™, NYC
Illustration from the Rider-Waite Tarot Deck® reproduced by permission of U.S. Games Systerm, Inc. Stamford, CT 06902 USA. © Copyright 1971 by U.S. Games Systems, Inc. Further reproduction prohibited. The Rider-Waite Tarot Deck® is a registered trademark of U.S. Games Systems, Inc.
golden retriever image: © Copyright 2013 by Paper House Productions, Inc., Saugerties, New York
Venice image: Rio della Fava, Rambling Traveler

cover designed by Kachergis Book Design
typeset by Diane Collins

Printed in the United States of America

Pamina and Papageno
Wir wollen uns der Liebe freun,
Wir leben durch die Lieb' allein.

Pamina
Die Lieb' versüsset jede Plage,
Ihr opfert jede Kreatur

Papageno
Sie würzet unsre Lebenstage,
Sie wirkt im Kreise der Natur

Pamina and Papageno
Ihr hoher Zweck zeigt deutlich an,
Nichts Edlers sei, als Weib und Mann.
Mann und Weib und Weib und Mann,
Reichen an die Gottheit an.

Emmanuel Schikaneder
The Magic Flute

We want to rejoice in love,
We live through love alone

Love sweetens every sorrow,
Every creature makes sacrifices for it.

It seasons all the days of our life,
It pervades nature's cycles.

Its highest goal is clear.
There's nothing nobler than wife and man.
Man and wife and wife and man,
Reaching to the divine.

Paolo
Vieni, vieni, Francesca! Ore di gaudii
lunghe ci sono davanti.

Tito Ricordi
Francesca di Rimini

Come, come, Francesca! We have many hours of happiness before us.

TABLE OF CONTENTS

CHAPTER 1

Many years ago, the *St. Petersburg Times* used to give away free copies of the paper the following morning if the sun didn't come all day, so rarely did this happen. But it looked like a real possibility the day I met Joyce Creighton to discuss the production of *The Magic Flute* that she had asked me to assist her with.

It had been pouring when I crossed the Frankland Bridge from Tampa with the rush hour traffic in the morning and it was still raining steadily when I headed back to St. Pete at 4:00, after my office hours. University of St. Petersburg, where I taught history, is three miles beyond the city, less than a mile from the Gulf.

Joyce taught in the theater department at Western Florida University in Tampa, where my wife Angela was an associate dean. After Joyce and I got together, she was heading over to St. Pete's Rafferty Theater to meet with Marge di Cosi, the director of Civic Opera of Tampa Bay. Then the two were going out to dinner with a couple of donors.

Joyce and I had had a long talk about *Die Zauberflöte* at a reception at WFU a couple of months earlier. The next day she had asked me to serve as "dramaturge" for the production, a kind of consultant, and we had already met once. I had no claim to be an expert on Mozart or the opera, but didn't try too hard to talk her out of the offer.

The plan this afternoon had been to walk and talk in Bayfront Park, but we decided to meet instead in the bar at the Vinoy

Hotel. I like the walk along the bay and don't mind getting a little wet, and I was early, so I parked close to the Art Museum, found an umbrella under the seat, and did the whole stretch. The white boats in their slips rocked slightly in the driving rain. The mottled ducks and mallards sheltered under the banyan trees. Otherwise, the park was deserted.

The director of *The Magic Flute* has some interesting decisions. A lot depends on the production's budget. Will there be a couple of trap doors in the floor? The libretto requires them for several entrances and exits. Two generations ago every theater had these, but not today. Will the three Boys descend from the rafters in some kind of flying vehicle? Easy as Sacher Torte in Mozart's day, but with the wages of union carpenters and electricians, the little balloon or dirigible might now cost as much as a private jet. And should three female sopranos sing the Boy's parts? They were likely to be a lot better singers and actors than a trio of pre-adolescents.

How much verisimilitude did you want in the production anyway? Was the serpent at the beginning of Act I going to be scary enough to frighten the audience as well as the hero, Tamino? How about the animals that the prince charms with his magic flute later in the first act? You could do 3D computer graphics or holograms for each, instead of stuffing people into costumes.

There are other, more troubling questions for a director in the era of political correctness. What do you do about Monostratos, the lustful Moor who threatens several times to rape the captive heroine Pamina? In his only aria, which might be moving if the audience hadn't gotten to know the guy already, he declares that *"ein Schwartzer hässlich ist"*–a black man is ugly. Generations of directors had no problem with a singer playing the Moor in blackface, but you wouldn't want to do that today. Good African-American tenors are not cheap, and even if you landed one, you'd have to alter the aria and some dialogue. Most directors simply make the Moor an ugly white guy and revise his lines.

The sexism, not to say the misogyny, of the libretto is so pervasive there's not a whole lot you can do. Tamino is ridiculed for trusting a woman, the Queen of the Night, and the unscrupulousness, weakness, and fickleness of women is something of a leitmotif. Some directors make cuts, and most try to do what they can via stage directions for Sarastro, the head of the brotherhood of priests and ruler of the land in which the opera takes place. He can be made to appear solicitous toward Pamina, who is, after all, initiated into the brotherhood in the end. But there's only so much you can change.

Then there's the famous *Bruchproblem*–the break problem. Critics have written about it for two centuries. In Act I, the Queen of the Night is a sympathetic character. Her daughter has been abducted by the evil tyrant Sarastro. In Act II, the roles are reversed. As Sarastro tells it at least, he has rescued the princess from the baneful influence of her mother. Tamino buys the story immediately, and so has nearly every director.

I was not so sure. Most custody battles are not clear-cut, after all. I'm no more anti-Mason than the next guy, but there are a lot of things that aren't terribly attractive about the brotherhood of priests. So the idea I'd thrown out to Joyce at the reception and that we'd worked on since was to dress the *Eingeweihten*, the initiates, in boots and brown uniforms. They would salute Sarastro with upraised arms, one hand clenched, the other open. There would be banners with the logo of the brotherhood, maybe a sun with a double bolt of lightning. Joyce didn't say right away, "Storm Troopers in the Temple of Wisdom. What a great idea!" But I could see she was intrigued.

The point was to make the audience think twice about the happy ending. The object today was to convince a couple of big donors to buy into the reinterpretation.

In the second Act, the Queen is a lot more like Lady Macbeth than a damsel in distress. Singing that a "hellish vengeance boils in my heart," she presents her daughter with a dagger sharpened for Sarastro. If Pamina refuses to kill him, the Queen will disown her.

We spent some time in the Vinoy talking about how to make the lady a little more sympathetic. The kidnapping of her daughter has pushed her over the edge, and we thought about ways we could suggest that to the audience.

Joyce had some novel ideas for costumes for the Queen and her three Ladies. In contrast to the totalitarian priests, they would be dressed as '50s rebels, in black leather jackets and pants, low-cut silver lamé tops, biker boots, tattoos, and lots of dangly silver jewelry. Their hair would be long, and they would wear black headbands embroidered with moons and stars.

We were so intensely absorbed in our discussion that we hadn't noticed that the sun had come out by 5:45, when it was time for Joyce to head over to the Rafferty.

❦

I liked Joyce a lot. She was not what many guys would consider attractive. Tall, thin, angular, with short blond hair, large, slightly bulging eyes, a small mouth, a round head and receding chin, she looked a little insect-like.

Joyce was from Nebraska, and I'd gotten off to a bad start with her when, after she told me, I said incredulously, "Omaha! Jesus, Joyce." She'd smiled and assured me there were lots of intelligent and interesting people there. Joyce had been married briefly right out of college, but had been single for many years.

You get close to people when you work side-by-side with them. Teaching is a solitary profession. There'd been a lot of noise recently about "learning communities" and "collaborative instruction," but, unsurprisingly, the experience had not been pleasant the two times I'd been talked into trying it. This was a whole lot different.

Stepping out of the hotel, we paused for a moment in the bright sunlight. The surface of the bay sparkled, the drops on the lawn glittered. Then Joyce stumbled on the first step and I caught her. It was one of those moments when you can cross from friendship into something deeper and more dangerous. We looked at each other for a couple of seconds, but then I released her and asked if she was OK.

I already had enough adventure in my life. I was sleeping with my brother's wife and my wife's sister.

PART I:
DRAMATIS PERSONAE

CHAPTER 2

Julie

Before the sisters-in-law came the cousins, and it may be best to start with them.

Identical twins are supposed to feel so close to their former womb-mate that they sometimes can't tell where their personality ends and their sibling's begins. Young lovers staring into each other's eyes also sometimes feel the boundaries dissolving between them.

That's the way it was with Julie and me. Even before we became lovers.

Julie Weiss was the younger daughter of my mother's unhappy little sister Jean. She was a year older than me, but we were the same size. Julie was skinny and fragile-looking, with curly black hair and tragic sea-green eyes. Her skin was eerily pale, and the veins under her arms looked like glaucous ridges. A forked vein on her temple throbbed when she was upset. Unlike her bubbly sister Cheryl, Julie was quiet and serious. Cheryl, I knew intuitively, was the cute sister, Julie the *jeune fille fatale*.

Jean and her husband Al, a cabinet-maker and carpenter, lived in a small house in Van Nuys, across the Hollywood Hills from my parents' home in LA's Beverly-Fairfax district. A stock video of Julie, aet seven: She's standing beside me in the bright sunlight

9

in the Weisses's back yard, next to a wading pool. "Stick out your arms, Jonathan," she tells me. "Now look up. Now we have to say the magic words. Double, double, toilet trouble, fire burn and cauldron bubble. Twirl, twirl, twirl!" Around and around we both spin. The clouds and little sycamores blur. We fall to the ground on top of each other, giggling.

Before we'd get up, one of us would sometimes say, "One eye." We'd slowly move our foreheads together until the eyes of the other merged into one. Sometimes we'd pause, a couple of inches apart, each looking at our reflection in the other's eyes.

One thing Freud may have gotten right was infantile sexuality, and there were other games where we touched each other.

When the girls were a little older, Al and Jean bought a larger, above-ground pool, and Julie and I would give each other porpoise rides. She'd get on my back, legs clenched tight around my waist, hands on my shoulders, then I'd get on hers, gripping her tightly.

Next to the pool was a redwood jungle-gym. We spent hours playing on it.

Once, when Julie was dangling upside-down from one of the horizontal bars across the top, her t-shirt down over her face, I started tickling her, then poked her nipples, first one, then the other. "Hey, buster," Julie said, and I stopped.

Most of the games we played in the Weisses' back yard were pretty innocuous. We put salt on slugs and watched as they excreted an iridescent froth. We pulled out the long white stamens on the gold shrimp plants by the redwood fence and sucked the nectar from the tiny bulbs at their base, pretending it was a magic elixir. We caught butterflies, studied the patterns on their wings, and made silent wishes. Then we let them go. Some butterflies were enchanted princesses and they would remember us with gratitude.

When it was cold or raining out, we went into the room Julie shared with her sister and discussed the meaning of "round yon virgin" and "my country tisovthee" and other conundrums. If

10

Cheryl was out, we'd play with her Ouija board. Abraham Lincoln told me to get a haircut. JFK told us he was in hell. Helen Keller admitted that she was not really blind.

We also deciphered messages in the ice cubes in our Kool-Aid. We'd spit the cubes into our hands, study the cloudy shapes and fissures, and tell each other our fortunes. These mostly involved romantic encounters with dark and mysterious strangers. One particularly informative cube, interpreted by Julie, predicted we would be rich and famous, but our lives would end tragically. We would be shipwrecked near the South Pole and die in the icy water, looking up at the moon and the stars.

Indoors or outdoors, we lived in a world of our own invention. Like a vivid dream that vanishes seconds after you wake up, that world is impossible to re-enter. It was peopled with witches and magicians, giants and dwarfs, princes and princesses, and talking animals, some of whom were wise and witty, particularly a kangaroo named Phyllis and an alligator called Samuel. We both narrated, picking up where the other left off.

The real animals at the Weiss's were a quartet of overfed cocker spaniels that my Aunt Jean doted on. Whenever we were over, she would be lying on an over-stuffed couch in the darkened living room. The curtains were never open. Jeanie was a chain-smoker, and the couch and curtains and La-Z-Boy reeked of menthol cigarettes, and the carpet of dog urine.

My aunt was a voracious reader, and next to the overflowing ashtrays and half-full coffee mugs would be stacks of paperbacks. There were piles on the floor as well, which the dogs would knock over. Jeanie loved Peter de Vries and S. J. Perelman, and plied me with their books. For my ninth birthday she bought me *A Tree Grows in Brooklyn*, and a year later gave me *Catcher in the Rye*.

Unlike my mother, Aunt Jean retained her New York accent, though she was just a little girl when her parents moved to LA, and she was an even more rabid hater of Southern California and the film industry than her big sister.

And unlike Mom, and every other grown-up I knew, Jeanie was frank and caustic. My brothers and I would listen intently as she dissed politicians, actors, and newscasters, and expatiated on subjects like puberty, zits, farts, and masturbation. Occasionally she read to us–Ambrose Bierce's *Devil's Dictionary*, Mark Twain's *Letters from the Earth*–but usually she just held forth. Julie and Cheryl were embarrassed by their mother's monologues, and never joined us as we sat on the floor at her feet, enraptured.

I can no more reproduce Jeanie's comic narratives than I can the stories Julie and I spun. A lot of the ad-libbing was on the theme of "just wait until you're an adult," and was, of course, self-deprecatory. Jean imitated and ridiculed her doctors and dentists. Another subject was the stupidities of the spaniels. We were often in tears.

But the giggling fits that left me gasping for breath and sick to my stomach were not provoked by my aunt but by her daughter, and Julie was a fellow-victim as well as the provocateur. A case of the hiccups could do us in. So could a belch. The most exhausting episode happened one evening when we were sitting at the dinner table at our house. Al, in a foul mood, said sharply to Julie, "I want you to eat every pea on that plate!" We went into convulsions for five minutes. Only when we'd finally recovered did Al explain to my father, "They thought I said 'pee on that plate.'" Of course this triggered another five minutes of hysteria.

Al's bad mood no doubt had something to do with Jeanie. It was obvious even to a child that they didn't like each other. He was often the butt of her sarcasm. But so were Cheryl and Julie. When Julie didn't reply to my dad's hearty, "How you doin', kiddo?" he said, "Still waters run deep."

"Don't count on it," said Jean.

Even physically Jeanie was like no other adult I'd ever met. She had a pretty, urchin-like face—she looked a lot like Liza Minelli—but her weight ballooned from under 90 pounds to over 200, and then back again. Thin or fat, she wore billowing floral muumuus and silver slippers. Her feet were tiny. We knew Jean had been hospitalized after a suicide attempt, and that she was on antidepressants–Miltown, in those pre-Prozac days. She was probably addicted to barbiturates as well. When Jean came over, she'd go into the medicine cabinet and clean out my mother's bottles of Seconal and Nembutal. Mom took to hiding the pills before her sister's visits.

⁂

Julie and I were always holding hands, but it was something innocent and spontaneous, like the ESP we shared. With boring frequency, we'd think of the same thing at the same time.

One afternoon, though, as we came in for lunch holding hands, my brother Danny yelled "faggot." I threw one of the dog's tennis balls at him, but I was a little more self-conscious about touching Julie the next couple of visits.

Then one day we went beyond hand-holding. We started playing a game called "put out the fire," in which we had to urinate on an imaginary conflagration. That led to "doctor."

Touching my penis, Julie observed unprofessionally, "It's so funny-looking."

"Well," I said, "having nothing there is funny-looking."

When I examined her vagina a little more closely, she said, "That's where babies come out." I must have looked puzzled, so she explained, "You stick your penis inside and squirt something and then nine months later a baby comes out."

I'd never been told the facts of life, and must have given her a skeptical look.

"You didn't think the stork brought it?" Julie asked.

"Can I touch it?" I asked.

I pressed hard and my cousin said, "Ouch."

"How is the penis supposed to get in there?"

"It gets hard. When you're a grown-up."

13

"It must hurt the lady."

"No," said Julie, "It's supposed to feel good."

"Who says?"

"Never you mind, my pretty," Julie replied, switching from urologist to the wicked witch in Sleeping Beauty.

If Jeanie sensed what was going on, she may have approved. But sometimes she seemed annoyed at how close Julie and I were. She would call us "the kissing cousins."

⁓

As we grew older, we had less and less in common. I was taking AP classes and planning to go to college. Julie had no such ambitions. When I sent her books I was enthusiastic about–*Demian*, *Steppenwolf*–she didn't read them. Jean tried to kill herself again and spent a longer time at Gateways. We didn't see much of the Weisses. Both Cheryl and Julie moved out before they'd finished high school.

The summer before my own last year in high school, Julie invited me to visit her at a new apartment in North Hollywood. She was working in a beauty salon, sweeping the floor, taking calls, and handling the register.

I hadn't seen her for months. I walked in the door and did a double-take. She'd become a hippie. Though the Age of Aquarius was long past, Julie's curly black hair was down to her shoulders, she wore a beaded red headband, dangling silver earrings, strands of multicolored love beads, and a necklace with a big crystal pendant in the shape of a heart. Julie was dressed in a short white halter top and tight cut-offs. A large vanilla candle was burning on the coffee table next to the lava lamp, and the smell suffused the room.

"You like?" she asked. She meant the apartment, but I was looking at her.

"You bet," I said. We gazed at each other for a long time. "One eye," I said, and we moved our foreheads together. Then I kissed her and we embraced. "Julie, Julie," I moaned.

14

She led me through the beaded curtains into her bedroom. I was a virgin. Julie already had had several boyfriends. She slipped off her top, undid her bra, and I stared at her breasts and then gingerly cupped them. I couldn't believe this was happened. We lay down on her waterbed and clutched each other tightly, and then got undressed and made love. She guided me into her, and I came almost immediately. When I apologized, she assured me that it would get better. And it did, half an hour later, after we'd had a glass of the Chianti I'd brought.

After we'd made love a second time, Julie smiled and asked, "Do you think it's illegal?"

"Having sex with your cousin? No, why should it be?"

"Still, my mother would kill me if she knew."

"Well, mine wouldn't be too thrilled either. So why don't we not tell them."

The rest of the summer I came out to Julie's as often as I could, after work at Cedars-Sinai and on weekends. At the end of July, I talked my parents into helping me buy a car, so I wouldn't have to borrow my mom's Impala. It was a six-year-old yellow Mustang convertible. The pretext was that I'd been accepted into the UCLA High School Honors Program and needed wheels to get out to Westwood.

The program permitted some high school seniors who lived within a certain radius of the campus and had passed a test to take classes at UCLA in the afternoon. The university then tried to recruit you, offering to let you retain your permit for parking lot 5, off Sunset, a privilege regular students would kill for.

It was a liberating moment to leave behind the bells and stupidities of high school and drive through the big gates on to Fairfax Avenue, past the ROTCies who had been ordered to swing them open for us. Then I'd head up to Sunset, put the top down, slip in a Beach Boys tape, crank up the volume, and take the curves as fast as the traffic would let me.

15

The first thing we did when we got to campus–it was all guys my year–was to head over to the top of the big hill that slopes down from the side of the library. We'd sit in the sun before our classes began and watch the gorgeous coeds walk by. Sometimes we'd grade the girls. I wasn't into this game nearly as much as the others. My mind was on Julie–pale, petite, no California girl, but intensely, insanely desirable.

In the summer I'd gone up Laurel Canyon to Van Nuys to see her, but when UCLA started, I took the San Diego Freeway over Mulholland. The descent into the Valley at 70 m.p.h. was always exhilarating. The guys I'd driven from high school were pissed off that I wasn't taking them back, but I told them I had a job at a restaurant in the Valley, and they'd have to make other arrangements.

I couldn't repeat the same story to my mother. I told her I was helping Julie with her homework. I'd convinced her to take a class at Valley Junior College, and she reluctantly agreed. I immediately regretted mentioning Julie, and switched the excuse, claiming I needed to study at UCLA's graduate research library.

Julie and I didn't do much besides making love and smoking dope. We'd listen to oldies from the late '60s and early '70s on her tape player as we'd pass the joint back and forth. One of Julie's favorites was "The Bright Elusive Butterfly of Love." After a few hits, the lyrics sounded poignant and profound.

❧

Before the second summer of our affair, I began getting bored. I loved Julie, and I loved making love to her, but there wasn't much to talk about afterwards. She'd tell me about the customers at the beauty salon that day and who wasn't getting along with whom on the staff, and why. I was headed to Reed College, and all incoming freshman were required to read the *Iliad* and the *Odyssey* over the summer. I couldn't discuss these with Julie, any more than I could the books and lectures in my German Lit in Translation,

16

Renaissance Painting, or Intro to Philosophy classes at UCLA. I was curious about Aunt Jean, but Julie didn't want to talk about her mom. She didn't seem all that interested in reminiscing about our glorious afternoons in the Weisses' back yard.

At some point Julie decided that junior college wasn't for her, and enrolled in a beauticians' school. I tried to talk her out of this, and we got into our first argument.

"Jonny, I'm not smart like you," she said.

"I'm not smart. Not like Carl." My precocious little brother. "I just like to read."

"Well you have to understand that I don't. You have to accept that. Please don't try to make me be somebody I'm not."

I changed the subject. "One eye," I said, and we slowly moved our faces together until our foreheads touched. We kissed and made love, and then listened to another favorite of Julie's, "Bridge Over Troubled Waters."

⁓

I flew up to Portland in August and didn't hear much from Julie. In those pre-cell, pre-texting, pre-Skyping days, you had to sit down and write a letter, and Julie wasn't much into writing. I'd expected to be swept into college life, but that didn't happen. The constant rain was depressing. The savvy New Yorkers and sophisticated San Franciscans were intimidating, and after my 3:00 German class, I'd rush to the mail room to see if anything was waiting for me from my cousin.

There was only the occasional insipid postcard from Julie, but one day I got a long letter from Cheryl. Julie, she wrote, had gotten married in Vegas to an Italian sculptor ten years older than her, Giovanni Villari. They'd moved to an apartment near Fairfax. She gave me the address and new phone number.

Cheryl was suspicious of Giovanni. He was handsome and charming, but had a vile temper. She didn't trust him. She thought he was using Julie to get a green card.

Cheryl knew a thing or two about men. She'd been promiscuous in high school, according to family gossip, and then had been sleeping with one of the vice-presidents at the bank she worked for as a teller. But she threw him over for a guy called Brad Maxx, the lead singer in a short-lived rock band, The Love Machine. The marriage lasted less than a year. Brad and she had just gotten divorced.

"P.S.," wrote Cheryl, "I know that you and Julie are lovers. She didn't blab. I guessed and she had to admit it. She's not a good liar. I think it's wonderful! I won't tell anyone. By the way, first cousins can get married in California. I don't think this thing with Giovanni will last."

✐

I called Julie as soon as I was back in LA for Christmas. She told me her husband was in Santa Barbara visiting a customer, and I could come over the next day.

As soon as she opened the door of the upper duplex on Blackburn, I could see Julie was pregnant.

"Jesus Christ, Julie!" I said.

"How about 'congratulations'?"

"Well that, too. When are you due?"

"The second of March," she said. "Don't worry, you're not the father."

I did a quick computation. "How can I not be?" I asked, "I can count backwards from nine."

Julie swallowed and looked down at the floor. The vein in her temple throbbed. "I started seeing Giovanni at the beginning of summer."

"You told me you weren't sleeping with anyone else."

"I lied."

I raised her chin with my hand and stared into her sea-green eyes. "I think you're lying now."

Julie started crying, then whipped her head back and forth. Glistening tears flew in both directions.

18

We sat down at the little formica table in the kitchen. Julie made some peppermint tea.

I took a sip. "Sweetie, you were taking birth control pills, right? You showed me the disk. What happened?"

"Well they're not foolproof. They don't always work. Maybe I skipped a day."

"Maybe you skipped a day?"

"Jonny, I didn't plan this. Believe me."

I took a deep breath and exhaled. "OK. I believe you."

"Once the baby was growing inside me, I couldn't get an abortion. I just couldn't. And that's what you would have wanted. That's what you would have forced me to do."

"I wouldn't have forced you, Julie."

"But you never would have married me."

I rotated the mug of tea and took a long swallow. "I would have. I love you, Julie."

Again her tears started up. "Don't you see? Don't you see?" she said. "You've gone off to college. You're going to be a doctor or a lawyer. How could I ever be your wife?"

"People get married in college."

"Don't bullshit me. You don't want to get married."

"Divorce this guy. I'll marry you."

"You're crazy. You don't know what you're saying."

"I love you, Julie," I said desperately.

She shook her head and the tears went flying off again.

I rushed around the table, knocking over my chair, and knelt at her feet. I was crying now. I hugged her around the waist, and put my head on her lap. Then I pulled up her t-shirt and kissed her swollen belly. I ran my hands over it and put my ear to it, as if our baby might have some words of advice. I reached around and up and unhooked her bra.

She pushed my arms down. "Jonny, I can't. I'm a married woman."

"You said Giovanni's in Santa Barbara. You don't expect him back anytime soon, right?"

19

Julie scowled. "No. He's staying through the weekend." Then she stood up. "You can't stay, Jonny. I've got to get on with the life I've got now."

"But Julie, I love you. I'm never going to love anyone like I love you. Never."

"Oh Jonny, Jonny, Jonny."

We held each other, our foreheads pressed tightly. We were both crying again.

Julie disengaged herself and stepped back. "Jon. If you love me, you'll leave me alone. Forget about me." Then she said very slowly, "Just let me try to make a life for myself with Giovanni and the baby. Please."

Her pleading look, her misery, our desperation will stay with me to the end of my life.

I wiped my eyes with my handkerchief, then blew my nose.

"OK," I whispered.

I walked to the door, then turned around and said, "Julie, promise me, if things don't work out with this guy, if you ever need help, you'll call."

Julie nodded and I left.

I'd made a copy of Julie's '60s hits and the tape was in the glove compartment. I shoved it into the deck and listened to "The Bright Elusive Butterfly of Love." I had to pull over and park. I put my head on the steering wheel and sobbed until the stupid song ended.

❧

Later, I would remind myself that I was only eighteen. I'd never considered the idea of being a husband and father. That was way over the horizon. I just wanted to be a freshman in college. I wasn't doing a very good job of that. There were lots of kids who were smarter and better read than me, and even more who were cooler. I didn't have any close friends. I wasn't the star of the classroom, like in high school.

I was only eighteen. I was selfish, weak, and frightened. Julie knew both sets of parents would be furious, and that my resistance would crumble. She knew she would never fit in with the Reedies and their successors, that she didn't share my tastes and interests. I knew Julie was right.

I hoped she was right about Giovanni. She'd slept with him, Cheryl later told me, just a couple of days after her period didn't come.

But for years I couldn't forgive myself for not doing the right thing, for not defying my parents and hers and convincing Julie to divorce Giovanni and marry me. Our son would eventually share my feelings.

∾

I came back to LA over spring break. Julie and Giovanni were still in the Fairfax apartment, though they would get kicked out within a couple of weeks. Julie had given birth a week early, and named the baby Jayson.

Giovanni was out in the double garage, which he'd converted to a studio, paying extra rent for the privilege. Julie took me out, with Jayson in a sling, and introduced us. Giovanni was holding a blow-torch in one hand and hammering fiercely with the other. What I assumed were a few finished sculptures stood at the back of the garage, assemblages of twisted metal that looked like the debris from a car wreck. Some had been stippled by a ball-peen hammer and spray-painted silver or gold. Giovanni went right back to work after giving me a half-wave and Julie and I returned to the apartment.

"So what are you supposed to do with a five-week-old baby?" I asked.

"Give him your finger," Julie said. "See if he grasps it." He did, and gave me a little smile. "He likes you."

She got up to make some tea.

"He's a blondie," I said.

21

Julie turned around and frowned. "Grandma Sophie had blond hair when she was a girl."

After she returned with the two mugs, Julie said, "Giovanni isn't the jealous type. And I'll never tell him. I'll never tell Jayson. I'll never tell anyone."

"Except Cheryl."

"I trust Cheryl."

I stood up and began walking around the little kitchen.

"Is Giovanni a good father?"

Julie smiled ruefully and shook her head. "Not really."

Jayson was fussing, and Julie rocked him in her arms. "He's into his art. Some people really like it. This rich guy in Santa Barbara. But until he gets a gallery, it's hard for him to make a lot of money. I don't care. I can bring Jayson to work. They don't mind. He takes long naps in the afternoon. And mom watches him almost every other day."

"Why did you spell his name J-a-y-s-o-n?"

"Because that's the way I wanted to spell it."

"Yeah, but you don't need the 'y.'"

"I like it."

"But it looks trashy."

"The people he's going to be around won't care."

"How do you know who he's gonna want to be around?"

"Jon, stop it. Please."

"I'm just saying, it looks trashy."

"I'm not taking the 'y' out."

And so we had our second and final quarrel. When I left a short time later, I'm sure Julie was more convinced than ever that she'd made the right decision.

∽

Giovanni was bad news. We heard from Aunt Jean that he drank heavily and was into hard drugs. He was also bisexual. He was sleeping with the Santa Barbara patron. One evening

Giovanni ran a red light, killed a young mother, and drove off. He was caught and went to jail. Within a year, Julie and Giovanni were divorced.

But Julie didn't leave well enough alone. She married a flaky French Canadian poet, Raoul Gervais. Poetry paid less well than sculpture, and they moved up to Sonoma, where Raoul's uncle owned a couple of dry cleaners. Raoul left Julie and she married a Venezuelan musician, Jorge Guzman. Then they got divorced. What these guys apparently all had in common, besides their passion for the muses, was their love of booze and extramarital affairs.

I didn't try to see Jayson again. I told myself that was what Julie wanted. I began sending a card for his birthday with a check for $25 or $50. But the third or fourth time, Julie pointed out that he would eventually start asking questions. So I'd send the check directly to my cousin. After I landed the job at St. Pete, I enclosed one for $1000. Julie sent it back with a note that said, "Were doing fine, Jon. We dont need your money. But thanks."

❧

I used to imagine reunions with Jayson.

We'd be hiking together in the eastern Sierra, on the Little Lakes Valley trail where my dad's partner Mel Kravitz had taken me a couple of times. We'd identify the trees and flowers together.

Then I'd say, "Jay, I have something to tell you. I'm your real father."

"You're kidding."

"Nope." And we'd hug each other, tears in our eyes.

Or we'd be walking on Venice Beach early on a foggy morning when I'd tell him. We'd have a big breakfast at Zoomba's, and I'd fill him in about Julie and me, how she'd just wanted to do the right thing for him, and I was too young and immature to marry her. I'd tell him a little about my life, and find out what he'd been up to.

In my fantasies, he was not especially into cars or sports, but loved to read. He felt isolated, alienated, depressed. I'd reassure

23

him. This was something a lot of bright, sensitive guys go through. Don't worry, I'd say. Be patient. It was a good sign. We'd stop in Small World Bookstore, and I'd buy him copies of *Demian* and *Steppenwolf.*

I'd give Jayson some advice about girls. If you have to ask, she didn't. Don't be yourself, be someone a little nicer. There are girls who adore fascists, but you don't want to sleep with them.

You'll be told love is a fever that has to run its course. You'll be told the heart always overrules the head, and what's called the heart is located behind your zipper, not your shirt pocket. Still, try to be a *mensch*. Try to leaven passion with a little compassion. It's not easy. It's always going to be more exciting to fall in love than to be in a relationship. And if someone should tell you "the road of excess leads to the palace of wisdom" or "he who desires, but acts not, breeds pestilence," turn around and walk rapidly in the opposite direction. Do as I say. Not as I do.

I'd come back to LA every six weeks. Jayson and I would go hiking in Malibu and Topanga Canyons. I'd pick up a boat, and teach him how to sail. He'd come out to Tampa and stay with Angela, Amy, and me. Everyone would hit it off. We'd go walking with the dogs in Wildwood or go out to Caladesi Island or Fort de Soto. The next time I was out in California, I'd buy Jay a golden retriever.

It never happened of course. After Angie and I moved to Tampa, I called Julie and asked if I could see Jayson. "We've got our life and you've got yours," she told me. I didn't call again.

What I found out about Jayson, I learned from Cheryl.

CHAPTER 3

Cheryl

Cheryl was six years older than me. She called Julie and me "the babies" and ignored us. Once, when I started to show her some stories Julie and I had written and illustrated about Phyllis and Samuel, she said, "Why should I look at that crap?"

By the time she was fourteen, Cheryl had stopped accompanying her family when they came over for dinner. She was never around when we drove out to the Valley.

After she wrote to me about Julie, Cheryl and I exchanged a few more letters. She said she was sorry she'd been so mean to her sister and me. She was glad I'd gotten involved with Julie. I was a good influence. She hoped her sister would see the light about Giovanni. Cheryl told me a little bit about her life, her wild high school years, her disastrous marriage to Brad, what the Sunset club scene was really like. She had some of her mom's sense of humor, and I enjoyed the letters.

Cheryl was writing from Las Vegas. She'd pulled her life together and was finishing nursing school. She'd married a guy named Steve Lloyd, a high school guidance counselor. Lots of normal people live in Vegas, she assured me.

It was another three years before I met up with her. I'd just graduated from Berkeley–I'd transferred there from Reed after my freshman year–and had to store my things. I was heading to Princeton. The Graduate College rooms were furnished and I wouldn't need most of the stuff in the fall. Friends who were leaving town sold everything, but I wanted to hang onto the furniture, lamps, prints, and rugs I'd collected. There wasn't any room at my parents' house, but Jack and Jean had an empty storage shed in the back yard.

So one Friday morning in early June, I headed out to the Valley to meet the van from Berkeley.

Jean was in the psychiatric ward at Cedars-Sinai, and was coming home the next day. Cheryl had arrived the night before. She was using vacation time to take care of her mom for a week.

I arrived at eleven, a few minutes before the van, and Cheryl helped me stash everything in the shed. She'd made a nice lunch–poached salmon, risotto, asparagus with mock-hollandaise sauce. Jeanie never cooked.

I'd bought some flowers for my aunt, big white stargazer lilies, with purple iris and babies' breath. Cheryl put them in a vase on the kitchen table, but then moved it when she brought out the salmon. "They're lovely to look at, but up close they stink," she said. "They should be the state flower."

We sat at the table and talked, finished the bottle of chardonnay and opened another. I learned a little about Jayson and Julie. They seemed to be doing OK, though Jay was not an easy kid. Julie had divorced again and remarried, but husband number three, though he was a musician, seemed like an improvement.

I learned a little about Cheryl. The rumors were true. She'd been a hellion and a slut in high school. But there were reasons. These had to do with her parents, and she would tell me more later, she said.

After leaving Brad, she'd gone to New York, lived in the Village, and worked in banks. But the City had gotten old quickly, and she'd come back, determined to be a nurse. She'd spent a day in the ER at Mt. Sinai after a friend was hit by a car, had admired the nurses, and had a long talk with one during her lunch break.

26

Steve had once helped Cheryl back to her apartment after she'd gotten plastered at a party. He'd been a gentleman. My cousin hadn't met one before. Cheryl kept his number, got back in touch with him, they dated and got married. When his mother's emphysema got worse, they moved back to Vegas. Steve's mom was well off–his dad had owned a big insurance company–and Cheryl was able to go to nursing school. But recently things were not going so well. Steve, like his dad, had an alcohol problem. He'd taken a semester's leave to go into rehab.

There was a long silence after Cheryl finished. We stared at each other, stood up shakily, and lurched into each other's arms.

Cheryl was only a little taller than Julie. She had short strawberry blond hair, a small retroussé nose, freckles, perfect teeth, and, it turned out, lovely, pert breasts.

She was very good in bed. I'd had some experience at this point. It was not hard to get laid in Berkeley after the '60s, and I'd had sex with some acrobatic performers. Of course I recognized that "good in bed" had something to do with your feelings for the partner, and the rush of affection and gratitude I felt toward my sexy cousin intensified the pleasure. She wasn't a soul-mate like Julie, but I adored her. She seemed so funny and shrewd. And, at twenty-seven, she was that mysterious and enticing individual, an older woman. She was also a married woman, and that fanned my lust.

Before Al came home, we made love again in the little bedroom that looked exactly as it had when Cheryl and Julie abandoned it in high school. Jean came back the next day, and I went out to the Valley to visit her. After I left, I checked into a Motel 6 on Sepulveda, as Cheryl and I had arranged, and she met me there an hour later.

There's a string of cheap motels along that stretch of Sepulveda and we tried three others during the week. We pretended to review the various rooms for the Triple A after we made love. I was supposed to start work at Cedars. My dad had gotten me a job in medical records my first year in high school and I'd worked in the hospital each summer since. I told them I needed to go back up to Berkeley to take care of some things.

Later in the summer, Cheryl was able to come out for a long weekend, and two other weekends I drove to a motel on the outskirts of Vegas and Cheryl met me there.

When my cousin returned to Southern California, we weren't about to spend the weekend hanging out on Sepulveda Boulevard. We found a motel in Venice, and spent our two days together wandering along the boardwalk, the beach, and the canals, when we weren't making love.

The Venice canals are now lined with expensive homes. There are little bridges over the water, and you can watch ducks paddle by beneath you. But in those days, the neighborhood, like a lot of the town, was pretty seedy. The canals were just big, sandy ditches with a little filthy water at the bottom. The motel had pictures of them in their glory days, and it was sad to think of how they'd ended up.

It was in Venice that I learned how crazy my aunt and uncle were.

I'd never been told any details about Jeanie's suicide attempts. My impression from my dad was that they hadn't been all that serious. This wasn't the case.

The first time, Cheryl had come back from junior high and found her mom lying on her back on the kitchen floor with a knife in her chest. There was a lot of blood. Cheryl took the knife out, pressed a towel against Jeanie's chest, and called 911.

It was Cheryl again who found her in the bathtub the second time. The gas jets had been turned on, the pilot light extinguished, and Jean had taken half a bottle of Miltown. There was a knife on the bathroom floor, but Jeanie had passed out before she could use it, or decided not to.

Then came an unhappy affair with a neighbor, a high school gym teacher. The guy wanted to leave his wife, marry Jeanie, and move to another city. Jean was wildly undecided, and called

28

Cheryl to ask her advice. It was very weird, my cousin said. She didn't know what to tell her mom. Later, she realized that Jean was just asking for her approval. "I wish I'd told her to go ahead," Cheryl said bitterly.

Mother and daughter met on Venice beach very early one morning, and walked back and forth. Jean was crying and trembling. Suddenly she twisted off her wedding ring and hurled it into the ocean. Cheryl and her mom spent an hour searching for it before giving up. Later Jeanie told Al she'd taken it off to wash her hands after she'd gotten tar on them, and it had slipped down the drain.

A few weeks later Jean took more pills and walked into the Pacific at dawn, not far from where she'd tossed her ring into the waves. Somebody saw her, dived in, and pulled her out.

Cheryl also had news about Uncle Al. "When I was fourteen, he got obsessed with me," she said. He kept quizzing her about boyfriends. "One afternoon when no one was home and I was taking a nap, he came into my bedroom. He said he needed to check and see that I was still a virgin. I was frightened and let him. Then he told me to give him a blow job. He explained how to do it. I did." Cheryl shut her eyes. "He swore he'd kill me if I told anyone. He said Mom hadn't slept with him in more than three years."

Over the next twelve months, she had oral sex with him several more times. Cheryl moved out the next year.

"Did he go after Julie?" I asked.

"No. I told him if he touched her, I'd call the cops."

"You know what's really sick," said Cheryl a little later. I couldn't imagine. "A couple of years after Mom threw her ring into the ocean, I slept with the neighbor, the gym teacher. He was a good-looking guy."

Cheryl slept with a lot of guys in those days. "I lost count," she said. Eventually she learned how to say no. "I made Brad wait a long time. It drove him crazy."

29

"I grew up in a nuthouse," Cheryl said. "Your parents seemed so normal. I envied you and your brothers so much."

"Believe me, things were not so idyllic," I said, then asked, "Did you ever try to talk to my mom about what was going on with your mom and dad?"

"How could I?" We'd reached the end of a canal and turned back. Cheryl took my hand. "I know she wanted Mom to get a divorce. She nudged her to get a job or go back to school. But then she got impatient. She just threw up her hands." Cheryl didn't say anything for a minute. "I'll tell you, the only person who was really kind to me was your Grandma Marike. I loved her." Suddenly my cousin's eyes were full of tears. "I used to wish she was my grandma."

"What about Grandma Sophie?"

"After you were born, she lost interest in me. She used to take me places when I was little. Even then Mom almost never left the house. We had fun. A couple of times we took the bus downtown and had lunch in this weird cafeteria she liked called Clifton's. It was like you were inside of a cave. It was cool. There were waterfalls, stalactites, and statues. I loved it. But then you came along, and the trips ended."

"Sorry," I said.

Cheryl smiled. "Not your fault, Jon."

"Well, I've done my bit to mess up your family."

"No, no," Cheryl said. "That's all on Julie." We sat down on the sand. "I have an IUD, by the way."

"I trusted you." I was actually too drunk to think about birth control the first afternoon.

A moment later, she added, "I'm keeping an eye on Jayson."

༝

I went east to grad school and met my wife. Things got better between Cheryl and Steve. They had two kids, Chuck and Hailey. It had been a one-summer affair. The next time I saw my

30

cousin was at Jeanie's funeral. I held her for a long time when we embraced. We exchanged a look, but when I chatted with her at the reception afterward, neither of us suggested getting together. The little bed we'd first made love on was still there, of course, and now piled high with coats and jackets.

CHAPTER 4

Wendy

And now the sisters-in-law.

My brother Danny met Wendy Huang when he was at UCLA Law School and interning his first summer with a big trust and estates firm in Century City, where Wendy was an associate. He'd had his heart set on sports and entertainment law, but so had ninety percent of his classmates. Danny and Wendy started getting together for late dinners on little Santa Monica after work. "He was the first guy who took an interest in me," Wendy said. "And he told me he wanted to have kids." I said I doubted that no guy had been attracted to her, but she ignored me. "Your brother can be very charming."

"So I'm told," I said.

After another moment of silence, she added, "Jon, he was very sweet and earnest and bright. He really wooed me."

"He's an impressive guy," I said. "Until you get to know him."

Wendy looked down for a second. "I'm not going to argue with you."

❦

Wendy had two older brothers who had gone to Cal Tech and MIT. The MIT brother taught at Cal Tech, the Cal Tech brother was a computer engineer in Massachusetts. "Yeah, it was always 'you get A-minus, you bring shame to fammery,'" Wendy said. "And I was always shaming the family. I even got a couple of B+s. And I wasn't pretty."

"But you are," I said a little too hotly. We were already lovers. Wendy just shrugged.

⁂

My sister-in-law had started at UCLA and transferred up to Berkeley. She was two years older than me, and our paths had never crossed, but we'd had a couple of professors in common, and could talk Berkeleyiana. We remembered the same Telegraph Avenue characters, had both bought bo buns from the same truck on University, browsed Moe's and Shakespeare & Co., hung out at Café Med, got stoned in Strawberry Canyon, and had coffee Sunday mornings at Peet's on the north side.

I'd missed the halcyon days of the Age of Aquarius, but Wendy had caught the tail end. They lingered right through the '70s in Berserkeley. There were even a few after-tremors, and I'd had a chance to see cops in full riot gear and had once stepped out of Nirvana on Telegraph, fragrant with sandalwood, and felt tear gas sting my eyes. Wendy had been more skeptical than me–I'd remained a Marxist into grad school–but even she had listened raptly to lectures by Abbie Hoffman, Jerry Rubin, Mario Savio, Tim Leary, Baba Ram Das, and other bearers of good news. And she remembered, better than I, some of the local politicos. In those days, on the extreme right of the spectrum were those hide-bound conservatives, the former McGovern Democrats. So we reminisced about Berkeley in its Iron Age, and shook our heads at our naiveté, our trust in the People, our faith in change.

I told her I'd seen the sign that heralded the end of the late '60s–though it was by now the end of the '70s. On a concrete wall on the south side of campus, there was a graffitied message in red letters a foot high: "Smash the State." One day someone crossed out the "the" and wrote above it "Ohio."

"It was probably just a stunt by the Athletic Department," said Wendy.

❧

There were a lot of little signs that all was not well in the Marcus household in West LA. But when I was around, at least, Wendy didn't respond to Danny's sarcastic digs and obeyed his orders.

Then one day as I was leaving—I had stopped by to drop off a belated birthday present for my niece—a neighbor called me over. I'd chatted with Mrs. Rosenzweig before, but this time she didn't want to talk about aphids or Jerry Brown. She motioned me to come into the house and I followed. We went into the kitchen and Mr. R. joined us.

"Jonathan, we hardly know you," Mrs. Rosenzweig said, "but we know you're a good person."

I didn't deny this.

"We're worried about your brother and Wendy." Max Rosenzweig nodded vigorously. "We almost called the cops once."

"What's going on?"

"There's no violence," Mrs. R. said.

"Yet," Max added.

"We just hear a lot of yelling. The language that your brother uses, Jonathan! Oy vey!"

"We were thinking maybe you could talk to him," said Max.

"Well, I can try, but he's never listened to me."

"Be firm," Mrs. R. admonished, shaking her fist at me. "Don't tell him we told you," she whispered as I left.

Of course I didn't talk to Danny, but I did bring the subject up with Wendy. And of course she dismissed my concerns. "It's Danny's way of blowing off steam. I don't take it personally."

"Yeah but he shouldn't be swearing at you. And he shouldn't be swearing at you in front of the kids."

Wendy was irritated. "Jonathan, please. Butt out."

Before I could reply, little Sam raced into the kitchen. He pointed a very realistic-looking pistol at Wendy and said, "Bang! You're dead." Then he helped himself to a popsicle in the freezer and left the room.

⌘

I first took a more than brother-in-lawly interest in Wendy the night I saw her performing with her string quartet at a home in Stone Canyon. It was an ambitious program. With a pianist who sometimes played with them, they did the Trout, and then an early Beethoven quartet, Opus 18, number 4, in D minor. Danny, no fan of classical music, was staying home with Sam and Ashley. I'd heard Wendy practice many times, but had never seen her perform.

Wendy, so stolid in real life, was one of those performers who emotes. From time to time she would shut her eyes and whip her head from side to side. Her expression suggested more pain than pleasure, even during the jolly Trout. I found myself staring at her knees and thighs, hugging the amber cello.

"You seemed very moved by the Beethoven," I told her afterward, as we walked together on the brick patio, away from the crowded catering tables.

"I know, I know. Ever since I began playing, I've been told to stop making faces. Obviously I can't help it. Was it really distracting?

"Not at all," I lied.

We walked down the steps onto the lawn.

"I mean it's the audience that's supposed to be transported, not the performer."

"It didn't diminish my pleasure, believe me. Actually, it increased it."

I looked out across the lawn at the dark canyon wall in front of us and back at Wendy, in her long strapless black silk chiffon dress. She took a sip of champagne.

An owl flew down from the top of a tall sycamore, seized something and soared up over the top of the canyon. Wendy turned to look and the light from the house caught her profile and her bare shoulder. I stared, transfixed.

Our eyes locked for a second. Then she took my hand and said, "Let's get something to eat." We walked back to the house.

⌘

I first made love to my sister-in-law in a room filled with cardboard boxes.

Two days after the concert, Wendy's father died. He'd lived by himself in a small rented house in Santa Monica. Wendy's mom had passed away ten years earlier from stomach cancer. The Huangs had owned a greenhouse on Sepulveda. When his wife died, Mr. Huang sold the family home and put most of the money in a trust for the grandkids. He'd been in pretty good health, but had had a massive heart attack during the night.

I was in LA staying at my parents'. I would come out every summer for a couple of weeks. After the first few times, Angela never went with me. She was OK with my dad, but never got along with my mom, disliked my brothers, and loathed LA. I always tried to get up to the eastern Sierra when I was out in California, but Angie didn't like the mountains any more than she liked Glitzburg. She was terrified of heights.

Wendy's brothers took off right after the funeral. The Massachusetts programmer went home and the Cal Tech brother flew to Chicago for a conference. Danny left the next day for Sacramento, with perfunctory apologies. So it was up to Wendy to clear out the house. Sam and Ashley were parked with the sister-in-law in Pasadena. The brothers told her they didn't want anything, not even photos.

There was a lot more stuff than I expected. Despite Wendy's pleas, her dad had hung on to almost everything, apart from the furniture and paraphernalia in the kids' rooms. A woman from an auction house had come out on Friday and found enough stuff to warrant sending a truck. This would be easier, though probably less lucrative, than a house sale.

So Wendy had to figure out what she wanted to hang onto, what should be auctioned, and what should be dumped. The guy who was going to haul off the trash was coming the next day.

Everything to be auctioned went into the living room, the stuff to be saved was moved into the bedroom, and what was going to be dumped we carried out to the garage, along with some things for the Salvation Army.

We hadn't finished by 9:00 in the evening. There was no central AC, so we'd taken turns standing in front of the window unit in the bedroom.

"That's it," said Wendy when I came in from the garage. "No more." We'd been thinking about take-out, but needed to escape the stifling house, so we walked to an Italian restaurant a couple of blocks away that was still open. We shared a bottle of Orvieto.

The Through-the-Looking-glass moment came as soon as we were back in the house. "Thank you so much," Wendy said. We exchanged a look and then we were hugging each other tightly. "I'm so sweaty," she said.

"So am I." I shut my eyes. "Wendy, I've wanted to hold you for so long."

"Me, too," she said, and raised her arms. I pulled her t-shirt up over her head.

❧

"Well, now I have something I can tell my shrink," Wendy said afterwards. "I slept with my husband's brother in my father's bed." She shook her head. "Five days after he died on it."

"You really see a shrink?"

She nodded.

"But Wendy, you're the sanest relative I've got. You're the only sane one."

38

"That doesn't mean I'm happy."

"Well I hope you're a little happier now."

She nodded again and bit her lip.

❧

We met the next morning for omelets at Zoomba's on the Venice boardwalk. We walked along the beach, empty at this hour, and onto the rocks of the breakwater. Wendy hesitated before one jump and I grabbed her arm when she landed. I held it a little too long, and she pulled away.

Back at the house, we went through the discard pile again. Wendy had been pretty ruthless. I suggested for a second time that she might want to keep a few of the boxes of slides her dad had taken on family vacations, but she shook her head.

"Who's going to look at them?" she asked.

"I don't know, my happiest memories as a kid were family trips."

"Mine weren't. My brothers made sure of that. And I don't want to look at myself as a plug-ugly ten-year-old or a surly adolescent. Anyway, how often do you look at your dad's slides?"

"I don't," I admitted.

"A vacation is special when you're on it. You're paying attention to everything."

"Well, there's pleasure in remembering something pleasurable."

"Not so much for me. But you're the historian."

"Trust me, most history is not pleasurable to contemplate. Unless you're a sadist. Or at least a Schadenfreudian. But don't you think Sam and Ashley might want to see pictures of their mom as a kid one day?"

Wendy gave a derisive snort.

❧

At one, as he'd promised, the guy who was going to haul off the junk showed up. Willie Clump arrived in an ancient, battered black Ford pick-up with a rusted-out body and splintering

39

wood slats that looked as if it had been driven off the set of the Beverly Hillbillies. The truck rattled as he backed it up the long driveway.

Willie was small, wizened, and coal black. He had a limp, but was very spry. He'd throw things onto the trailer bed, and from time to time hop up and rearrange the junk. We handed him boxes of tax returns, antique computers, and the slide carousels. He came back to the edge of the truck bed once, brandishing some photo albums, and later a couple of oil paintings by Wendy's mom. "You sho' you don't want these? Don't want you t'have a change a heart tomorrow."

Wendy shook her head.

"When they's gone, they's gone."

After Wendy paid Willie and he pulled off, she sat down inside the garage and slumped forward. I sat next to her. "Willie Clump gets everything in the end," she said quietly.

"Yeah."

"All those possessions you wanted so badly. All the pictures you took, diaries you kept, paintings you did, everything."

"Well, you're hanging on to a few things. And your dad's clothes, the lamps, and other stuff is going to get recycled."

My sister-in-law just shook her head. "Willie Clump gets everything."

Afterward Wendy threw a blanket on the bare mattress and we made love again. Then we pulled the mattress out to the garage for the Salvation Army.

∽

We sat on the wood floor in front of the AC, side by side, knees drawn up. "You know what I spend my day doing?" Wendy asked.

"I have a rough idea."

"I draw little crosses on trust documents. Or little tablets with a Star of David for Jewish clients."

40

I gave her a puzzled look.

"On the timeline in the summary section at the beginning. So they can focus on what happens when one of them dies, and then when the other dies. How the trusts convert. It brings the reality home to them. And to their kids. It sobers them up."

"So what if it's a mixed marriage?"

"Then I draw both, twice, side-by-side."

"What if they're atheists?"

"They still get a cross. That's what I did for my parents."

"They were atheists? Really?"

"No, not real atheists. They were just areligious. Like a lot of Chinese. The Chinese have never been into religions."

"Too reasonable?"

"Too materialistic. The religions they've adopted, they've picked up second hand. Religions are something Indo-Europeans and Semites come up with."

Wendy closed her eyes.

"Anyway, you'd think dealing with death in the office every day, you'd get inured. Of course it doesn't work that way."

⁂

I started going out to LA more frequently, and staying longer. That seemed to be fine with Angela.

Wendy and I got into a routine. In the early afternoon, I'd check into a motel in Venice, she'd take a half day off, we'd make love and walk along the canals until it was time for her to go home. We figured Wendy was not likely to run into anyone she knew in the scruffy parts of Venice we walked through.

But other times I would accompany Wendy officially as her brother-in-law. I started going to rehearsals. I admired and envied the camaraderie among the members of her quartet, how they worked so hard to create something beautiful together, and the pleasure they took in accomplishing this. At rehearsals shortly before a performance, when they'd mastered the score, it was

41

exciting to hear the music, sitting just three feet away. And I loved watching Wendy play.

One day after a rehearsal of Haydn's third "Sun" Quartet, she said to me on the drive back, "Jon, you've got to stop staring at me. When you were in the bathroom before we left, Liz told me, 'I think your brother-in-law has a little crush on you.'"

"Perceptive girl."

Wendy smiled. "Well please try to restrain yourself."

"Liz isn't going to pass that intelligence on to Danny."

"Just do it, Jon."

"Sweetheart, you have such beautiful eyes," I told her the first time we made love at a Venice motel. I brushed my finger along her epicanthic folds, then over her high cheekbones. "Your skin is so nice. So clean and tight."

"You just love me because I'm Asian."

"Come on Wendy, don't say that."

"I hope it's not because I'm Danny's wife."

"Wendy, please. I love you because you're you."

Ten years of psychoanalysis apparently hadn't done all that much for Wendy's self-esteem. And if her shrink had discovered why a kind and reasonable woman had married, and remained married, to my brother, he wasn't telling her.

CHAPTER 5

Danny, David, and Carl

Danny is the next oldest of my three brothers, a year younger than me.

I grew up with "Leave It To Beaver" re-runs and idolized the Cleavers.

Whatever the producers may have imagined, kids didn't care much for the Beave himself. We didn't think the little twerp was cute or endearing. It was June and Ward we were in love with, so reasonable, so mild-mannered, so attractive, so charming, so wise.

But I took a shine to Wally as well. He was the ideal big brother, exactly what I wanted to be. Sometimes he was exasperated by the Beave's antics, but he was always there to bail out his kid brother by the end of the episode, or at least not squeal on him. Theodore was always grateful, even if he didn't say so in as many words.

Unfortunately, my relationship with Danny was more like Cain and Abel's than Wally and the Beave's.

There was some pushing and shoving over trucks and planes and yo-yos when we were little kids, but the real violence began half a dozen years after David was born. Oddly, it often seemed to come over David.

The first fight took place late one summer. Danny would have been eight. He and David were sitting on the brick patio in the back yard, under the jacaranda. "Get me the chocolate chip ice cream, slave," Danny told David. "And a spoon."

I stepped into the sunlight, closed the sliding glass door behind me and told David, "You don't have to do anything he tells you."

"Ignore him, slave," Danny commanded. Then he turned to me and glared. "Mind your own business, asshole."

I couldn't come up with anything better than "You gonna make me?"

Danny charged me, head lowered, and knocked me down. But I grabbed his collar as I fell and pulled him with me. We rolled down the two patio steps to the grass below. I knew what was at stake and was able to get on top of him and pin his arms with my knees before Mom came running out. But I was surprised at how powerful Danny was, and that he hadn't hesitated for a second to answer my question in the affirmative.

Danny was shorter, darker, hairier, more muscular than me. People couldn't believe we were brothers. I had a lot of trouble myself.

I'd tried to be nice to him. I was told repeatedly how charming I'd been at a year and a half when I'd suggested to my parents, while my brother was crying inconsolably, "Maybe Danny want some applesauce."

I'd shared toys, as instructed by my mother. It didn't work. If I had something, he wanted it. If I built something, he'd knock it down when my back was turned. Later, he found he could push my buttons by pretending to crash land one of my model airplanes, rearrange the books on the shelves above my bed, or hide the agates in the collection on my dresser.

༄

My pinning him on the lawn should have been the end of it. Bullies are supposed to be cowards. If you fight back and whip them, they won't bother you anymore. No one told that to Danny.

He kept coming after me. Sometimes it had to do with his master-slave relationship with David, but other things set him off.

"Pass the potatoes. Non-stop!" he said one night.

I helped myself to a spoonful. "I didn't hear a 'please,'" I said.

He gave me the finger.

Later, when we were clearing the table and loading the dishwasher, he said mellifluously, "Oh, Jonathan," and when I turned around, he shoved a handful of mashed potatoes into my face. I pushed him against the double oven, but he bounced off and kicked me hard on the shin. I fell over the open dishwasher door. He was on top of me in a second, and had gotten one knee on my back when Mom came into the kitchen.

"Get up!" she yelled. "I can't leave you two alone for a minute!"

The next day I asked my mother if I could take karate lessons—not so popular then. She refused. "I don't want you breaking Danny's neck."

"He's more likely to break mine," I muttered. I took out books on karate from the library, and practiced kicks on my own.

When David was the victim, he was not grateful for my interventions. He and Danny would team up. A couple of times David crouched behind me while Danny pushed me in the chest. I'd fall back over David. The third time I sensed him behind me and kicked him hard in the ribs. After that I was his enemy, too.

Once, when I came back early from a rehearsal after school, I must have been in the 10th grade, I was about to knock on the bathroom door when Danny came out, adjusting his fly. He pushed past me. I was about to go in when David emerged. "What are you two doing in there?" I asked.

Danny turned around. "None of your fucking business," he said.

Another time I saw them come out of the bedroom together and I knew they'd been up to something. I didn't say anything. Then, again returning from a rehearsal, I heard the shower running in our bathroom. A few minutes later I was getting a towel from the linen closet in the hall and saw first David and then Danny come out of the bathroom. Danny glared at me. "Spying?" he said.

"What would I be spying on?" I asked.

Danny of course started picking on Carl, our youngest brother. I came in the back door one day and saw Danny sitting on the yellow metal chair by the washing machine and Carl kneeling at his feet, tying Danny's shoe. "OK, now lick the sole." Carl refused. "Did you hear me, you little shit?"

I grabbed Danny from behind and got my arms around his neck, pulled him out of the chair, and twisted him to the ground. When his face turned red and his eyes widened, I released my grip. "Don't ever do that again," I said, my voice shaking. "If he ever messes with you, you tell me," I said to Carl.

I never got a thank-you from my little brother, but it was understood from then on that we were on the same side. In our tackle football games in the back yard, it was always D and D against Carl and me. We didn't fare well; little Carl only wanted to get out of the way.

There was more violence. On a family vacation at Lake Arrowhead, Danny tapped me on the shoulder. I turned around and he punched me in the face, knocking me out. My dad took me to the emergency room at the little hospital, but everything checked out. Back home, after dinner a couple of nights later, I kicked Danny in the stomach, a karate move I'd worked on where you whirl around, flex your knee, and connect with your heel. "Just practicing," I said. Danny started vomiting all over the floor. Mom wasn't pleased.

At some point, my brother and I reached a modus vivendi. We would exchange insults but not blows. One of the attractions of going off to college was not having to deal with him. Then, as adults, we tacitly agreed to forget the past. Danny was even capable of sentimental expostulations about the fun we'd had together, playing football in the backyard, building model planes, collecting agates, warming ourselves in front of the heating vent on cold days, and stuffing envelopes side-by-side at the Fairfax Democratic headquarters.

✍

Danny became a personal injury lawyer. He joined a big firm downtown, but quit after a couple of years and hung up his own shingle. His true vocation was always politics.

During election campaigns, we'd volunteer at our precinct headquarters. But while I was content to bask in the ambience, listening to "Hap-py days are here again" blaring over the loudspeaker, and collect buttons and bumper stickers, Danny was interested in the maps on the wall with the pins stuck in them and the clipboards with the lists of numbers next to the bank of phones on the big table in the center. I was bored after an hour, but he could spend a whole Saturday there.

Danny made himself useful. Unlike me, he was well organized, and liked to organize others.

In high school and college he worked for Tom Bradley, and eventually moved into the mayor's outer circle. He became something called "Assistant Director of Youth Outreach" while he was in law school, and then got a chance to manage a district campaign headquarters of his own. After the election, he got some kind of position with Parks and Recreation. Whatever he was doing paid well: a couple of years out of law school, he had a swanky condo in the Marina and drove a BMW.

One of his duties was being in charge of a youth basketball league that the city ran. He bought into an agency that arranged travel for the all-stars, and for the baseball and track athletes in the city's programs. He had married Wendy by this point and they moved from the Marina to Beverly Glen, above Sunset. My mother was floored by the 5,000-foot home and by the then-astronomical price they'd paid, over $250,000. My parents had bought our house for $35,000.

47

But Danny had a falling out with the mayor's people. Someone may have been troubled by the conflict of interest. He got involved in lobbying in Sacramento for the Association of Trial Lawyers of America (later "The American Association for Justice" and maybe now "The Association for Truth, Justice, and the American Way"), and did some consulting for the California Department of Aging. He bought a condo near the capitol.

Next we heard, Danny was running fleets of vans in LA and Sacramento providing blood pressure testing and eye exams to Medicaid and Medicare patients in public housing. But apparently he and his partners in Cal Medi-Serve were double-billing and after several years they got caught. One of them went to jail, but Danny got off with a reprimand from the ABA and a year's probation. He still had his travel agency, and still bought or leased a new Mercedes or Beamer every two years.

Wendy didn't want to talk about what Danny was up to, but he evolved into something like what would have been called, in Chicago or New York, a "fixer." He had an enormous Rolodex, and when someone wanted something from City Hall or Sacramento, they'd give him a call. Right out of law school, he cottoned onto the fact that you didn't need to know the statutes, that's what your paralegals were for. You needed to know the judges, and the city, county, and state department heads and their office managers. His brushes with the law didn't seem to have hurt him with any with his friends in high places. He still had access. When you paid to play, you paid Danny.

Helping my brother with his fixing and his bundling was his associate Unique Beazley. The statuesque consultant was always by Danny's side at fundraisers, and no one doubted she was his mistress. But he also had a girlfriend in Sacramento, Wendy told me, a tall, willowy African-American lobbyist called Deleese Duchamps. And they'd each had predecessors. Unique wasn't.

∽

48

Deliberate, plodding, cautious, myopic, David was Danny's opposite. He wouldn't have crossed a deserted street against the light at 3 a.m. But David would never have been out after 10, and the doors would be securely locked, and the locks triple-checked. And tall, athletic Black women were not to his taste.

By the 7th grade, David had secured the position of class nerd. He had the leather briefcase, the glasses, the plastic pocket pen-holder. But he was of the priggish genus. David was a meticulous dresser. His checked shirts were ironed, his creased pants didn't ride up above his ankles, and the nose-piece of his metal-framed glasses was never taped. The nerdish look and manner were deceiving. It came as a disappointment to successive teachers that David was not a stellar student. He got nearly as many Bs as As. But he always turned in his homework on time and had a perfect attendance record.

David went to UCLA, living at home, and then to the UCLA Library School. He was interested in school libraries and worked at a high school in Northridge for half a dozen years shushing Valley Girls before landing a job at a community college.

One of the assistants was a woman named Karen Kent.

We'd always assumed David was gay, though certainly of the costive, well-closeted sub-species. But no one passed their suspicions on to Karen. One day David announced, after they'd been dating for only a few weeks, that he and his girlfriend were getting married.

If you were gay and wanted to get married, Karen was a good choice. Flat as a board, skinny as a toothpick, she looked like a prepubescent boy. Karen had lank blond hair and a fetus face–a fetus with gas. She had two expressions: distress, with her mouth half open and lower teeth protruding, and disapproval, her thin lips turned down and a scowl creasing her forehead. Karen wore granny glasses, baggy khaki pants or long denim skirts, peasant blouses, and Hush Puppies. Looking at them together, no one would fail to guess that David and Karen were librarians.

But Karen didn't have her MLS, and spent the first years of the marriage pursuing one. We heard long stories about the problems with each of the distance-learning programs she entered, how they were too technology-oriented, even then, and indifferent to art and literature.

Wendy and Angie kept their own last names and had polite but distant relationships with my parents. Karen became Mrs. Marcus and cultivated my mother. She seemed to regard Mom as an arbiter of culture and good taste, and parroted her opinions about the concerts we attended and the books they both read. Mom's opinions dutifully reflected those of the L.A. Times' reviewers Robert Kirsch and his successors and Martin Bernheimer. So we were treated over dinner to two reverent précis of the assessments in the *Times*.

But, not surprisingly, my mother seemed to like Wendy and Angela more than clingy Karen. Long after Angie became disaffected and stopped coming out to LA, Mom had kind things to say about Professor Salvucci's growing oeuvre, in which she took a maternal pride. Being a lawyer didn't have quite as much cachet, but Wendy was a lot friendlier to my parents than Angie was, and both Mom and Dad were astonished and grateful that Danny had married somebody so reasonable and civil. Wendy was first off the starting block with kids, and this didn't hurt.

The day came when David announced that he and Karen had "amicably" agreed to separate. I learned later from Wendy, whom Karen confided in, that she and David, both virgins of course, had carefully researched sex and only attempted copulation after studying books and manuals for a week. The hard work apparently didn't pay off. Karen's perpetual frown deepened. She consulted Wendy about techniques and strategies. They even purchased some sexy lingerie together, but David was apparently unmoved.

⌒

Later that year David announced that he was going to bring Richard over for Thanksgiving. Richard and he would be living together at the beginning of January. This didn't work out, though the lover appeared to be cut from the same cloth as David. Polite, quiet, shy, and yet another librarian, he apparently had a roving eye. My brother forgave Richard when he discovered first one and then another teenage boy in his bed, but after the third time he gave his roommate the boot. Danny helped David buy out Richard's share of their modest two-bedroom house near Pico and Bundy.

Karen and David remained "good friends" as well as colleagues, and she continued to turn up at the occasional wedding, bar mitzvah, and funeral.

I didn't keep up with all of Richard's successors, but David was the monogamous type and eventually found a cheerful, heavy-set older guy named Gordon, a jewelry store manager, and their relationship seemed to prosper. Gordon even hit it off with Karen, which was more than any of us had done.

✍

Especially Carl. My youngest brother could be scathing toward people he didn't like. This included all of humanity minus about a dozen individuals. I was not among this company. But whereas Carl loathed Danny and despised David, he tolerated me.

He referred to his two other brothers collectively as "the schmucks." They called him "brainiac" or "R2D2," and later "the idiot-savant."

Carl was particularly incensed by David's conversion from agnosticism to Conservative Judaism. Oddly, this happened just around the time David emerged from the closet. Conservative rabbis at that time opposed homosexual unions, so the choice was a little mysterious. The only thing David said to me was, "I've returned to my people."

With one exception, my convert grandmother, his people had all been agnostics or atheists. But Carl was the most militant among them. At age seven he announced he was an atheist and would not be participating in the family Seder. As the youngest at the table, he was supposed to read the four questions. Mom told him that if he wasn't going to take part, he wouldn't get dinner. "Fine," said Carl, and stomped off to his bedroom.

It was not as if we used a traditional haggadah. It was the product of Shalom Sunday School, where Danny, David, and I were sent. The school provided a secular Jewish education. We were taught that to be a good Jew was to be a liberal Democrat. We learned about the Triangle Company Fire, the Pullman Strike, and the Hollywood Ten. God was never mentioned. The Shalom School haggadah carefully excised all references to miracles. Moses and company crossed the Red Sea at low tide. They escaped when the tides came in and the Pharaoh's chariots got stuck in the mud. Mixed in with tributes to the workers of the world and to the heroes of the Warsaw ghetto uprising were paeans to the coming of spring, which, said the haggadah, the holiday had originally celebrated.

I had already learned that Carl was not a typical kid, and certainly not a typical Marcus. When he was six, I taught him chess. I knew he was a bright little guy, but I didn't expect to be beaten in the first game we played.

"I wouldn't do that," he said when I was about to move a knight.

I studied the board. "I don't see why not."

Carl didn't reply, but checked me two moves later.

"Beginner's luck," I said. But I never beat him, and he quickly got tired of playing me.

"You're scary, Carl," I told him, after he checked me in four moves. I'd had no trouble whipping Danny and David.

∞

To no one's surprise, Carl got into programming. After graduating from Stanford, he entered their Ph.D. program in computer engineering. But he left after a couple of years. I asked him why he was dropping out.

"I don't want to waste my time three days a week trying to teach dummies," he said.

"You're talking about computer science majors at Stanford, right?"

"Yeah, and some wannabes."

"I don't think most people would consider them dummies."

"Why should I care what most people think?"

"You should try teaching intro to world history some time."

"I'd rather slit my wrists."

Carl joined a couple of guys who were producing educational software. He designed a program to teach math to K-6 students, and it was hugely successful. The partners bought out a rival that produced children's games, and scored with a couple of these. Carl loaded up on the shares of other Silicon Valley companies he liked. I never discussed his income with him, but it was pretty obvious from his lifestyle that he'd become not just a multi-millionaire, but a rich one.

Carl had a mansion in Los Gatos, a house in Laurel Canyon, the rent from which was probably double my salary, half a condo at Lake Arrowhead, and a farm house in Provence. But his real passion was food and wine. His cellar in Los Gatos would have been the envy of many upscale restaurants. While Carl was an excellent chef, he was passionate about fine dining. With fellow-foodies, he visited France each year, eating at several Michelin three-stars. He thought nothing about flying anywhere in this country for dinner.

One year, my wife's sister Donna and her husband Nino invited Angela and me to join them for a weekend in Vegas. They'd cover everything. I hadn't been there since I was a kid and Angie was mildly curious, so we flew out and stayed with the Corellis at the then-new Venetian. The last night we had an early dinner at B & B. Everyone seemed to know Donna and Nino, including the maitre d', who explained that Mario Batali was out of town and would be sorry to hear he missed them. When the entrees had been cleared and what seemed like the tenth woman had come up to our table and shrieked, "Di! You look marvelous!", I spotted my brother wending his way toward the back.

"Carl," I yelled. "What are you doing here?"

"What are *you* doing here is the question."

I reintroduced him to Nino and Donna. They'd met at our wedding reception.

He explained that he and his friends, two guys and a woman who had walked on to their table without waiting to be introduced, were eating at Mario's tonight and Bouchon tomorrow. He wanted to see how Batali stacked up against Thomas Keller. I didn't tell him that someone else would be doing the cooking at B & B.

In a fraternal mood, I phoned Carl the next day while we were in the airport.

"So how was your dinner last night?"

"Great. It better have been. We spent over $5000."

I was floored. "How can you spend over $5000? There were just four of you, right?"

"It's not hard if you choose the right bottles of wine. I've seen parties of four spend twenty-five, thirty thousand."

"God, Carl, that's more than some people make in a year."

"Those people don't eat at B & B or Bouchon."

❧

Carl had walked into B & B–and presumably Paul Bocuse's and Alain Ducasse's eateries in France–dressed as he always did: jeans, a t-shirt, and sandals. As a concession, his curly, shoulder-length blond hair was tied back in a pony-tail, and he had slipped on a sports coat over the t-shirt. The sandals were a particular point of honor. Carl had gotten kicked out of high school for wearing them, and had countered with letters from doctors and lawyers, and of course had gotten his way.

My brother made it his business to be truculent with any authority figure, especially one in uniform. At least twice he'd been detained by TSA.

Carl was, of course, a self-proclaimed Libertarian, and I'd overheard a couple of exchanges with Danny over the years. Danny was an organizer, not an ideologue, but occasionally he'd rattle off a line or two from the Democratic playbook. Carl would cut him off with a single sentence.

When Danny once started going on about empowering the disempowered, Carl announced, "The masses are asses." When Danny started extolling Clinton-care, Carl listened for a minute, then asked, "You want hospitals to be run like the post office?" Once, when I was speculating on what it was exactly that Danny did for a living, Carl jabbed his hand impatiently. "Look," he said, "he's just another red-white-and-blue collar criminal."

The encounters between the brothers were few and far between. Carl boycotted anything that took place in a synagogue or church, so he missed the occasional wedding, bar mitvah, and funeral the rest of us attended, though he'd show up once in awhile at the reception afterward. He went to the brunch my parents threw for Angie and me after we got married, but took a pass on the shmucks' receptions. The last time we were all together was when he stopped by the house briefly after a memorial service for my dad. I heard him exchange unenthusiastic "Hey, how you doin's" with D and D.

There'd been no wedding reception for Carl. We speculated about his sexual orientation and tastes, but the evidence either way was pretty meager. We never heard about a girlfriend or boyfriend. He looked like a lot of computer guys, half-biker, half-nerd. No tattoos, no chains around the neck, but you might give him a wide berth crossing the street at 3:00 a.m. He was short, stocky, and troll-like, and had an intimidating stare. It could just mean that he was concentrating on some programming problem

55

from earlier in the day. Or it could mean that you'd picked up a scallion instead of a shallot, as he'd requested.

I tried to coax him into explaining how he had gone about programming Math Gremlin and Zambonis, but he refused to try to simplify what he did. I learned, however, that Larry Ellison was an asshole, Steve Jobs a jerk, Scott McNally worse, but Bill Gates was OK, though Carl couldn't say the same about Bill's software.

CHAPTER 6

Leonard and Ruth, Sophie and Marike

What kind of parents had raised such an unattractive brood?

Dad and Mom were Leonard Marcus, a cardiologist, and Ruth Stern Marcus, a former high-school English teacher. Leonard was tall, thin, scholarly-looking, and detached. The scholarly look was deceptive. I never saw him read a book, only medical journals.

I have no doubt he was an excellent doctor, but the Law of Fathers before the '80s decreed that the last thing you wanted to do was talk to your kids. We respected him, but didn't like him much.

Dr. Marcus was a busy guy. He bolted down his food in silence, a habit he'd acquired as an intern, and retired to *JAMA* and *The Lancet* in his study. Before dinner started, he always called his exchange and told them "Hold it for 'e's," emergencies. Dad was jovial over the phone, unlike in real life. When we got a call during dinner, we were taught to spring up and get it, and quiz the woman at the other end to make sure it was indeed an emergency.

Leonard was uncoordinated–he never tossed a ball with us– uninterested in sports, and uninterested in literature or history, though he dutifully went to plays and concerts with my mother. The Mark Taper Forum and the Dorothy Chandler Pavillion were his schul. But culture was my mother's religion, and dad just went along. He lived for his work.

As long as we were getting good grades and staying out of trouble, he was not curious about us. And yet I have photos of him when I was one, two, and three, where he seems happy to have been a father. In one I'm up on his shoulders, and he's holding my hands and beaming up at me.

∽

Unlike my brothers, I had a surrogate dad for several days a year. This was my father's junior partner, Mel Kravitz. Mel's father, Sol, had founded the firm right after World War II. A burly, shaggy-haired, outdoorsy guy, Mel had married the office's stunning receptionist, Charlene. Sol was furious. Mel and Charlene had two girls, and the ex-receptionist, a Baptist from Little Rock, raised them as Jewish princesses. Debbie and Lisa weren't about to get dirty or wet.

So I was invited to go hiking with Mel in the Hollywood Hills, in Bronson, Topanga, and Malibu Canyons. He taught me how to sail, off Marina del Rey. For some reason, Danny, David, and Carl were never asked along. "Dr. Marcus," Mel would say to my dad, "I'm going sailing Sunday, and I'd like to borrow Jonathan for the day." Twice we went camping in the Eastern Sierra and one July we did the Yosemite High Camp loop. Mel knew all the birds, trees, and wild flowers, and tried, without much success, to teach me the calls and how to identify the flora.

Mel didn't talk a lot on the trail, except to point things out. But once when we were camping at Lake Ediza, at the foot of the Banner and Ritter range, he told me that when his dad had been diagnosed with cancer of the gallbladder, Sol had taken a dozen cyanide capsules. Mel said he had his own bottle at the office in case he ever got a similar diagnosis, but that he'd prefer to die in the Sierra, under the stars. He didn't like the idea of rangers having to haul his body out, but that's the way he wanted to go.

And so he did. When he saw the scans showing that he, too, had advanced gallbladder cancer, he drove to the Shadow

58

Lake-Thousand Island Lake trailhead and managed to walk to Ediza. From there he continued up to Iceberg Lake, just below Mt. Ritter, took the cyanide, plunged into the chilly water, and swam to the middle of the lake. His body was never recovered.

I learned this plan in a sealed letter he left for me, along with his worn copies of Starr's *Guide*, Philip Muntz's *California Mountain Wildflowers*, and Genny Shumaker's *Mammoth Lakes Sierra*. Charlene also forwarded to me Mel's Eagle Scout badges and a certificate from the Sierra Club, whose board he'd served on in the days when the club was interested only in preserving the Sierra. Mel's note also urged me to become a doctor, "a most rewarding vocation." The advice, which he'd given me a couple of times sailing and hiking, came too late. I was already a grad student in the history department at Princeton.

My mother had given me a push in that direction. When I'd developed a passion for biographies of historical figures, Mom supplied me with books. She encouraged me to read the great Victorian novelists, and their Russian and French contemporaries. Sometimes she'd read them along with me. Several times she helped me write English papers in high school: "Nature in *Return of the Native*," "Whiteness in *Moby Dick*." Most things are learned best by working alongside someone who knows what they're doing, and this is true of writing. She'd ruthlessly critique my drafts, pointing out what was redundant, illogical, ambiguous, or clichéd.

The obverse side of Mom's love of literature and biography was her hatred of Hollywood. Her dad had been in the film industry, and she'd been an extra in movies and had small speaking parts. But her face reddened and her eyes narrowed when she spoke about the vulgarity of the people she worked with and the trash they produced. We never went to movies together as a family. She didn't enforce her boycott on us, and my brothers and I were permitted to go to most of the movies our contemporaries saw, but it was made clear to us that the actors were nothing like the characters they portrayed, and that most were shits in real life. The Marcuses were the very last among their friends and relatives to get a TV, and the hours we could watch were rationed. We were each allowed three shows a week.

Dad was always disengaged, but mild-mannered. Mom swung from intimacy to coldness. One evening on a vacation, I think everyone else had gone out for ice cream, my slightly drunken mother started telling me about her two half-brothers from her dad's first marriage. They'd moved to upstate New York. She was very fond of the younger brother. He was so witty, she said, so droll. Then she got going on all the men who had proposed to her. I asked why she had said "no" to each. "Because I wanted to have you, sweetie," she said, hugging me tightly.

But these moments were few. For days on end I would be frozen out. Ruth would become furious over some transgression—spilling my milk, being late for a flute lesson, getting a B- in math—and the hostility would linger. Sometimes the rages seemed to be connected to Mom's quarrels with my grandmother.

Sophie Stern was the next to youngest child of a Viennese journalist, the son of a rabbi. He had married the daughter of a prominent Catholic politician. The reb and the *Ratsherr* had both forbidden the match, and the couple had eloped to Paris, and then headed for New York. Sophie's curly blond hair came from some Polish cavalryman. Her mother was a brunette.

Sophie's pretty little sister Selena married into the Schenk family. Nick ran MGM and Joe United Artists and then Twentieth Century Fox, so every unemployed relative got a studio job during the Depression. My grandfather held out until his company went belly-up in 1936.

Mort Stern had owned a firm that manufactured women's lingerie. Even after he had a dozen employees and his own sales rep, he still went out on the road himself, telling my grandmother he wanted to keep up his personal relations with some of the buyers. No doubt he did, said my mother, and with plenty of other

60

women. He sent my mom postcards of himself from studios in hotels in Cleveland, Chicago, St. Louis, and Kansas City.

Once upon a time Mort had sent postcards from the same hotels to Sophie. On the back were scrawled passionate declarations of his love for her, sometimes in rhyming couplets. This was a little indiscreet, as he was still married to his first wife. When my mother once asked him why he'd stopped writing cards to her mom, he'd told her, "After you catch a streetcar, you stop running."

Mort took to showbiz. My grandfather was assistant director for a few Fox films–the guy who yelled "quiet on the set" and "cut." Eventually he was allowed to direct some Spanish-language pictures and a couple of low budget Westerns.

He divorced my grandmother within a few years after moving to LA and married a Latina starlet a month later. When Mort died a year before I was born, having choked on his vomit, he was about to head to Vegas to marry wife number four.

Despite Mort's bad example, Leonard and Ruth never dispensed any wisdom themselves, never told us what was right and what was wrong, what was good and what was evil. This was left to Shalom Sunday School. Getting "A"s was good. That was about it.

The grandmas, on the other hand, were always offering advice, Sophie in particular. I didn't mind. It was gratifying. Sophie wanted me to be the first anarchist President of the United States, and inflamed me with her hatreds. Destined for the inner circle of hell, or already residing there, were the triumvirate of Adolf Hitler, Richard Nixon, and Louis B. Mayer. But there were plenty of other evil men, Joe McCarthy, J. Edgar and Herbert Hoover, Huey Long, Martin Dies, and gaggle of other southern politicians, Henry Ford, Henry Frick, John D. Rockefeller, and other assorted plutocrats, mostly deceased, and of course the antisemites, the doubly-damned Henry Ford, Father Coughlin, Charles Lindbergh, George Lincoln Rockwell.

And there were heroes and heroines: John Reed, Emma Goldman, Eugene Debs, Norman Thomas, A. Philip Randolph, and Martin Luther King. But more important were the martyrs, Sacco and Vanzetti, Julius and Ethel Rosenberg, Alger Hiss, and the Hollywood Ten.

Sophie gave me *Spartacus, Citizen Tom Paine, The Proud and the Free*, and *The Passion of Sacco and Vanzetti*, so I learned American history, and a little Roman history, from the winner of the Stalin Peace Prize. When she came over for dinner, Grandma would bring issues of *The Nation* and *The Progressive*, the articles she wanted me to read and discuss with her highlighted with a red ballpoint pen.

I always imagined Sophie had inherited her radicalism from her journalist father, but at some point my mother set me straight. Her grandfather had been a litterateur and aesthete, the translator into Yiddish of Mallarmé, Huysmans, and Maeterlinck. It was her own flirtation with the left in the '40s, Mom claimed, that politicized my grandma. Ruth had joined the Young People's Socialist League in college, but her zeal rapidly cooled. It was Grandma Sophie who turned into a crusader, an apostle of the religion of politics.

On walks along the Pacific Palisades and over hamburgers at Fisher's in the old Town and Country, she set me straight about who ran the country and in whose interest, and why wars were fought. She also warned me about our family. You have bad genes, she said. Your great-grandfathers and their fathers were politicians and rabbis. Phonies. Grifters. Con-artists.

But I would be different. I was going to be someone important, someone who would change the world. My scalp tingled.

My other grandmother, Marike Maan, had no such grandiose plans for me, but I loved her just as much. Her father had moved from Antwerp to Denver, and owned an upscale jewelry store. Originally from Hasselt, he'd married into one of the Jewish families of Antwerp's *Beurs voor Diamanthandel*. My great-grandmother was baptized before her marriage, but when her daughter Marike married the handsome Jewish medical student she'd met as a young nurse at the National Jewish Hospital for Consumptives, she converted to his faith. My grandfather, however, was only nominally Jewish and didn't much appreciate his young wife's enthusiasm.

Nate Marcus's father and grandfather had been Hassidic rabbis—more bad blood. But after arriving in New York, Nachum, as he was called then, had gotten hold of Voltaire, Darwin, and Spencer, Charles Bradlaugh and Robert Ingersoll, and turned violently against religion. God was an unnecessary hypothesis. Nachum no more, my grandfather vowed to dedicate his life to science, not superstition, and, with like-minded friends, celebrated Yom Kippur by going out to a restaurant and ordering a ham sandwich. When he came down with TB, he was sent to a sanatorium in the Rockies, and so impressed the doctors with his intelligence and zeal, according to family legend, that he was able to get into medical school without having gone to college.

As one of a dozen or so doctors in Denver serving the Jewish community, and then the only one in Salt Lake City, Nate knew he had to be outwardly observant. He didn't mind that his wife was president of Haddassah and a pillar of the temple's sisterhood, though he wished she would leave her Judaism at the door when she returned from Temple Emmanuel.

But Grandma Marike kept a kosher home and insisted on a conventional three-hour seder with a haggadah in which God parted the Red Sea for Moses. Unlike my taciturn grandfather, Marike was outgoing and gregarious. She was also a fabulous cook, and it was a treat to go over to her house each Sunday for dinner. Her secret was lots of butter. After noodle pudding and baked chicken with corn-flake crust, we'd return home with tins of fudge squares, almond crescents, walnut meringue kisses, and orange date bars that would disappear long before we would return the cheery Christmas containers the following Sunday. The Sterns were all indifferent cooks.

While a devout Jewess, Grandma was also a Belgian nationalist and taught us the *Branbançonne*. Each Sunday, while she accompanied us on the piano, we would cheerfully pledge to give our blood "*voor Vorst, voor Vrijheid, en voor Recht,*" for king, for freedom, and the law. The song was in Flemish, Grandma told us, but she herself was not a *Vlaming* but a Limburger, and she would correct anyone who mistook her for one. Then we would sing "Hatikva."

What especially endeared her to me was that she didn't seem to care about our grades. When I got the B- that infuriated my mother, Grandma said, "That doesn't sound too bad to me."

Not that she didn't have ambitions for me. I knew she wanted me to become a doctor, like her husband and son. But she didn't push the idea. After my dad was in school, she'd resumed work as a nurse for my grandfather. His office was in the back of the house, and he remained a general practitioner when everyone else was becoming a specialist. "He was interested in g.i. problems," Grandma said. "But he didn't want to give up delivering babies."

If she didn't tout the calling, she did have a few words of advice. Small nations surrounded by menacing neighbors deserve your sympathy. Be a nice person. Make other people happy and you'll be happier yourself. Be honest. It's easier.

It all sounded simple and practical.

Above all, she always seemed so happy to see me.

When Grandma Marike died, I cried for the first time since infancy. I'd always been a stoic kid. I was in a production of South Pacific–I was one of the Frenchman's two bi-racial children–and I was standing in the bathroom trying to get the makeup off my face. I thought of how good and kind Grandma had been, and that I was never going to see her again. The tears began streaking down my cheeks.

"A man who has been the indisputable favorite of his mother keeps for life the feeling of a conqueror," says Freud. I was never sure about Mom, though she seemed to be more angry and impatient with my brothers than with me. But I knew I was the favorite of both grandmothers. The consequences, however, were a little more equivocal.

CHAPTER 7

Laura

The first time I made love with my wife's youngest sister, Laura Salvucci, it was also on a bare mattress surrounded by cardboard boxes. Laura was moving to a new apartment in Providence. This was something she seemed to do every six months.

Occasionally the move was a dramatic upgrade. This happened if she found a single professional woman looking for some help with the mortgage payments on her harbor condo, or some empty-nesters in Newport looking for a surrogate daughter. Laura seemed bright, cheerful, and amusing when you first met her. But inevitably there would be a falling out, and my sister-in-law would have to look for some less upscale digs in a hurry. Several times she wound up living out of her car for a week or more.

This move was another downgrade. Laura had been renting a nice apartment in Federal Hill, the city's Little Italy, where the lines for wood-fired pizza and roasted wings snaked around the block. She'd had a job for a couple of years as a secretary in the Brown Medical School. Laura had begun proofreading grants, then helping edit them, and her boss had encouraged her to take a class in grant-writing. But midway though the course, there'd been some rupture and she'd stormed out of the office and emailed an irate letter of resignation.

As Laura told it, her supervisors were, one after another, capricious, irrational, arbitrary, and temperamental. They made sexist remarks, even, especially, the women.

It was always a bad sign when Laura started talking longingly about the Southwest. Her recurring daydream was to move to Arizona or New Mexico. She had actually gotten out to Flagstaff once, in college. She'd returned bitterly disillusioned in two weeks. There were sexists in the Grand Canyon State. But the fantasy persisted. Santa Fe, she decided at some point, was much more *gemültlichkeit*. Then she got fixated on Sonora. When she started waxing eloquent about life among the cacti and Joshua trees, it usually meant a crisis was approaching.

Laura was an early and tireless blogger. She originally wrote under the name "Miss Divine Providence," and then switched her handle to "Lorelei." I don't know how many readers she had, but they were advised each day about the health hazards of various foods and supplements, and warned about mold and pollen, about menacing weather patterns over the Atlantic, and about the latest tactics of con artists, muggers, and rapists. Laura also passed along information she thought would amuse or enlighten. I happened to check her blog one Valentine's Day. She informed her readers that the shape of the heart derived from the head of a penis or a spread vulva. Laura also read tarot cards and cast horoscopes, and occasionally discussed the significance of the signs and symbols in the deck and in the night sky.

Though an ardent feminist, Laura's politics were not always predictable. For several weeks she was incensed about female genital mutilation in Muslim countries, and linked articles and petitions. Multiculturalism did not trump women's rights for my sister-in-law. One year, in January, she became exercised by Martin Luther King's plagiarism, and more links followed. Usually she was outraged by more conventional bête noirs: off-shore drilling, unexploded land mines, high-kill shelters, baby seal hunters, and pedophile priests.

Laura was of the school of feminism that disparaged marriage. Her "wit and wisdom" page included several cynical quotations about the institution:

"Marriage, in life, is like a duel in the midst of a battle."

"It doesn't much signify whom one marries, for one is sure to find out next morning that it was someone else."

"Marriage is the only adventure open to the cowardly."

"Love is blind, but marriage restores its sight."

"The one charm of marriage is that it makes a life of deception absolutely necessary for both parties."

Angie and I would go to Providence for a week at the beginning of each summer. A few days before one flight to PVD, Laura blogged about an article in *Parade* extolling Albuquerque as America's most livable city. "Check out the pollen count!!!" she told her readers.

So I wasn't surprised when Laura announced over pizza at my in-laws' that she was leaving her crummy apartment in a neighborhood infested by late-night revelers for the quiet and seclusion of a place in Pawtucket overlooking a cemetery.

Angela got along with Laura no better than she did with her other sisters, and didn't offer to come with me when I said I was helping Laura move the next day. Angie was meeting a friend from Brown for lunch and they were going to an exhibit at the RISD museum.

Laura and I loaded up the Impala I was renting and headed to Pawtucket. Suspecting a move might be in the offing, I'd thought about upgrading to a van.

"Of course it's not as light and spacious," Laura warned, as we pulled on to I95. It wasn't. She was renting a basement apartment across from Notre Dame Cemetery. There was a strong odor of cat piss as we clambered down the rusted iron steps to a subterranean concrete storage area. Next to Laura's door was a row of garbage cans and a rack with mops, rakes, and snow shovels. The wall was mossy and there were puddles on the ground. The interior was just as depressing. Sunlight filtered through only the upper third of the dingy windows. There was a distinct fetid smell, and I gave Laura a quick look as we put down our boxes.

"First thing I'm going to do is paint over this pukey green paper," she declared. "The landlord said it's OK."

"You might want to strip it first," I said, tugging on a detached piece next to the door.

"And pick up some lamps," she said. "I can turn this place around in a weekend."

Laura was silent on the way back. Overhead, dark clouds began rolling in. The storm broke just as I pulled into the nearest available space. Parking was the big drawback of the place in Little Italy, and the closest space was three blocks from Laura's apartment. "I should have dropped you off," I said, as we stepped out into the driving rain.

"No, no, I love storms," she shouted. Thunder crashed directly above us, and Laura grabbed my hand. "Let's go."

We were both soaked by the time we got back to the apartment. Laura turned on her boombox. "White Bird in a Golden Cage" started up again. A favorite of hers, this was the anthem we'd packed to.

"Listen," she said, "I think I've got something you can change into. There's a pair of baggy overalls in one of these boxes."

I laughed. Laura was about 5' 2". "I doubt very much if they'd fit," I said. "Don't worry, my clothes'll dry after awhile."

"Well, I'm gonna change. Shut your eyes. Or don't."

"I'll just go into the living room," I said. She grabbed my hand and pulled me close. And the next second we were over the edge. I was holding her tight, my mouth pressed against hers.

Of course I saw the red warning lights flash. Of course I heard the good angel on my right shoulder expostulating furiously. But the devil had slid down my wet shirt and was tugging on my fly.

I helped Laura peel off her blouse. She reached behind and undid her bra. "You like?" she asked.

"Sure," I said.

"Jon," she said, "you're the love of my life. You know that, don't you?"

I gulped.

We embraced, sat down on the edge of the mattress, then lay down, still clutching each other tightly. We were both frantic with desire, but there was a slow, surreal feel to the lovemaking, as if we were underwater. I barely had the presence of mind to ask if she was using birth control. She nodded.

I came first and helped her come afterwards. Her orgasm was the loudest and longest I'd ever provoked.

Did she look like Angela? Of course, even if she didn't sound like her. Laura had the same large, heavy-lidded eyes, but they were a little too close together and she was slightly cross-eyed. She had the same features, the small Roman nose and large elfin ears. Laura was shorter than Angie, and heavier, with wider hips and thicker thighs, though smaller, more spherical breasts. She wore her thick, lustrous black hair in a long shag cut, where Angela's was short. Even with her salmon pink plastic glasses, Laura looked waif-like. My wife always looked as if she was about to make a wisecrack. And Laura was six years younger than her sister.

I noticed blood on the mattress. "Your period?" I asked.

"I'm a virgin. Or was."

"Jesus Christ," I whispered. "You seemed tight, but I thought...."

I'd never slept with a virgin before. They were few and far between at Berkeley. My high school girlfriend had been one, of course, but I had barely rounded second base with Helene. On top of everything, this was not especially welcome news.

"But you said you're on birth control."

"I am, but it's for my auto-immune system."

We stared at each other, our foreheads touching. Laura had the most beatific smile. "Oh, Jonny, I've wanted this for so long."

71

"Me too."

I'd be lying if I said I hadn't contemplated sex with Laura, but, I'd always thought, in an idle, dispassionate, academic way. Angela was the junior high school boy's daydream: the cute, skinny girl with large, pendulous breasts. But at some point I'd acquired a taste for less well-endowed *belles laides*, and had occasionally caught myself staring at my sister-in-law when Laura–and Angie–weren't looking.

"You're wonderful in bed. You have such a nice body," I told her as I admired it. "So why haven't you shared it til now?"

I'd asked lightheartedly, but she scowled and I could see this had not been a good question.

"I frighten men," she said.

"I don't see why," I said quickly. "You're bright, funny, pretty."

Laura just shook her head.

"Well, you don't frighten me," I lied, and kissed her.

We embraced and began caressing. "I can't," I said after a few minutes. "Maybe ten years ago."

Laura laughed. "OK, I'm hungry anyway. Let's get some dinner."

"Sure. But let me call Angie."

At the mention of her sister's name, Laura looked serious.

When I got off the phone, she hugged me tightly and whispered, "How long should we wait to get married after you divorce Angela."

I must have looked stricken.

Laura smiled brightly and said, "Just kidding."

We had dinner at Andinos. I could do a short guidebook on romantic Italian restaurants to take your sisters-in-law to before and after you sleep with them.

"I can't move into that place," Laura told me over the antipasto.

"Of course not. Did you sign a contract?"

Laura nodded.

"OK, let me talk to the manager tomorrow. How much do you need to stay where you are?"

"Jonny, I would never ask you for money!"

But we talked it over, discussed her job prospects, and by the time the zabaione arrived, not only was my sister-in-law my lover, she was my mistress.

⁓

After dinner, we retrieved the stuff we'd brought to Pawtucket and made love again.

This time I took a shower afterward.

Laura had started to unpack her books while I was in the bathroom. In our violent embrace before I left, I bumped the little case beside the door. From among Laura's feminist classics, *Sisterhood is Powerful* tumbled to the carpet. I slid it back between *Our Bodies, Our Selves* and *Sexual Politics*.

⁓

I can't calculate the exact proportions of dread, terror, and desire in my relationship with my bi-polar sister-in-law. Wendy was reasonable, discreet, careful. Laura was none of these. I sometimes thought that a part of me wanted Danny to know I was sleeping with his wife. Naturally, no part of me wanted Angela to know I was having sex with her little sister. I was riding the tiger with Laura. I couldn't get off. But this didn't mean I didn't enjoy the ride when I shut my eyes. Which was most of the time.

Was it simply that the forbidden fruit was sweeter? Was danger an aphrodisiac? But I'd always considered myself risk-aversive. What had happened?

And the attraction didn't fade over time, as I thought it would. The honeymoon can go on and on for adulterers who live a thousand miles apart.

I joined the New England and Mid-Atlantic Associations of British Studies and the Victorian Studies Society, and started going to their conferences. I had no professional reason to go to a conference, and hadn't been to one in years. I told Angie I wanted to see Lee Matlock, a grad school buddy, and Marv Pasternak, a friend from WFU who'd gotten a job in Boston, as well as my ancient dissertation advisor Warren Kipper, a dutiful conference attendee. I revised a couple of papers so old and boring that no one would possibly remember them. I even went to the AHA when it was in the northeast, something I vowed I'd never do after I landed the job at St. Pete.

So our rendezvous were usually in New York or Boston. Though she lived only three hours away by train, Laura had been to Manhattan just once, to see the Rockettes with her Girl Scout troop. I had the pleasure of introducing her to the Met and Frick collections, the Morgan Library and the NYPL, Central Park and Fifth Avenue, the Cloisters, the Village, etc. I tried not to play the pedant and truly enjoyed Laura's exuberance. Her responses were sometimes flaky, sometimes acute, seldom predictable. We were always tourists, people with no past and no future.

I tried to discourage public displays of affection, but this always upset Laura and I gave up after awhile. Angie and I didn't know anyone in New York, and Laura's few friends never ventured into the city. Ange refused to read her sister's blog, and so missed Laura's aperçus on New York and Boston, which roughly coincided with my conferences.

⁂

One bright, cold January day, we went for a long walk in Central Park. Laura was in particularly high spirits, prancing along the trail that snaked up to the base of Belvedere Castle. When we climbed to the upper balcony, we discovered that we were the only people on the terrace. Laura and I embraced passionately. An older couple came up and beamed at us. My sister-in-law always wore a gold band on her ring finger for our assignations. When she suggested we go shopping together for a ring, I turned her down.

We stopped for hot chocolate at the Loeb Boathouse restaurant, and sat hunched over an outdoor table, watching the ducks. "Obviously they stick around for the winter," Laura said. "Holden was wrong."

"He was wrong about a lot of things," I said.

We sipped our hot chocolate in silence for a minute.

"You ever wonder what ex-rock stars do all day?" Laura asked.

"Not really," I said. "I suppose most of them hang in there. Even if it means a gig at a Holiday Inn in Indianapolis. What else can they do? But I guess the supernovas just sit by the pool and track their investments."

"What about prostitutes?" said Laura. "What do you think happens to them when they hit their sixties?"

I told her I had no idea, but that, like the rock stars, they could probably hang in there, especially with the internet. Then I said, "I suppose the brighter ones get married at some point."

"Not necessarily the brighter ones," said Laura. "You have some whipped cream above your lip." And she leaned over and licked it off.

❦

We headed for the Frick. We'd been there before, but it had always been crowded. Today, a late Thursday afternoon, we had the Fragonards to ourselves.

"The Progress of Love" is not overtly sensual. If Boucher had painted the panels, there would have been a lot more pink flesh. The lovers in the four paintings are like little porcelain figures in shimmering silk against the dark, billowing foliage. After "The Pursuit," where the frightened girl rises from her bench in alarm, arms raised, comes "The Meeting." The maid has been dismissed, and the would-be lover is perched on the wall of the garden, about to hop down. The girl, arms outspread again, but lowered, glances anxiously back to make sure no one is looking. In "The Lover Crowned" the girl holds a laurel wreath over the boy's head. He looks up at her adoringly, hands on her lap. The garden bursts with flowers. In the final scene, the lover, now clad in white, leans up against the girl, his head on her shoulder, his arm around her waist.

Laura bought a post card of the last panel, pulled a pen out of her bag and wrote something on it. She handed the card to me as we walked out of the Frick. "Brother in law. Lover in life." We kissed in the bright sunlight and walked hand in hand to Fifth Avenue.

As we waited for the light to change, I dropped her hand to put on my sunglasses. A taxi screeched to a halt next to us. Laura's sister Donna lowered the rear window. "Laur, Jon, what are you dong here?"

"I'm here for a British Studies conference," I said. "Laura came in for the afternoon."

The conference actually was in New York, and I'd told Angie that her sister was coming into the city after lunch, and having dinner with me.

Laura hadn't put on her gloves yet. I saw her thrust her left hand into her jacket pocket. Had Donna noticed the ring?

"Can I give you guys a lift somewhere?"

"No, no, we're fine," I said. "We were about to walk in the Park."

"Great. Well, enjoy the Apple."

Laura waved as the taxi pulled away. She turned back to me. "I want to live in a Fragonard painting."

I exhaled. "Don't we all."

When she grabbed me around the waist after we'd crossed the street, I looked behind before I put my arm over her shoulder.

∽

Did Laura feel toward Angela anything like the antipathy I felt for Danny? Not quite, but she didn't have fond feelings for her sisters.

76

She'd been a mistake, born six years after what was supposed to have been the last child. Did her mom lose the rhythm? Or did her dad want to take one last shot at having a son, and fail to pull out as he'd promised? These were not questions I could ask the Salvuccis.

But rather than treat the new arrival like a living doll, someone to fuss over and play with, the older sisters, each less than a year and a half apart, ignored her, according to Laura, and when they didn't ignore her, they tormented her.

She had a lot of grievances. "They were always playing tricks on me," she said. "They tried to get me to eat yucky things. They used to dig holes in the back yard and cover them with branches and leaves, and try to get me to step on the leaves. They called them Laura-traps. They made me act as a croquet wicket when they played. Once they made me hold up the side of the badminton net."

There were other complaints. "They'd take something I really loved, Alex, my Teddy Bear, and toss it back and forth. I'd run from one to the other like some crazy animal. They would say I had the cooties and would run away from me. I'd chase after them, but they were too fast. Thanks to them I was really unpopular at school. The other kids called me the cootie bug." Laura was almost crying.

She blew her nose. "And they were always reporting me to Ma. Like when I wet the bed. I'd beg Angela to help me change the sheets, but she would always go right to Ma first thing in the morning and tell on me."

"Well, how about when you reached puberty," I asked. "Didn't they help you out, you know, offer some sisterly advice?"

She shook her head. "They were so mean. Once, when I was twelve, Angie and Donna told me to go up to this guy down the block I had a crush on, Tony Ferrara, and ask him if he wanted to see someone named Mike Hunt. Tony was sitting on his porch steps and I went up to him and said, 'My sisters want to know if you want to see Mike Hunt.' He gave me a funny look and asked me to repeat what I'd said. Then he started cracking up. 'Sure,' he said. I didn't get it. I didn't know the word 'cunt.' I kept saying 'What's so funny? What's so funny about Mike Hunt?'"

"That's so nasty," I said. "It's hard to believe."

"They made me feel ugly. They called me the Kookalootz. I think they still do."

Laura was right. Angela had told me how crazy her sister had been, racing around like a little fury, and always a pariah at school. She hadn't described any incitements.

Laura later gave me this analysis of her sisters: "Marie was the conventional one, Donna the pretty one, Angie the smart one, and I was the weirdo."

It turned out each of the Salvucci girls had a different take on her sisters.

Marie: "I was the only responsible one. I still am."

Donna: "Marie was the good girl. I was the bad girl."

Angela: "Donna and I got out. Marie and Laura never left home."

If leaving home meant leaving the Church, this was not quite accurate. Marie went to St. Adalbert's every Sunday and Donna went to church on Easter and Christmas and when she was back in Providence. It was Angie and Laura who were lapsed. But whereas Ange was a laodicean ex-Catholic, Laura railed against the Vatican in her blog, and excoriated predatory priests and corrupt bishops. I'd heard lovers whisper " Jesus" when they came, but no one, before Laur, had ever bellowed "Jesus, Mary, and Joseph" five times.

∽

Laura seemed to be doing better after the affair began. I'd worried that the mood swings might become more frequent and violent, and, of course, that there might be high melodrama: threats, rages, tearful reconciliations. But there weren't–for awhile.

I urged her to write a letter of apology to her supervisor at work and to meet with the woman. She did, got a decent letter of recommendation, and was able to get another secretarial job in someone else's lab at the med school.

I nudged her to resume the grant-writing course, but this didn't appeal to her. Laura had majored in poli sci at University of Rhode Island, but had taken a lot of math and science and decided to go back part-time and get a BA in biology. She got all As in her classes. But then she seemed to lose focus. I tried to interest her in graduate programs. I brought her information on the GREs. I suggested that she apply for an internship or volunteer to work in a lab, so she could get some experience and a line on her c.v. She seemed uninterested. I wrote to programs in New England. The catalogues and applications wound up in a shoebox in Laura and Angie's old room at her parents', the envelopes unopened.

There came a moment, inevitably, when Laura seriously asked me to divorce Angela and marry her. Unfortunately, it took place in Knave, the swanky bar at Le Parker-Meridien in Midtown. Conversations stopped at the tables around us even before Laura referred to Angie as "my sister." I quickly paid—in cash—and pulled her back to our hotel around the corner. There were tears, accusations, recriminations, and then apologies and passionate love-making.

I encouraged Laura to go out with what were once called eligible bachelors. I wasn't prepared to leave Angela. But I couldn't let Laura go. I was hooked.

Seeing her walk down the platform at Grand Central, with her slightly pigeon-toed gait, drove me into a frenzy of lust. And Laura loved me. And when I was with her, I was convinced I loved Laura, too. I couldn't say the same about Angie. As for her love for me, I was pretty sure it had expired years earlier.

✍ ✍ ✍

CHAPTER 8

Angela

Angela and I had gotten married when we were both graduate students at Princeton. I'd been living with a shy, earnest, sandy-haired girl with wire-rim glasses, Tassie Radford. Her dad was a chemist and her mom a biologist. She'd been christened Kay, but had always been called "Tassie"—short for potassium. The two professors had not been pleased when their daughter had majored in English, and were even less thrilled when she started dating a Marxist historian with long hair and an attitude. We met at the Graduate College, the grey limestone castle Woodrow Wilson had built—no expenses spared—on a bluff overlooking a golf course. Modeled on an Oxford college, with oak-paneled studies and a dining hall that looked like the interior of a gothic cathedral, the GC was, for a devout Anglophile like Tassie, the perfect backdrop for a student romance.

We moved off-campus the next year, to a little apartment on Allen Street. Then one day at an English department party I met a first-year Ph.D. student called Angela Salvucci. She seemed everything Tassie wasn't, short, dark, wiry, sensual, and dangerous. When I asked her how she liked Tigertown, Angela laughed and said it spooked her. All that orange and black everywhere—every day seemed like Halloween.

One night I left Firestone early and had a drink with Angela in Debasement Bar at the grad college. We wound up back at her room and made love under the moonlight pouring through her dormer window. Eventually, there were terrible scenes with Tassie. I vowed never to go through a break-up again.

Angela and I tied the knot the next year and moved into married student housing. The stresses of combining grad school and marriage created a certain camaraderie among the harassed denizens of Butler apartments, the spartan barracks build for returning veterans in the late '40s and never replaced. Angie completed her general exams on schedule. I took an extra year. We moved to London to research our respective dissertations, she at the British Library, then still in the grand rotunda in the British Museum, and I mostly at the LSE. We fell in with a group of entertaining American grad students and hardly ever talked to any English men and women—they were still thick on the ground in London then—apart from archivists, shopkeepers, and barmaids.

After two years of academic vagabondage, where we each had adjunct positions, we both managed to land tenure-track jobs in the Tampa Bay area, she at Western Florida University, me at University of St. Petersburg. We bought a home in Elysium Hills, over the border in Packer County, where the developers were opening up a new subdivision every month and prices were reasonable. It meant that while Angie had a twenty minute drive south—it became forty minutes after the pastures along the route turned into mini-malls—I had an hour's commute over the Franklin Bridge, beyond the city of St. Pete to USP, close to the Gulf.

The plan was that I would publish my way over to WFU. I got to know some of the historians, taught a continuing ed course there, and things looked promising. But when the British historian, Ben Carter, retired, the College of Liberal Arts closed the line. I was offered a job at a branch campus, but turned it down. The commute was well over an hour. When the position did reopen at the main campus, I still hadn't published a book, and had no real shot at the job.

Angela, meanwhile, had crossed to the dark side. After getting tenure, she'd become chair of the department, then was appointed an associate dean, teaching one class a year. Though she could still occasionally laugh at the bureaucratese of memos from the WFU ayatollahs, being an administrator seemed to scotch her sense of humor.

Then there was the time apart. Between the commutes, her meetings, and my teaching schedule, we may as well have been living in different cities during the week. After Amy was born, Angie went right back to work, and, as soon as Aim was eligible, we enrolled her in Discovery Day Care in the School of Education at WFU, where she was peered at all day by education majors sitting in a viewing pavilion behind a one-way mirror. The toddlers, doddering around under their own power, seemed incredibly gifted and mature. When Amy became one herself, we sent her to a nearby Montessori school, where she became a friendly, helpful Montessori child, a whiz on her abacus and an eager reader by age four.

Angela's work at the dean's office increasingly encroached on our weekends. We stopped going to concerts and operas at the Performing Arts Forum. We stopped sitting together on the lanai after dinner, admiring the lurid Florida sunsets. Sex became infrequent and perfunctory.

⟡

But what really drove us apart was the dogs. Amy had been pleading for one for years. I'd grown up with dogs, and vigorously seconded the motion–something not appreciated by Angela. Eventually Aim wore her down, and we adopted a golden, Nick. Angie and Amy had carefully researched the breeds. I'd suggested a German shepherd but was outvoted. Angela was not happy with an animal in the house, and for at least a year Nick had to stay in his crate when she was home. "Why does he have to watch me all the time?" she complained. "Why does his breath stink? Why does he have to breathe so loudly?"

I fell in love with Nick and with goldens. He and I spent hours together in the back yard and the lanai. He was an eager retriever of tennis balls and would charge after twenty-five throws before looking at me pleadingly, holding the ball in his mouth instead of dropping it at my feet. When I swam, he would race back and forth, lunging at the spray. I'd let him take a lap at the end.

I got involved with a golden rescue group and Amy and I began fostering homeless dogs. We eventually adopted a couple of our fosters, Molly and Lucy, a mother and daughter. Molly was an affectionate, overweight couch potato, but Lucy must have taken after her dad. Part sight hound, she was a more avid retriever of tennis balls even than Nick. No golden I'd seen had been half as speedy and tireless as Lucy. She was also an enthusiastic greeter, bounding up to me whenever I returned home and planting wet kisses on my face. Lucy was also a petty thief, raiding Amy's room to steal socks, flip-flops, and the occasional bra, which she brought back to her dog bed, but never chewed up. There was also no counter-cruising, no jumping on the furniture, no destruction of cushions and pillows, and regular and orderly pooping. The goldens may as well have been Montessori graduates. Even Molly would not touch food on the coffee table. It had just taken a few stern "no"s and some heartfelt "good dog!"s.

Angie was not happy with the fostering, but was again moved by Amy's pleas. Aim had taken a short course in dog-training and swore she would assume full responsibility for the fosters. We had Nick certified as a therapy dog, and Amy and I would take him down to the children's wing at St. Joe's on Saturdays. I told Angela that all the dog work was good for Aim's self-esteem and c.v. Still, we'd occasionally have two fosters at a time, and with five large dogs in a less than 2000 square-foot house, it sometimes felt like wall-to-wall goldens.

Unfortunately, Lucy started taking exception to the fosters, nipping one and getting into a ferocious fight with another. I got an ultimatum from Angela: if I brought another foster home, she was moving out.

✌

When unadoptable goldens were brought into the county shelter, I'd pull them for the rescue group. Shortly after Angela's démarche, three huge siblings turned up. They'd escaped their yard a couple of times and had killed several cats and a small dog. The owner didn't want to pay the fine. My rescue wouldn't touch them. I went down to the shelter and took the dogs outside on a leash, one by one. They were sweet, friendly guys, two brothers and a sister. I was sure the killings had been pack behavior, and when they were separated, neutered, and trained, the dogs would be great companions. I called and emailed around the Southeastern golden rescue network and a couple of other rescues eventually came through.

Then I worked on transportation. I pulled the last dog out the day before he was going to be put down. It was two days before Thanksgiving, there was no space at any kennel or vet, so I bought a crate from Petco, gave the dog a Capstar, and stuck him out on the lanai. Our dogs got along splendidly with the visitor, even Lucy. But Angela was furious and spent the night at the home of another associate dean, Sara Wexler. We had a frosty Thanksgiving, and afterward Angela told me that if the dog wasn't out of the house on Monday, she would be staying with Sara. "But Ange," I said, "you never go out on the lanai anymore." Watching sunsets after dinner in the summer, sipping cognac (me) and amaretto (Angie), used to be the prelude to love-making.

I was able to board the dog on Monday, and transferred him to another rescue a couple of days later. But I stayed on Angie's shit list. We didn't go to Sarasota over Christmas as we usually did. We didn't make love for several weeks. Angie seemed abrupt and short-tempered. We spent less and less time together.

When Amy went off to college the next year, Angela began sleeping in her room. I was snoring too loudly, she said, and thrashing around in my sleep. It was probably not a good sign that I didn't mind. The pluses, the chance to sprawl across the center of the queen bed and leave the toilet seat up, outweighed the goodnight kiss and hug. Spontaneous love-making late at night or early in the morning was only a hazy memory.

⁓

But Angie and I had once been so much in love. The year we were in London, we took three trips to Venice. Ange was working on William Morris, but had always been interested in John Ruskin. That demented genius was addicted to the *Serenissima*. With a tattered copy of *The Stones of Venice* and a new *Blue Guide*, we headed south in October.

Neither book had prepared us for the breathtaking splendor of the city. We were exhilarated by the fairytale palaces along the Grande Canal, the shimmering light on the water, and the wondrous stillness of a world without cars, without trucks, without velos.

Early most mornings we would walk in Piazza San Marco. Sometimes it was just us and the pigeons. Of course we couldn't afford to sit down at Florian or Quadri later in the day, but twice we had drinks by the windows in the second floor bar of the Correr Museum at the far end of the Piazza, with a magnificent view across to the basilica and the Doge's palace. The setting sun turned the Palazzo walls a luminous pink and we'd take a vaporetto across to San Giorgio for the best view.

We began eating dinner at one of the *touristica* pizzerias on the riva degli Schiavoni, across the Grande Canal from San Giorgio and Salute. It was all we could afford, but the pizzas were good and where else could you eat in Venice with such a magnificent view? Like so many waiters in Venice, our *cameriere* was fluent in five or six languages. We would talk to him in French and

German for fun. His French and German were a lot better than ours.

We couldn't get enough of the vaps. We'd ride from dawn until late at night. Once, after sharing a couple of bottles of wine, we went all the way out to the Lido. Bladders bursting, laughing hysterically, we dashed into the first bar to relieve ourselves.

Of course we saw everything we were told to by the *Blue Book*. We had the treasure room of the Basilica to ourselves late one afternoon, and admired the monstrances, chalices, and crucifixes the Venetians had stolen from Byzantium. One piece was particularly entrancing. It was an inlaid enamel bowl on which muscular, well-proportioned nude figures rested against pedestals or brandished spears. Yet it was from the 6th century AD. In a world of glittering mosaics with full frontal views of stern saints, some Byzantine artist was still paying homage to Hellenic canons, to nature, beauty, and *areté*. But we loved the mosaics, too. Standing in the center of the basilica, gazing up at the golden cupolas, and across to Jesus and the Apostles and the lovely angels with their long wings dangling, you could imagine a Christian Europe, reverent, pious.

Venice was the beneficiary and eventually the successor of the Byzantine Empire. It was by monopolizing Constantinople's trade and providing it with a navy that the city acquired its wealth. Even after it conquered the capital, Venice was still dominated by Byzantine culture. Everything in San Marco that wasn't stolen from the Greeks was designed and executed by Greek craftsman, and for centuries art in the *Serenissima* faithfully reflected Byzantine models. But then Venetian painting came into its own in the 15th and 16th centuries. We admired the Bellinis and Giogiones, but were blown away by the Tintorettos in the Scuolo San Rocco. This was before the Scuolo provided large mirrors to look at the panels on the ceiling. We lay on our backs and admired them, until the guards yelled at us.

Most of all, we loved getting lost. The *via touristica* in Venice runs from the Rialto bridge to Piazza San Marco. But if you stray from it even a few hundred feet, you can suddenly be by all by yourself. Especially wandering around the Dorsoduro, on the island across the Grande Canal, you come out onto tranquil little canals spanned by bridges with baskets of hanging flowers. The water laps against the pastel-colored buildings.

And of course we made love. Once we were inspired by the curious 18th century painting "*L'indovina*," in which a young woman appears to be explaining the facts of life to two boys, using as a model a buxom friend, with legs spread. We left the Accademia and rushed back to our hotel.

Angie and I tried to return to Venice as often as we could, avoiding the *Bianniale* years. My study was a little shrine to the *Serenissima*, with photos of San Marco at sunrise, the lion on his pedestal, gondolas in front of Salute, anonymous canals at dusk, and Tintoretto's St. Mark swooping down to free a slave.

CHAPTER 9

Marie and Donna

Angela had as little in common with her older sisters as she did with Laura. Marie was a dutiful, doleful B student, but teachers expected the worst of Angie after a year of trying to teach Donna. A shameless flirt, trailed by a pack of guys drooling over her, Donna boasted that she hadn't opened a textbook once her last two years in high school. There were a couple of decent students among her entourage, but Donna disdained to copy their homework, and when they copied it for her, didn't bother turning it in. The teen rebel was suspended several times for truancy and expelled for smoking. At home, Donna violated curfews and talked back to her parents. She left school at sixteen and moved to Manhattan. But Donna chose her lovers skillfully–the high school romeos never scored–and was able to break into modeling.

She changed her name to Diana. "'Donna' says 'white trash' or 'guinea,'" she explained. "'Donna' lives in a trailer park or a row house."

Diana Salvucci's first big success was in an ad campaign by *Seventeen* imitating the old back cover of *Cosmo*–"I guess I'm just that Cosmopolitan Girl." In a purported monologue by a typical *Seventeen* reader–who happened to look like a stunning model–advertisers were made aware of exactly how much disposable income the silly girl was prepared to throw around.

The highlight of Donna's career was probably the "Live the Fantasy" campaign of a famous perfume-manufacturer. In TV commercials and in full-page ads, she and a blond model took part in Felliniesque dream sequences, wearing very little, and sometimes no, clothing.

Donna had a strong streak of common sense and recognized that modeling careers could be short-lived. The work was grueling and not exactly intellectually challenging, and Donna was bright enough to be bored. She'd always been interested in design, worked hard on a portfolio, completed her GED, and was accepted at FIT.

The sportswear designer Nino Corelli gave a guest lecture her second semester, they spoke afterward, and Donna got a position that summer as an intern at NC, Inc. She was offered a job, and she and Nino got married less than a year later.

People not in the fashion industry assumed that Nino Corelli, like Giorgio Armani and Guccio Gucci, was Italian. But though he looked as if he'd just stepped off the via Veneto, Nino was born on Long Island, the son of a banker, and was known as Tony until his senior year at Haverford. Nino had lived in Rome for several years, and rolled out authentic-sounding "*buon giornos*" and "*arrividercis*." He and Diana had a flat there, near the American Academy, on the hill above Trastevere. They sold their enormous condo on the Upper Eastside and moved to Stamford, but Nino hung on to a rent-controlled apartment on 26th and 5th Avenue.

The conversations between the small, dapper Nino and his bulky brother-in-law Vinnie Perrino were short and sweet. "Yo, Nino." "Ciao, Vin." Vinnie was a former auto mechanic who now installed security systems.

Visits to Providence always included a barbeque at the Perrinos' and Vinnie would be turned out in a torn wife-beater and a pair of baggy shorts. Nino often came directly from work, and would show up in a $1000 linen suit. "Vinnie, put on something decent," Marie would yell, and Vin would set down the lighter fluid, trudge into the house, and return sporting a pink and green Hawaiian sportshirt over the wife-beater.

Though they collaborated against Laura, Marie and Donna had been bitter rivals growing up. At some point Marie recognized that she couldn't compete at the most important contest, the great man-hunt. She put on weight and starting wearing headbands and love beads and loose cotton dresses. Donna and Angela called her "the Hippio." Marie was notorious among her sisters for her cheapness, and the soubriquet was expanded to "the Thrifty Hippio." She began Community College of Rhode Island, but was wooed and won by Vinnie, and left to start a family.

Like Vin, I didn't have a lot in common with Nino. He was a bright guy, he'd gotten an MBA from Wharton after graduating from RISD, but as far as I know he never opened a book or went to a concert or a museum. The one thing we shared was a passion for musicals. Nino had acted right through college. My career as a "drahmie" ended before my senior year in high school. But we'd both been in productions of *My Fair Lady*. In my one starring role, my junior year, I'd played Professor Higgins. Even in high school I looked so professorial that I was cast over a couple of better singers. I'd wanted to do nothing but imitate Rex Harrison. The director had other ideas, and there was a tug of war. Nino and I enjoyed irritating the Salvucci girls by singing "I Will Never Let a Woman in My Life" and "Why Can't a Woman Be More Like a Man." In the latter, Nino, who'd actually played Freddy in a Haverford-Bryn Mawr production, bellowed the responses of Colonel Pickering perfectly.

The fashion industry is volatile, and Nino's fortunes waxed and waned. The apartment in Rome was sold, but then another was leased a year later and the Stamford palace remodeled for several hundred grand. Once Nino was approached by Sears and they discussed the possibility of a Corelli line for K-Mart. He turned them down. "For the rest of my life," he said, "everyone would spell my last name with a 'K'."

91

There was one thing missing in the glamorous life of the Corellis. I'd always imagined Donna didn't want kids, but one day Angie told me they'd been going to a fertility clinic for several months and were ready to try in vitro. This didn't work. Nino and Donna went though three more rounds, dropping another $50,000 at least, but had no luck. Angela reported that Donna had told her the nightly injections in the butt were the most painful and humiliating thing she'd experienced as an adult.

Had one or both picked up a nasty STD in their wild early 20s? Or was it some genetic defect? No one said anything, and I could no more ask than I could question the Salvuccis about the accident of Laura's birth.

So, by her own lights, Marie won in the end. She and Vinnie had four kids, Vinnie, Jr., the twins Gina and Tina, and Mikey. Apart from the personal tragedy, it seemed a loss for the human race that the handsome and clever Corellis would not reproduce themselves.

CHAPTER10

Marie and Karen

I had fallings out with Marie and with Karen. When the events I'm going to describe began, both had severed relations with me. Donna was the only sister-in-law, or ex-sister-in-law, who was speaking with me but not sleeping with me.

Mea culpa, in Marie's case. On one of our visits to Rhode Island, most of the family was gathered in Old World Pizza waiting for our order. Marie was sitting next to me and was describing in excruciating detail the Perrino vacation to the Grand Canyon. She decided that she needed to check with Mikey about when his Little League game began. She'd left her phone in the car, locked in the trunk with her purse, and I handed her mine. Instead of just punching in the number, she looked for it in my address book. There she came upon the entry "Hippio" and her home phone.

I apologized profusely. I explained that Angela had just happened to mention the old nickname to me before I'd entered her number, and so I'd written "Hippio" on the spur of the moment. I already had another "Marie" in my address book, I lied. I assured her that we never, never referred to her by this nickname. Hippio seemed mollified, and we went back to her house for dessert.

I was sure she was still out in the yard—I had just heard her order Vinnie to pick up some more ice cream—when I dumped her sickeningly sweet white cake with orange and green frosting into the kitchen sink. Angie was standing beside me as I turned on the faucet, and I said to her, "Hippio's cake is even more disgusting than usual." But Hippio had been in the little downstairs bathroom and had yelled to Vin out the window. She'd stepped into the kitchen a second before I spoke, and was standing right behind me, as I could tell from Angela's pained expression.

Thereafter I was never addressed by Hippio. She would refer to me in the third person to Angela, as in "Tell your husband we'll all meet at the DQ after Mikey's game."

"Welcome to Marie's dog house," said Vinnie.

❧

For awhile I tried to get Wendy to come with me to Mammoth Lakes, but fate always intervened. The two of us could hardly go off together by ourselves, but I'd hoped we might get some time together if we were to spend a week at Lake George with Amy and Sam. Even if Wendy and I didn't manage to make love, it would be fun to show her the trails Mel and I had hiked. It looked as if it was about to happen one June, but then Sam, who was accident-prone, broke his big toe and Wendy herself came down with the flu. Somehow David and Karen got wind of the trip and asked if they might take their places. What could I say?

I gave David a list of things he should bring and warned him there was a heavy snowpack, and he and Karen should make sure they had good, waterproof boots, and some reliable poles. When Amy and I met them at the cabin, they were both wearing bright yellow galoshes. I told them I'd meant waterproof hiking boots.

Even though we took it easy the first day, David came down with serious altitude sickness. When he developed heart palpitations, I took him to the hospital. They were pretty sure it was just the altitude, but they wanted to do an EKG and keep him overnight. David insisted Amy, Karen, and I hit the trails. We took a couple of hikes the next day without incident. Karen chattered gaily with Amy about recent novels she'd read.

The hospital wanted to keep David a second day. There was some irregularity in the EKG, and they were going to test him again. With his blessing, we headed for Little Lakes Valley early the next morning, an hour away. When we began the hike, Karen tried David on her cell. She knew he was asleep, she said, but just wanted to leave a message. She hadn't bothered trying to reach him the day before. Of course there was no signal. Karen was distressed. I told her it was hard to get a signal in the mountains. She wanted to return to Mammoth immediately. "I'd be happy to drive back here in the afternoon," she said brightly. I tried to reassure her. I told her that David knew where we were, that he was in good hands, and we should carry on, just as he'd wanted. We would go half way to the end of the trail, to Long Lake, and be back at the car before 11:30.

Karen seemed to accept this and immediately headed off down the trail. Amy and I stopped to identify wild flowers, and soon Karen was way ahead of us. There was no sign of her at Long Lake. We walked passed the lake, and I scrambled up a snowbank to a ridge to get a look ahead. A hiker on her way down assured us she'd seen no one in yellow galoshes, and we headed back.

After a couple of fruitless detours, where the trail forked to other lakes, we spotted Karen on the main trail. She'd taken a little fisherman's path to one of the lakes off the trail.

My meek and mild sister-in-law was enraged at us. We'd forced her to go on a hike she didn't want to go on. It was a perfect example of my passive-aggressive behavior, she said. I hadn't responded when she'd offered to drive back. I told her that if you head down a trail after someone reassures you, you shouldn't be surprised if they assume that you're reassured. If she wanted to go back, she should have stayed at the trail head and told me. I might have tried a second time to reassure her, but if she was not persuaded, we'd have headed back.

95

But her fury continued. I'd told her we could get a signal on the trail, she said. I looked over at Amy. Of course I had said no such thing. When I asked why she didn't wait on the trail and explain her feelings, she said first that my telling her we would be looking at flowers was a coded message that we wanted to left alone. Then she said she just wanted to get it over with. Then she said, "I thought about asking you for the car keys, but I knew what you'd say."

She raged at me all the back to Mammoth. "David and I aren't family to you," she kept yelling. "If Amy had wanted to go back, you'd go back in a heartbeat." Her long chin quivering, she told me that I'd bullied David as kid, but I was not going to bully her. Then she started telling me, for some reason, how fond she was of Angela, who despised her.

Amy had said nothing on the way back, but I could see she was appalled. After we dropped Karen off, I told her that it was the polite, obsequious, self-effacing people you had to watch out for. Doormats like Karen are seething with resentment.

David and Karen returned to LA the next day. I called, sent her a couple of emails, and then a birthday present, but got no response.

❧

A month later Wendy phoned and asked if I was OK.

"Sure," I said. "Why?"

"Well Karen told me you'd been diagnosed with a brain tumor. You had six weeks to live."

"News to me," I said.

"I didn't think so. What a sick fantasy."

Another couple of months passed, and I spoke with Wendy again. At the end of the conversation, she said, "Guess what the diagnosis is now?"

"I can't."

"You're supposed to have had seminoma and gotten a double orchiechtomy."

"What's that?"

"Removal of the testicles."

"OK," I said, and made a note to give Karen a wide berth at the next wedding, bar mitzvah, or funeral.

∾ ∾ ∾

CHAPTER 11

USP

My messy present and sordid past might have been a little easier to deal with if I'd had a real job. But I was a professor of history at a liberal arts college.

Like a lot of its counterparts, the college had given itself a promotion. Having launched graduate programs in marine biology and creative writing, it had christened itself the University of St. Petersburg.

The campus sits at the end of the western edge of the long, double-lobed peninsula that forms Tampa Bay. From the south quad you can look out over the Bay and across to the islands and keys along the Gulf Coast. Elysium Hills is northeast of Tampa, just over the Packer County Line. I must have had one of the longest commutes in the Bay area. After I got onto I275, I'd scan the horizon each morning for the traffic choppers. If one or more of those birds of ill-omen were hovering over the infamous "malfunction junction" downtown, it could be two hours.

When I started at USP, the president was a formidable woman named Margaret Hancock Van Vlack. Her reign had begun in the early '60s and she remained in charge for over three decades. Dame Margaret, as she was called, was a regal figure. Her blue-grey hair was swept up into a stiff coiffure, and she favored dark floor-length skirts, ruffled blouses, and double strands of pearls.

But there was something reassuringly grandmotherly about the half-glasses perched on the end of her patrician nose, and she took a liking to me. Though she'd acquired the Anglo-American drawl of the country's upper classes in the days of her childhood, Dame Margaret was from LA. She'd grown up in the tony Hancock Park district, east of my parents' house. She was a niece or cousin of the oil man and philanthropist Alan Hancock.

Margaret's fondness for me had its down side. She was always proposing new classes. I learned to dread a certain dreamy look in her eyes.

"Jonathan. The Byzantine Empire," she'd exclaim.

"What about the Byzantine Empire, Margaret?"

"The grandeur, the decadence." She sighed. "We must offer a course on it."

"Well it's much closer to Frank's field."

"Ah, but Jonathan, it continued until the 16th century. That's the remarkable thing about it."

"Well, the 15th century. But still, it always considered itself the Roman Empire. And its glory days were a lot earlier. Besides, I don't know any Greek, and I'm sure Frank still does."

Margaret tilted her head and gave me a confidential smile. "Jonathan. You know exactly what Frank will tell me. I would never ask him. I'm sure everything worth reading is in English."

Frank was Franklin Hutchins. I liked Frank, but Margaret was right about his range and ambitions. He was an historian of the final centuries of the Roman Empire, long before the subject came into vogue as "Late Antiquity." By then Frank had developed an obsession with the Vikings. It was a popular topic and he offered a class every year. His office was cluttered with replicas of helmets, shields, and swords. A small Viking longboat sat on top of one bookcase.

Meanwhile, Frank kept scaling back the first half of the European survey. "Well, m'boy," he'd say. "I've taken 'em to the 12th century."

"To or through, Frank?" I'd ask. Once upon a time, the second half of the course opened with the Renaissance.

The past semester, when I ran into him a couple of days before finals week, he winked and said, "Doin' the Norman Conquest tomorrow." Then he whistled a few bars of the William Tell Overture.

If Frank's slow progress meant his students were acquiring a deeper appreciation of Ancient Greece and Rome, I never saw any evidence of this. I did hear about elaborate re-enactments of Viking raids, which were always popular with the boys in class.

Frank's real interest, apart from collecting Scandinavian paraphernalia, was in constructing doll houses in his basement. Over the years, he'd put together a small village. Frank and Dottie had no granddaughters. With his white hair, bushy moustache and pink cheeks, Frank, I'd thought when I'd arrived at USP, was in his early sixties. In fact he was in his late forties and it looked as if he had no intention of retiring and devoting himself full-time to his dollhouses and his Viking hardware.

Frank and I were the European half of the history department. As at a lot liberal arts college, there were four historians. The two Americanists had to cover about 300 years, during most of which time the country was a provincial backwater. We Europeanists were responsible for closer to 3,000 years. We had to cover Ancient Greece and Rome, and now the Byzantine Empire, Medieval Europe, the Renaissance and Reformation, the Age of Exploration, the Scientific and Industrial Revolutions, the Age of Absolutism and the Enlightenment, the French and American Revolutions, Imperialism, Romanticism, Nationalism, and the rest of the unlovely 19th and 20th century isms, and a couple of world wars. Not surprisingly, Europeanists tend to view their U.S. colleagues as overprivileged and underworked. And for some crusty Europeanists, Medievalists in particular, anyone teaching 20th century America was little better than a jumped-up journalist.

Americanists are never fazed by the resentment. When the possibility of a fifth position in the department was broached, the two historians of the U.S., Emma Priestley and Richard Head, lobbied hard for a third Americanist.

Technically, Frank and I already had a third colleague, as Emma and Rick pointed out. He was Margaret's husband, Everett Van Vlack. Van taught a single course. Originally it was called "World War II," but Van focused entirely on Europe and even here he gave short shrift not only to the German conquest of the continent and to the Nazi-Soviet War, but to the Allied invasion of France as well.

Van had served as a junior staff officer under Mark Clark, and, before long, he began devoting the entire course to the invasions of Sicily and Italy. It got renamed "World War II: The Mediterranean Theater." Generations of students referred to it affectionately as "My War," then "Mark and Me," and finally, "Me and Mark." Van, who had served as a special correspondent for *Stars and Stripes* and had a fund of anecdotes, was devoted to his former chief. Students left the course with the impression that Clark had won World War II virtually single-handedly. His capture of Rome was a brilliant strategic move and broke the spirit of the Nazis.

While Van's students were learning about General Clark's preferences in toothpaste and razor blades, my responsibilities proliferated alarmingly. It didn't take much to inspire Margaret. I think the Byzantine Empire proposal was based on a coffee table book she'd idly opened at the house of one of the trustees. After a trip to India, she insisted on a course on the subcontinent. A piece of cake for any British historian, she assured me. Then Margaret caught an exhibit on Suleiman the Magnificent at the Met, and a year later I was teaching a class on the Ottoman Empire.

When Margaret retired at last, taking Van with her back to California, I was among the most relieved. She was replaced by a former Professor of Business Ethics from WFU, Guy Piccone. His trophy wife Cynthia was installed as first lady. Despite Margaret's annoying mid-Atlantic accent, she had had perfect diction. Guy had a gravelly voice and tended to mumble. He was known as "the Godfather." President Piccone, it turned out, had a little more in common with Vito Corleone than the faculty wits imagined.

A state university always has to be building something, and the Godfather was panicked by the absence of cranes and hard-hats at USP. He hit on what seemed like a brilliant scheme. USP would construct luxury condos on adjacent land along the Bay and lure wealthy retirees from the Northeast to purchase these. The selling point was to be the rich cultural environment USP provided. Residents of University Condos would have free passes to all concerts, lectures, plays, poetry readings, etc. that took place on campus.

The writing program and the music and theater departments benefitted from the Godfather's largesse. But the real estate was pricey and construction costs spiraled. These were paid for out of the university's slender endowment, and the Godfather bought near the top of the market.

It got sleazier. There were rumors about bribes to zoning com-missioners and kickbacks from contractors. The trustees had been uninquisitive. The guy had a Ph.D. in economics from Yale and an M.B.A. from Wharton, but also an M.A. from Union Theological Seminary. He must have known what he was doing, and maybe had a little help from the Fellow Upstairs. But at some point someone noticed that the endowment was about a third of what it had been when the Godfather took over. Piccone had overestimated the appetite for culture on the part the snowbirds. There was apparently not a lot of enthusiasm to see college pro-ductions of *Death of a Salesman* or to listen to the orchestra blast the *1812 Overture*, and the condos had few takers.

So the Godfather resigned under a cloud. The university cov-ered for the miscreant, and no charges were pressed. The trustees were clearly interested in getting someone as unlike Piccone as possible, and hired a whifty sociologist and ex-volleyball player named Suzanne Quiller. Her field was women in sports. Suzy Q, as she was called, had been an associate dean at a state college in Maryland. She was placed on leave after several times unintentionally sending personal emails to everyone on campus. Suzy became a humble sociologist again, more or less mastered the art of emailing, bided her time, and became a VP for Academic Affairs at a liberal arts college in Virginia. The ex-volleyball star still occasionally clicked the "reply all" button by mistake, but after Dame Margaret and the Godfather, ditziness was appealing.

Suzy wore shorts on campus and was popular with students, alums, and the trustees, who appreciated "the new enthusiasm," "the spirit and energy," and "the fresh face" in Coon Hall. No one said "the great pair of legs," but that had to have been on the mind of a few trustees.

The faculty was a little more ambivalent. Suzy's most controversial initiative was a new sign in front of campus. It was a large orange heart. In green neon above was written "University of St. Petersburg," and across the heart, in florid green script, were the words "SP i luv u." The dot on the "i" was a smiley face.

The memo announcing the sign declared that "in the age of smart phones and social media, we need to show the community and prospective students that we 'get it' and that we are a tech-savvy and forward-looking institution."

Faculty comments were predictable: "It would look vulgar in Vegas." "Next year they'll put up a cowgirl in a bikini and boots. She'll be winking and gesturing with her thumb at Coon Hall."

It's not as if the campus wasn't already an eyesore. The main building was a former luxury hotel, the Royal Moroccan. It was built in the 1890s by the entrepreneur who extended the train line from St. Petersburg to the Gulf. Now called Coon Hall, it had high, sand-colored walls, and a couple of tiled courtyards with fountains. At each of its four corners was a pseudo-minaret. But towering above the front of the building were two *Zwiebelturme*,

104

onion-shaped domes copied from the Kremlin. The architect had let his imagination run wild.

Frank Lloyd Wright had been commissioned in the '30s to design a cubist building on either side of the former hotel. These were painted to match the Moroccan, but were wildly anomalous, and their leaky roofs cost millions to repair. Still, they gave the university the right to a second entry in the National Register of Historical Places. To compound the chaos, the library, built in the '50s, was a Greek temple. This was at the insistence of its donor, the owner of a local drugstore chain.

USP was unlucky in its donors. Campus buildings included the Moody Student Center, the Kroch Gymnasium, and Cocke Hall. The latter was the location of the Women's Studies Program and its director labored manfully to switch with the Diversity Office, housed in Coon Hall. But Diversity had a suite of spacious rooms overlooking the bay, and was loathe to move. The university attempted to use the full names of the donors to designate the buildings. Coon Hall became the Charles and Merrie Coon Hall. But this was cumbersome and not much of an improvement. Finally, in internal memos, the controversial buildings were designated simply "the Humanities Building" and "the Administration Building." But the heirs of the donors were still alive and giving, and there was only so much the Godfather and Suzy Q could do.

The name of the college's athletic teams was even more distressing to the politically correct. For decades the teams were called the Moors, or the Fighting Moors, and no one had a problem with this. But by the '70s, the name had become as embarrassing as Monostratos's aria and was changed by fiat to the Moorhens. Even without the internet, St. Pete's rivals soon discovered that moorhens were also known as "river chickens" and "skitty coots." Our students agitated for a change.

Faculty members were upset that they hadn't been consulted about the name change. Dame Margaret was more careful the next time around, and the faculty meeting to approve the new name included a passionate debate that was still recalled years later. The choice in the end was between the Water Moccasins and the Saints. A theologian made an eloquent plea against the Saints, with a lengthy excursus on the boundaries between the sacred and profane. But a herpologist just as vehemently opposed the alternative. Apparently as a grad student he'd witnessed a co-worker bitten to death by several cottonmouths, and strongly objected to naming St. Pete's teams after the lethal reptile. Despite its potential to be more controversial, Saints won out in the end, and local sportswriters were pleased by the possible wordplay in future headlines.

More bitter and protracted were discussions over new grad programs. There hadn't been much controversy over the decision to convert the college's two flagship departments. St. Pete's location made it a natural for marine biology. And T. J. Birdsall, the head of the writing program, had been lucky in his protégés. He'd had a student who wrote some hugely successful vampire novels and another student who became the H. D. Thoreau of western Florida, meditating on the fauna and flora of the Gulf coast and the splendor and cruelty of nature. Another student made a name for herself as the Cindi Lauper of American poetry. She introduced orange hair and nose rings to the 92nd Street Y and pioneered the punk sonnet. Billed as "Alan Ginsburg on ludes," she sold like Rod McKuen for a few years. Still another Birdsall disciple gave the world the textbook and accompanying anthology *Writing the Female Orgasm*, still widely used in colleges and universities across the country. Generations of USP students referred to at as *Writhing the Female Orgasm*.

Best of all was a student who became an editorial assistant at the *New York Times* and wrote a long feature article extolling the writing program at St. Pete as the cradle of genius, and Birdsall as personal obstetrician to the Muse. Even Margaret recognized that an MFA program would be a money-maker, and hastened to establish one. These were then sprouting like poison toadstools across the country.

Ted Birdsall married the first and third of his famous students. Two subsequent ex-student wives didn't enjoy the fortunes of their predecessors, but the reputation of the program had been established. Ted was paid like a marine biologist. He was the only professor in the arts, humanities, and social sciences with a six-figure salary.

Birdsall's own recondite meta-fictions, and the poems and stories of his disciples, including Cindi after her reputation went into eclipse, were invariably published by Southern Indiana University Press, where Ted had an old drinking buddy. Otherwise, the press was famous for its Indianaiana.

The competition for a new masters program was between Queer Studies, Climate Change, and Colonialism/Decolonialism. I was urged to contribute syllabi to the proposal for the latter. But I wasn't interested and wanted no part of a certification process that meant working with SECCS.

SECCS was the Southeastern Consortium of Colleges and Schools and was a holy terror for faculty at USP, as it was for every other college, university, and school district in its region. Every two years institutions had to have their credentials approved. Universities were able to hire administrators who dealt exclusively with SECCS, but USP didn't have that luxury.

Richard Head's wife Lorraine, a professor of education, was in charge of collecting the documentation that "learning outcomes" met the "compliance certification" and the "quality enhancement plan" that every school was obliged to submit months in advance of the assessment. After approval by an "Off-Site Reaffirmation Committee," an "On-Site Reaffirmation Committee" visited the campus and poked and prodded further before the institution was re-accredited. Everything emanating from SECCS was written in the most opaque and verbose educationese, and translating it into English was migraine-inducing work. As an education Ph.D., Lorraine was incapable of doing this herself, and instead inundated colleagues with cheery memos urging them to get their reports in promptly and not be a "SECCS offender." My documentation would come back several times with "non-compliant" scrawled by Lorraine in red pen.

The whip that SECCS cracked was that an institution had to be compliant for its students to be eligible for federal funds under Title IV.

The SECCS deviants made a point of not accepting grades as a means of "assessing learning outcomes." You may have spent hours designing and correcting tests and grading papers in order to evaluate what your students had learned, but to determine how well the young scholars had mastered your course material, the educators did not want to know anything about the grades you'd assigned.

At WFU, each of the six colleges had a compliance officer, with a couple of secretaries, a brace of work-study clerks, and an office manager. Multiply that by twelve, the number of state universities in Florida, and you see what great job-creators the SECCS fiends were.

∾

Suzy Q's flakiness didn't interfere much with day-to-day operations of the university. The president is there to raise money, and the real business of USP was discharged by the provost, Bob "the Shark" Clarke. But Bob had no academic counterpart. Normally this would be a dean or a vice-president for academic affairs. The last two incumbents, however, had each been driven out by the faculty a year after his arrival, and a well-organized campaign, orchestrated by Richard and Lorraine Head, convinced the board of trustees not to do another search. The Dean of Faculty–Rick himself–would handle the work normally undertaken by the veep. And so at USP the inmates ran the asylum.

When he arrived at USP, before the national tide of vulgarity flooded its banks, Richard was called Dick. Some time after the Moors became the Moorhens, he let be known that he would prefer Rick. Richard was also from LA, the Pacific Palisades, and he, Margaret, and I formed a little circle of expatriate Angelenos, complaining about the humidity and thunderstorms in the rival paradise. But they weren't sympathetic when I held forth to them once about how Florida and California, including Vegas, were both aberrations. "You're driving west or driving south and then suddenly you're not in the West or the South any more. You're in fantasy land." They disagreed. Neither had been to Vegas and both remembered another California and another Florida.

I took a lot of ribbing from Richard and Lorraine for living all the way up in "Cracker" County. When I confessed to Lorraine once that I liked to shop at the Walmart Superstore that opened nearby on Brewster, this was regarded as a wild eccentricity. "Jon shops at Walmart," Lorraine would tell visitors to campus when she introduced me. It may have been a test for candidates interviewing for positions. If the observation didn't get a rise out of them, they were blacklisted.

The Heads had a rival for influence at USP in the chair of the econ department, Ed Schultz. Ed appeared to have inadvertently wandered onto campus from the real world, and sometimes looked a little bewildered. A former Eagle Scout and troop leader, a church-goer, a board member of local charities, Ed was nicknamed "The Voice of Reason."

One or two other members of the humanities and social science faculty appeared equally misplaced. There was Catherine "Betty" Crocker in the political science department, who looked and acted like a blowsy June Cleaver. Her enthusiasm grated on her perpetually disgruntled colleagues. As in a lot of small politics departments, the scientists appeared to have nothing in common. Betty had written about voting trends in six rural counties in Missouri during the 1950s. Her two lefty colleagues, Alan Weiner and Mike McCarthy, specialized, respectively, in decolonialism in Central Asia and anarchism in the American South, while Roger Moncrief wrote about Italian Hobbesists and English Machiavellians.

109

When Roger and Mike had a serious falling out, and Roger objected to reading emails with smiley faces from Betty Crocker, The Voice of Reason was asked to take over the department for a year. Ed was also requested to serve as chair of the fractious foreign languages department and then the philosophy and religion department, keeping the logical positivist and the neo-pragmatist from strangling each other. (They were both OK with the theologian, a Nietzsche scholar.) There was such a paucity of reasonable faculty members that Ed oversaw as well the two graduate programs and the international studies program.

His own four-member department included Frieda Reinhardt, who did feminist economics, and Dieter Fleisch, a Marxist. This left surly Bert Grecco to handle all the micro and macro courses, with a little help from Ed when he could spare the time.

I tried to avoid evening events at USP, but when I was obliged to stay late, Ed and Holly would put me up in their sprawling home on the bay. Holly was Ed's counterpart, a PTA president, a deacon at church, a tutor in the St. Pete ghetto and soup-dispenser at the homeless shelter, and a tireless baker of chocolate chip cookies and brownies. Their two strapping sons, Troy and Wayne, were rapidly accumulating merit badges and always said "yes, sir" and "no, sir."

During a period when I was frequently having to spend the evening on campus, I flirted with the idea of renting an apartment in St. Pete. Ed had a few suggestions about landlords. I tried out the idea on Angie. "It's OK with me," she said. "But if you to turn it into a little love-nest, just make sure you pick somebody I don't know."

CHAPTER 12

WFU

Scholars peering at one another's name badges at a conference may not have heard of Western Florida University, but were not surprised that there was one. Every self-respecting state should have a full complement of institutions of higher education, one at each point of the compass.

With University of St. Petersburg, it was a slightly different story. Of course there was University of Chicago and NYU, but then there was something of a falling off. Still, every major American city was entitled to its own university, even if it had once been a small Catholic college, or something worse.

At WFU and its counterparts, not only did the on-campus construction projects continue non-stop, but the university, between recessions, was continually colonizing. WFU had seven branch campuses to the north, south, and east. It had long been verboten to refer to them as such. That was a derogatory, Tampa-centric term. For awhile they were known as "satellite campuses," but this was hardly more respectful. They'd finally been renamed "galaxy campuses." Each was its own star in the WFU universe.

The object of recent WFU presidents was to snatch sites within a rival's sphere of influence. Above all, this meant marching across the state and seizing territory increasingly close to the home base of University of East Florida, outside Orlando. A second campus was opened in neighboring Polk County. UEF was apparently preoccupied with colonizing the Space Coast, and not paying attention to its rear. WFU then crossed into Orange County, buying a condemned bowling alley in El Encanto and an adjacent pasture. Plans were approved for a second Orange County campus. According to rumors, there were pins on a map in the president's office tracking the march eastward. The object apparently was to close in on the Mouse Ears, the big landmark along I80—greeted with exuberance and relief by children and parents hurtling eastward toward the theme parks. Then, in two pincer movements, Orlando would be surrounded and WFU would strike at the heart of the Eastern Empire and swallow UEF whole. Tomorrowland belongs to me.

But UEF retaliated.

President Beryl Brannigan, the Wicked Witch of the East, announced one day that a UEF college of veterinary medicine would be opening in Clearwater. Later in the year, UEF struck again. The Houghton Estate, a nineteenth century manor house in Packer County, was transferred from the state to UEF. It would become a conference center and hotel. WFU and FSU had been dickering for years over the ownership of the historic Valencia Theater, purchased in Spain by a railroad magnate, transferred brick by brick across the Atlantic, and reconstructed in Sarasota. It was suddenly seized by UEF in a lightning coup.

Stung, WFU unfurled an enormous banner beside the entrance to the library. "Western Florida University," it proclaimed. "Third Largest Research University in Florida." Take that, UEF. But it was cold comfort after the brazen raids.

President Brannigan and her archenemy Barbara Bunyan, President of WFU, were former legislators. Fund raising for WFU and UEF and their ten siblings meant lobbying in Tallahassee. No group of donors was ever going to come through like the Florida House and Senate. Brannigan had been a Republican member of the House and a former Commissioner of Education. Bunyan

112

had been a Democratic state senator. The ebb and flow of the fortunes of the two universities had something to do with which party was in power.

The battle of the killer Bs was observed with a jaundiced eye by my friend at WFU Jerry Bender. Jerry taught German history, and we had both been part of a small group that gathered each month in one of the restaurants along Fraser Boulevard in front of campus. We called ourselves the Young Fogeys. Before we got around to updating the name, the other members had dispersed.

Departments, schools, and colleges within WFU fought each other for money and status even more bitterly than the university battled its Orlando rival, and the Fogeys told stories about the machinations.

There was a lot of unhappiness when the College of Education got a lavish new building with a glass enclosed atrium, a plush library with thick pile carpets, floor to ceiling windows, and automatic doors. Resentment focused on those doors. Most of the divisions in the College of Arts and Sciences were housed in Stalinist bunkers from the 1970s. The style was known on campuses across the U.S. as Isla Vista Modern, after the home of U.C. Santa Barbara. When rioters smashed windows in the student village in 1970, the university and businesses went in for poured concrete structures with tiny slits for windows, and some formidable defensive features. At WFU, the social sciences building was surrounded by a moat. A concrete bulge extended six feet out over the moat, to discourage anyone from wading across it and scaling the walls. There were no windows on the first two floors. To add to the warm, personal tone of the campus, all the buildings were designated by three letters, announced on large signs at each entrance, and were always referred to by these initials. Jerry worked in SOC, Barbara Bunyan in ADM, and Angela in CAS, HQ of the College of Arts and Sciences.

Now the denizens of every building demanded automatic doors. A memo was circulated by the provost claiming that "there were more differently-abled individuals in Education than in other colleges."

"You bet," said Jerry.

Apparently Jerry had made other derogatory remarks about the college–no doubt during the SECCS season–and when a bomb went off in the atrium, injuring no one, he was questioned by Tampa police investigators and the FBI.

"Look," said Jerry, "there are at least half a dozen people in every department who've said nasty things about the College of Education."

"Could you give us their names, please," said the FBI agent.

It was eventually revealed that a grad student in education had planted the bomb.

The "Open Sesame" competition was followed by the "Cargo Cult" contest.

A visit from the governor was canceled after he'd landed at Tampa International, owing to an accident that clogged I275. President Bunyan then promptly authorized the construction of a helicopter pad on the roof of the administration building. The College of Business followed suit. Visiting politicians should be able to meet directly with the college's honchos without having to talk to other administrators first. There followed serious proposals from several other colleges to make their roofs helicopter-friendly, so that the guys writing the checks would have direct access.

A lot of buildings got automatic doors, but no other college got its own helicopter pad.

Another controversial WFU initiative was the Institute of Traffic Management, which included a couple of engineers and several sociologists and psychologists. Everyone had appointments in other departments, but the Institute had a nice suite of offices, with staff, a munificent travel budget, and other perks for its scholars. The Institute was home to the scholarly journal *Traffic*. The professors were permitted to experiment with the signals on campus. How long will people wait at a red light, a couple of researchers wanted to know. After five collisions in two weeks, the project was terminated. But the sociologists got a couple of papers out of it, and were once again pleased to have proven the obvious.

PART II:
THINGS FALL APART

CHAPTER 13

The deadline for proposals for the next New England Association of British Studies meeting was approaching. It was going to be in Boston this year, and I decided I'd give a paper. Though I'd registered and picked up my name tag the first evening, I hadn't otherwise put in an appearance at the last three conferences I'd attended. Presenting a paper would let me apply for a stipend and maybe get $500 out of the Heads, co-chairs of the Grants and Prizes Committee. ("Two Heads are better than one.") They were stingy with senior faculty, but then not many were interested in giving papers. And I'd leave the program, open to my panel, on the dining room table, where Angie would spot it.

I decided to take a look at the old Deceased Wife's Marriage Bill question. Students were always amused by the topic. Marriage to your sister-in-law after your wife had died was made illegal in England in 1835, and, starting seven years later, critics at nearly every sitting of Parliament tried to overturn the law. It took them more than half a century. So why was there such fierce opposition to the idea of marrying your wife's sister?

The phone rang as I was writing down the names of some pamphlets from an article I was checking online. It was Wendy Huang. Wendy and I exchanged emails every couple of weeks, but she didn't call often.

"Jon, I have some bad news," she said. "Your mom's in the hospital. That cough she had a month ago came back, and she had some shortness of breath and chest pain. Anyway, she got a CT scan and now they're saying she has lung cancer."

"Jesus."

"I'm so sorry. I just talked with Vera."

Vera Shalamov was my mother's caretaker. Three years after my dad died, Mom had developed something diagnosed as spinal stenosis, which put her in a wheelchair.

I'd always assumed she'd cut loose after my father was gone, travel, join a book club, volunteer at schools and libraries. Dad had been out of it for a long time after a series of strokes, and Mom didn't disguise her relief when he died.

But she immediately became morose and withdrawn. She still read some and went out to dinner occasionally with friends, but she now had all kinds of physical complaints. Her days revolved around appointments with doctors. Then came the paralysis, which mystified all the specialists she consulted.

Vera had cared for my father and one of the last lucid things he'd said to her was that he wanted her to look after his wife when her time came. With her bulging eyes, flaming red lipstick, untidy hennaed hair, and tight, low-cut blouses, Vera didn't look much like your professional home nurse, but she'd been excellent with my dad.

I called my mother a couple of times a week and had heard about her bronchial infection. But she hadn't mentioned it the last time we'd talked. Now I dialed my mother's number and spoke with Vera. She'd been told that Mom would be discharged later in the day. David was going to bring her home. I asked her to have him give me a call when he got back, and said I'd book a flight out.

Then I got down on my knees in the study, always a sign for Lucy to rush over and nuzzle me. This time Molly clambered off the couch and joined her. She had a sixth sense about when there was trouble. I hugged both goldens and wondered, not for the first time, how people handled bad news when they didn't have large furry dogs in the house.

I canceled my Thursday afternoon class and was in LA that evening.

David hadn't called back and I tried him and Danny from the airport, got their voicemails, and texted each.

My mother was asleep when I arrived. Vera said that Mom had been told they'd found a malignant tumor. They hadn't gone into any details, and, uncharacteristically, she hadn't asked questions. My mother needed someone at night now, Vera said, and suggested Craig Barr, the stocky African-American guy who had been my dad's night nurse.

I tried Danny and David again, got their voicemails, and then called Craig. He could do three nights, and gave me the number of a couple of Philippina sisters. They were able to cover the rest of the week.

This didn't sit well with David when he called back an hour later.

"We were very happy with Craig," I reminded him.

"Mother isn't Dad," he said cryptically.

I didn't respond.

"We need to consult on everything, Jonathan."

"I called and texted. You never replied."

We discussed my mom's lack of interest in the diagnosis.

"If that's how she wants to deal with it," I said, "that's OK for now."

David disagreed. She needed to get past denial and grapple with her own mortality.

"If you're hoping for a deathbed conversion, it's not going to happen," I told him. "And I really don't want to go with hospice again."

We'd had a bad experience with my dad—at least I had. The hospice nurse seemed overeager to usher my father into the hereafter. "Let go. Let go. Let go," I heard her yelling at him one morning.

"He'll go when he's ready," I told her when we'd left the room. "Please don't do that again."

121

I'd asked Vera to double-check the doses of his meds.

But David was already looking into hospices.

"We've got Vera and Craig," I said. "We don't need anyone else."

My brother shook his head. "They don't have the same kind of training. They don't know the death and dying literature."

"Thank God," I said.

⁘

Mom's grey hair was brushed straight back, and without her glasses, her beaked nose, hooded eyes, and high cheekbones made her look eagle-like. Cancer seemed to have shrunken and bleached her. She felt brittle when I gave her a hug.

"Mom, I'm so sorry," I said.

"Sorry?"

"The diagnosis. The tumor. That's why I'm out here."

She closed her eyes and flicked her hand. "It's nothing," she said. "But I'm always glad to see you. Whatever the pretext." She asked about Angela and Amy. Then my mother started coughing, quick staccato barks that ended with a couple of long gasps. She took an inhaler from the cluttered top of her night stand, knocking over a bottle of yellow pills, shook it and took a hit.

"Isn't that for asthma?"

"It works."

I gestured at the canister of oxygen standing next to the night stand. "You don't want to use that?"

She shook her head.

I sat down in the brown leather recliner beside the bed and looked around the room. On the walnut bookshelves and coffee table beside my dad's armchair were African masks, Balinese puppets, and a couple of miniature totem poles. Next to the poles was a crude Intuit abstract sculpture of a man, consisting of six grey stones, and then three Mexican paper maché Dias de los Muertos skeleton figures—two grinning mariachi guitarists and a dancer in a red dress slit to her crotch. The Third World artifacts looked particularly hideous this morning.

I noticed a book spread open on the bed, *Jackie O*. "How come you're reading that?" I asked.

"Oh, Vera lent it to me. It's entertaining."

"You've got a lot more interesting books right here." I stood up and walked over to the hanging bookshelves facing the bed. I pulled down *Brothers Karamazov*. Mom winced and shook her head. I grabbed at random *Eugenie Grandet* and *Mansfield Park*. My mother wasn't interested in either.

"I just want fluff, Jon. That's all I'm in the mood for."

Both doctors had spoken with David a few days earlier, and neither was particularly happy to see me. I asked the internist if he thought that my mother's stenosis might have been a tumor. Mom had never smoked. He looked irritated and said that wasn't likely. She'd had a section of one lobe removed ten years ago, he reminded me. My dad had made light of the surgery. He'd said Mom had a small spot on her left lung and they didn't want to take any chances. Then a year later they found a tumor in her left breast, and she'd had a partial mastectomy. But the internist hadn't ordered any CT scans for a couple of years, and I kicked myself for not having considered the possibility that the stenosis was related to the earlier tumors.

The oncologist had grim news about the prognosis. Three months at the outside, probably less. He showed me the scans and explained why. Surgery was not an option, he said. He was willing to try a combination of chemo and radiation, but we ought to think about palliative care.

Both doctors' offices were in Cedars Medical Building, south of the hospital, and instead of returning directly to my mother's, I parked on Sixth Street and took a walk around the La Brea Tar Pits. We'd lived in an apartment close by when I was little, and Mom used to bring me there. The pits themselves, which had trapped Pleistocene mammals 10,000 to 40,000 years ago, were fenced off, but hadn't always been. A couple of boys had drowned in them before I was born, Mom once told me. "I don't know what I'd do if I lost you," she'd said suddenly, clutching me tight.

Years later, after dinner and a movie, I'd walked there one foggy night with my high school girlfriend, pre-Julie, Helene Fein. Helene was the intellectual cheerleader. There used to be one on the squad in every class at Cromwell High. There was also at least one slutty cheerleader, and I was often sorry, at the end of my dates with Helene, that I wasn't going out with Tracie Dalrymple. But that night was special. The dense fog was magical, and Helene and I walked hand-in-hand earnestly discussing Life, Love, and Death.

Now I sat on a bench in front of the biggest tar pit and thought about the oncologist's death sentence. The pit features a life-sized sculpture of a wooly mammoth sinking in the tar. On the shore is her baby, trumpeting at her plaintively.

∽

My mother was reading *Jackie O.* when I came back.

"Mom, can I talk to you for a minute?" I asked.

She put the book down.

I picked up a device from her night stand, a clear plastic tube with a ping-pong ball at the bottom, to which a small hose and mouthpiece was attached. "So what's the new toy?"

"It's a spirometer. They want me to blow into it and raise the ball to the top."

"Sounds like fun." I sat down in the leather chair. "Listen, Mom, I've just come back from your doctors. They say you have a non-small-cell lung cancer. Adenocarcinoma. You have to think about your treatment."

My mother stared at me bleakly.

124

"The cancer is sensitive to radiation. You can get radiotherapy, maybe in combination with chemo. Or they can just make you comfortable and see what happens."

"Let's see what happens."

"I understand, but..."

"Jon, I don't want those other things. Let's just see if it doesn't go away by itself."

I tapped the spirometer against my left palm. "Mom, it's not going to."

My mother was silent for a moment, then said, "I don't want to talk about it any more."

"OK," I said. "OK."

Danny had been in Sacramento at the end of the week, and though he returned on Saturday, I flew back Sunday morning without having seen him. Carl was apparently in Provence. I tried his European cell number, but either he hadn't switched it on, or hadn't activated his voicemail. It just rang. I sent him an email. Not how I'd like report news like this, but I assumed he'd be checking every day. I told Mom that she should think over what we'd talked about. I'd give her a call that evening and see her in a couple of weeks.

"Where are you going?" my mother asked.

"Back to Tampa."

"Ah, yes," she said, and closed her eyes.

I was sitting at a little round table in the Southwest terminal in LAX, pulling apart my croissant and sipping my coffee. I started thinking about the many times I'd been in the airport with my daughter Amy when she was small. Aim often got airsick, and I'd crumble a dramamine and later half a promethazine into a bowl of ice cream for her, a ritual she always looked forward to. She didn't often get a scoop of rocky road in the morning.

Suddenly I felt like something was uncoiling in my chest. I put my head down. The pressure increased. Then I began coughing. I headed to the men's room across the corridor. The coughing subsided, but the tightness didn't go away. I picked up some cough drops at a shop and went into the sports bar next door and downed a brandy and soda. It seemed to help. The bartender was a short guy with curly red hair, a snub nose, and freckles. I noticed he was left-handed, and had a tattoo on his upper arm of a grinning skull with a crown of roses. "Truckin'" was playing quietly over the speakers.

"Not what you usually hear in a bar at LAX," I said.

"You do on my shift." He looked at me harder. "You OK, man?"

"Yeah, I'm fine. Just a little congestion." I patted my chest.

The bartender came back after a couple of minutes and asked if I wanted another. I shook my head. He winked when he wished me a good flight.

"You, too," I said.

A couple of uniformed pilots were passengers on my flight. This is usually reassuring, but somehow this morning it wasn't.

CHAPTER 14

Monday evening, the day after I returned to Tampa, Angie announced that she was heading to North Carolina the next day to interview for the position of dean at a small liberal arts college.

"I had no idea you were applying anywhere," I said.

Angie shrugged. "You know the game. Showing them another offer is the only way to get more money out of the bloodsuckers in ADM." She poured herself a glass of Chablis. "If St. Jude really wants me, they'll find something for you."

"I wouldn't count on that," I said.

My daughter also had some unsettling news.

After getting a degree in biology from University of Chicago, Amy had entered the Ph.D. program in genetics at Stanford. Ever the good Montessori child, Amy had always done well at school and had lots of friends. When colleagues complained about their teenagers, I had nothing to say.

Angie and I spoke with her several times a week, and felt we were still an important part of her life, as she was of ours. The only thing Aim seemed to be lacking was a steady boyfriend. I wasn't concerned about this, but I didn't imagine she shared my indifference. When Amy discussed the subject at all, it was with Angela. She'd had a casual boyfriend in her IB program in high school for a year, but he wasn't replaced when they broke up. U.C. was IB squared, and her demanding major apparently wasn't conducive to a flourishing love life. Angie blamed the U.C. boys. She called them "social retards." We'd hear about some guy from time to time, but no relationship caught fire.

Amy looked nothing like Angela and had none of her edginess. With her blond hair, high forehead, and long, pale lashes, she looked like the daughter Tassie and I might have had. Amy didn't share Angie's taste in clothes. She favored an outdoorsy L. L. Bean look, with muted earth-tones, and she resisted Ange's attempts to get her into contact lenses.

When Amy called Tuesday evening, the first thing she said was, "Guess who friended me on Facebook."

I gave up.

"My cousin Jayson," she said.

"Well you can unfriend him. He's bad news."

I regretted this as soon as I said it. I'd had no contact with Jayson since I saw him at Julie's apartment off Fairfax. When emailing took off at the turn of the century, Cheryl and I had gotten back in touch, and she'd occasionally tell me what he was up to. It was often no good. He'd been arrested for DUI. He'd already had a couple of speeding tickets, and lost his license for six months. Then he was caught with a carton of Percocet in his trunk, and was lucky to get probation. Another DUI followed, but again, miraculously, no jail time.

Jayson had wanted to be an artist and had moved from Sonoma to San Francisco, took some classes at SFAI, and then moved to Santa Cruz. He drew caricatures for tourists on the wharf and worked odd jobs. He had long hair and a beard. But then he underwent some kind of anti-spiritual crisis, cut his hair, shaved the beard, and began working at casinos in Vegas. Cheryl was not sure this was a good move. "I'd feel a little better if he was on the Strip," she said, "but he's over on Fremont Street." She didn't see much of him.

I asked Cheryl if Jayson had any inkling that I was his father. She said no. He had only one or two memories of Giovanni, who was deported after his sentence was up. But that was the guy he thought was his dad. "It's better that way, believe me," Cheryl said. I wanted to.

I didn't like the idea of Jayson getting in touch with Amy, but thought maybe I was over-reacting. After all, I didn't know the guy.

∽

I spoke with my mother later that evening. I asked her if she'd given any more thought to chemo or radiation. "The drug they have in mind is called Tarceva," I said. "They've had good luck with it."

"I don't like the name," said my mother.

"You could go with radiation therapy alone." I summarized what the oncologist had told me and what I'd gleaned online. "It's six weeks and you'll feel tired, but it should relieve your symptoms. And you won't have the nausea you might get with chemo."

My mother didn't reply.

"Mom?"

"I'm really tired now, sweetheart," she said. "Talk to Vera."

Vera took the phone into the den and told me that David and Danny had signed Mom over to hospice. The nurse had been by this afternoon. "Eet eez not easy to vork viz her," Vera reported.

I called David. This time he picked up.

"I thought we were going to consult about everything," I said.

"Well, we got your input. Majority rules."

"How about Carl?"

"What about him?"

"Has anyone been in touch? He still has a vote, too, right?"

David said he'd tried to call him during the week, but his voice mail didn't pick up. He'd sent an email, too, but had gotten no reply.

"I think he's abstaining," said David.

I always had trouble telling whether or not my brother was kidding. Usually he wasn't.

∽

129

The next day I was supposed to have lunch with a job candidate. Bert Grecco had mercifully decided to take an early retirement, and the university–or at least Ed Schultz–was looking for a sober, affable mainstream economist. Attending the 4:00 p.m. talks of the candidates was de rigueur for all faculty. We were supposed to give the impression that USP cared about their research.

The ubiquitous Lorraine Head joined us for lunch. She introduced me to the candidate. "This is Jon Marcus, our resident reactionary. He has a soft spot for rednecks." She sniffed. "Jon shops at Walmart." The guy didn't betray much of a reaction, no doubt earning a black mark in Lorraine's book. With Selma Armstrong, the theologian, we headed over to Finney's, a fish restaurant favored by the senior faculty.

Lorraine started complaining about her adjuncts. Among Professor Head's many positions was Director of Composition, and apparently one of her peons kept straying from the syllabus. To illustrate the parts of speech, the young woman had put a joke up on the screen:

Mickey Mouse is on trial for killing Minnie Mouse.
Judge: "You claim you murdered your wife because she was crazy."
Mickey: "No, I said she was fucking Goofy."

The idea was to get the students to see that the humor consisted of a verb and noun being interpreted as an adverb and adjective.

"In the first place," said Lorraine, "I've told Marcia more than once we don't teach parts of speech at USP. No one's done that for decades. In the second place, it's incredibly insensitive. We do not use the f-word in the classroom at USP."

The candidate was no doubt regretting that he'd laughed so loudly at the joke.

"What if this gets reported to SECCS?" Lorraine fretted. "A pretty kettle of fish."

"I don't think that's likely," I said.

I got the candidate going on the marginalist revolution. I'd been warned by Ed not to do this, since Frieda Reinhardt already taught her version of the history of economic thought, but the guy had written a paper on the subject and I was curious. He brightened up and explained that the revolution really was a shift in how economists understood the human psyche.

For the classical economists, people were addicts. They always wanted more of what they liked. But the marginalists recognized that this wasn't always the case. After a few minutes, you get bored with even the most spectacular sunset. All little kids know that seconds are never as good as firsts. People won't pay the same price for a second watch, or a second head of lettuce. So demand curves slope down, at different rates, and you can use differential calculus to figure out economic outcomes. The bottom line: there are diminishing returns on nearly everything in life.

"What's the slope look like for marital felicity?" I asked.

This was greeted by silence. "I'm sure someone's working on it," the economist said after a moment.

"Does the curve ever pop back up?" I asked quickly. "I mean, when you get near the end of that second bowl of ice cream, when you're down to a couple of spoonfuls, you start to savor it again. And those last seconds, before you go back inside, you take a good look at the sunset."

"Those feelings don't count in the market," the economist said. "They're like seller's remorse."

Lorraine had her own questions. "What would you do tomorrow if you were appointed Chairperson of the Fed?" she asked.

∽

One part of my life was going swimmingly. Marge di Cosi and the two donors had been enthusiastic about our plans for *The Magic Flute*, and so had several other supporters with deep pockets. The opera had been scheduled and the casting completed eighteen months earlier, but it was now going to be our subversive version that would be staged. The first rehearsals were to begin at the end of the month, and we would get a couple of trap doors and a floating cloud for the *Drei Knaben*.

⚬

That Sunday, for the first time in awhile, I went out to the Packer County Animal Shelter. In the course of pulling stray goldens over the years, I'd gotten to know some of the staff and would volunteer once in awhile on weekends to walk the dogs, something the employees didn't have time for. The supervisors were off over the weekend, and the head animal care tech, Terry Peterson, was usually in charge of Building C. The C dogs were strays and owner turn-ins, and most were waiting until their hold time was up. Then, if no rescue group took them, they would either cross the parking lot to the Adoption Center or be euthanized. Volunteers normally weren't allowed to walk these dogs, since most weren't legally owned by the county. Some were sick or injured, some were vicious, and some were in quarantine. But I convinced Terry I could read the cage cards and would stay away from the dubious customers, and he let me walk the C dogs.

A lot of the animals were frightened at the shelter. Some had to be coaxed out of their cages. Others wouldn't budge. Apart from the constant barking, the building had no AC, and it could get pretty stifling over the summer. There were no assessments on the weekends, and I could see from the cage cards who was going to be put down first thing Monday morning. It was these dogs I'd try to take for a last walk. If they had fleas, I'd slip them a Capstar. They'd get re-infested, but at least they'd have a few hours of relief. If the dog was interested, I'd take it for a run.

Angie thought the whole routine was bizarre. "Not only do you waste hours every week throwing tennis balls to the dogs and taking them for walks, you drive twenty minutes to walk dogs you don't even know and you'll never see again."

⚬

I was calling my mother every couple of days. Mom seemed listless and didn't want to talk for long. She used to describe her symptoms in great detail, but now, when I asked about her breathing, she'd say things were OK, and change the subject.

A few times she sounded out of breath. There were occasional bouts of coughing. Two weeks passed.

An hour after I'd booked a flight for the following weekend, I got another call from Wendy. More bad news. After a violent headache and vomiting, Mom had had a brief seizure and had been given a second scan. They saw a small tumor in her brain, on the periphery of the cerebellum.

I called the oncologist again and asked about surgery or radiation for the tumor. With a radiation-sensitive primary tumor like small-cell lung cancer, stereotactic radiosurgery was a possibility. This would be a palliative measure. It wasn't likely to buy my mother much time. The doctor was meanwhile giving her corticosteroids to relieve the swelling. He described SRS briefly–he would use a Gamma Knife–and asked us to talk it over with my mother and get back to him.

CHAPTER 15

Saturday morning I met with David, Danny, and Wendy around the breakfast table at my mother's. My brothers didn't want to discuss radiosurgery with Mom. I explained that this wasn't some risky, heroic measure, but might bring a little relief. D and D weren't buying this. I told them that it was Mom's decision, and I would be talking to her.

Carl had finally gotten in touch and was supposed to be coming out in a couple of days. But then he was flying back to Lyons the following evening. He and some friends had been planning a three week gastro-tour in southern France for over a year.

Danny and David went out to get something to eat. I hugged Wendy tightly after they left. It had been nine months since we'd been together.

"Listen," Wendy said when we detached ourselves. "I think you need to get a lawyer."

"I've got one," I said.

"Seriously, Jon. Danny and David are up to something with your mother's trust."

"You're kidding. What?"

"I don't know. But you need to talk to your mom, and get some good legal advice."

"But you're the one who wrote the trust for Mom and Dad."

"Yes, but your mom as sole trustee can always amend it. I shouldn't be involved at this point. I'm an interested party. I'll give you the names of a couple of good people in other firms."

We gazed at each other for a moment in the dining room, my hands on her shoulders, hers around my waist.

"Of course I've told Danny he shouldn't touch the will or the trust," she said. "It's absolutely not right."

I pulled up her smoky sunglasses and kissed her again. "Is there any way you can come to Park Plaza?" This was the nearest motel, a couple of blocks away.

Wendy shook her head. "I have to pick up Ashley in an hour. And it's way too risky."

"What about this evening? Somewhere out near you."

Wendy shook her had again.

I looked at her a little more closely. "Wen," I said, "what happened to your eye?"

The skin under Wendy's left eye was slightly bruised. There was a yellowish semi-circle below the lower lid, the way a shiner looks three or four weeks later.

"Nothing. I stepped on a rake in the garage last month. It was stupid. I'm fine."

"Did Danny hit you? Tell me the truth."

She didn't say anything. Then her eyes filled with tears.

I was suddenly enraged. I grabbed her shoulders. "If he touches you again I'm going to kill him. I swear to God." I was trembling with anger.

"Jon, please, let go. You're hurting me."

"I swear to God, I'll kill him."

❧

I spoke with Mom after she woke up from her afternoon nap. I told her about the scan. No one had mentioned it to her, or she didn't remember. She shut her eyes and sighed, but didn't say anything. I described radiosurgery and the possible benefits. Not too many weeks earlier, she would have jumped at it. Now she seemed not to be processing the information.

136

"How's that hospice nurse working out?" I asked finally.

Mom looked at me blankly for a moment. "I want Cheryl," she said.

"She's in Vegas, Mom," I said. "Listen, can you promise me something? If Danny and David try to get you to revise your will or amend the trust, tell them that you need to talk to Wendy about it, OK? Make sure Wendy's there. She wrote the trust, remember? She went over it with all of us."

My mother nodded, then closed her eyes.

CHAPTER 16

When I called my mother the day after I got back, Vera picked up and went into the den. She told me the hospice doctor had upped the Oxycontin dose. "Do you think Mom's in any more pain?" I asked.

She didn't think so. The doctor had never come by. He'd just ordered the change.

"Keep the dose at 10 milligrams," I told her. I faxed her a note that said, "All medications for Ruth Marcus are to be administered by her private nurses."

I googled oxycodone and took a closer look at the side effects. I'd seen the usual "nausea, vomiting, constipation, headache, dry mouth, lightheadedness," etc., but now read how it depresses breathing and should be used with caution in patients with serious lung disease. Once more I kicked myself for not having done some basic research.

I called the hospice doctor and left a message.

Then I called one of the lawyers Wendy had recommended, Mark Rosenblatt. He told me there wasn't much I could do about David and Danny's machinations with the trust unless I had Mom certified as non compos mentis.

"She's not," I said.

"Then the best option is to get a signed and notarized statement from your mother stating that she won't alter the will or trust without your consent."

I faxed a statement to Vera and negotiated with the manager of my mother's bank to have one of the officers who was a notary come over to the house and witness Mom's signature.

Then I emailed Carl: "Please call."

Two days later I got a call from him.

"Look," he said, as soon as I said hi, "I don't want to get involved."

"Carl, she's your mom, too."

"Did you not hear me?"

I hung up without saying goodbye.

Later that week Joyce and I met with the chorus, while the principals watched and listened on Skype. Joyce introduced me as the dramaturge, and mentioned what I'd been up to. If the singers were dubious, they didn't say anything.

She explained the way the opera was going to be staged. Joyce told Sarastro she wanted him to strut. Think Mussolini, she said. The Queen of the Night was going to be the most sympathetic Queen ever to hit the top F. And Monostratos would be a little more ingratiating. He was to come to the front of the stage and sing his rewritten aria directly to the audience. Tamino, dressed in a pink candy-striped suit, floppy bow tie, and spats, was to imagine he was Bertie Wooster. Pamina was told to keep her distance from Sarastro, and dramatize her confusion and despair. Papageno can be played various ways, and Joyce opted for a more Chaplinesque, down-and-out bird-catcher, rather than the exuberant clown of some productions. In a lot of recent Flutes, Papageno and Papagena are virtually having sex on stage by the end of their duet in scene 29. Joyce didn't want this. On the other hand, there was going to be some violence. In the finale, the ex-Moor and the Queen and her Ladies would be cut down by a machine gun before they could fire their Lee-Enfield rifles.

When I called my mother after the meeting, Vera picked up again. She told me the hospice doctor had ordered a nasogastric tube and IV hydration.

"Mom isn't eating?" I asked.

Vera told me the Oxycontin had killed her appetite. She'd refused food for forty-eight hours.

"Are you giving her the Oxy?"

"No," she said. "I show your note to nurse, she give it to Danny, and Danny tear it up."

I called my brother. When the voicemail beep sounded, I said, "Call me back when you get this and tell me what the fuck is going on."

On Sunday I went out to the shelter, and when I came back I got a call from Craig. He was at home and told me Danny and David were going to have the hospice nurse remove the NG and IV tubes on Tuesday. He and Vera were to stop the formula and fluids immediately.

I sat down on the sofa. "I just talked to Mom on Friday. She was tired, but she seemed to understand what I was saying."

"She understands OK," said Craig.

"Look, you have my permission to give her food and water. And tell Vera. I'm calling my lawyer first thing tomorrow."

"Good. Thanks."

When he returned my call, Mark Rosenblatt promised to send what he called "a strongly worded letter" by special delivery advising my brothers that his client was prepared to sue them if they authorized any changes in Ruth Marcus's diet or medication without his consent.

I spoke with Danny that evening. He called Rosenblatt's letter "bullshit" and "a bluff," but food and water were restored. "If you want to micromanage Mom's care, you need to be out here," he said. "You talk to her for two minutes."

"I talk to Vera," I said. "And it's not like you're sitting beside her all day."

I told him I was flying out the coming weekend, and that I wanted to cancel the contract with hospice immediately.

"No can do," Danny said. "Obviously you didn't read the fine print. It's till death do us part. Once you're in the program, you can't opt out."

"I'll check on that with my lawyer."

"You can't win this, Jon. You need to accept the fact that Mom's going to die."

"I don't have a problem with that," I said. "I just don't want her to be killed."

I should have predicted what happened next. Vera called me in tears the following day. "Your brozzer fire me. And Craig."

I got Danny's voicemail when I called and repeated my earlier message. David didn't pick up either.

CHAPTER 17

I still hadn't heard from either of my brothers when I flew out again on Friday. I got to my mother's house around 10:00 p.m. and stuck my key in the lock of the redwood gate in back. It didn't go in. I looked down at the key. The lock had been changed.

I walked to the front, opened the wrought iron gate, and tried the door. Of course its lock had also been changed. I rang the bell twice and knocked a few times, but no one came to the door. Maybe the new care providers had been told not to let anyone in.

I did what we used to do when we'd forgotten or lost our keys. I walked up the neighbors' driveway alongside the house and hoisted myself over the wooden gate into our back yard. I went up the steps of the patio and tried the sliding glass door to the den, but it was locked. So was the kitchen door.

I went back down the brick steps to the lawn and peered into my parents' bedroom. There was a lamp on beside the bed. I could see my mother was asleep.

I was about to tap on the window when I heard the sliding glass door open. Danny came out. He held a leveled pistol.

"Danny," I said, "It's me. Put that down."

He crossed the patio without replying.

"I rang the bell. No one answered."

When he still didn't reply, I said, "Danny, put the gun down please. It's not funny."

"It's not supposed to be."

I decided to tread lightly. "Didn't anyone ever tell you not to point a gun at someone unless you're gonna use it?"

"Who says I'm not."

We stared at each other in the dark for several more seconds. Then he lowered the pistol.

"Are you crazy? What the fuck was that all about?"

"So who are you looking for?" he asked.

"What you mean? I'm here to see Mom."

"Ah," said Danny. "Well, Mom's unconscious. She's in a coma."

"All the same, I want to see her."

We glared at each other. Then he smiled. "So, does Wendy make little cooing noises when she comes?"

"How would I know?"

"You mean you don't give her an orgasm."

"I don't know what you're talking about."

I followed Danny back into the house. My hand was trembling as I shut the kitchen door. My brother seemed to want to treat the confrontation as a joke. There were no rounds in the pistol, he told me, and promised to make me a set of keys the next day. Changing the locks was a reasonable precaution when you switch care providers. Vera and Craig both had had copies of the house keys.

"You're afraid they might sneak in and give mom some extra Ensure?"

"Jon, we're following the instructions of her doctor to the letter."

"A doctor who's never seen her."

We went into my mother's room. She was breathing quietly, at wide intervals. Danny introduced me to the new night nurse, a small Philippina woman named Olympia.

I asked her when my mother had last been conscious. She glanced over at Danny before saying that Mrs. Marcus had never been awake since she started work.

144

I called Wendy after Danny left and described our encounter in the back yard. She was incredulous. "I've never told him anything. Never. I didn't even know he had a gun."

"Maybe he borrowed it from one of his girlfriends."

She didn't reply.

"Wendy. Leave him."

Again she said nothing.

"Sweetheart," I said, "Meet me tomorrow at the Holiday Inn Express." We'd used the Santa Monica Boulevard motel a couple of times.

"Jon," Wendy said, "I'd love to, but I can't."

⁓

Saturday I sat beside my mother most of the day, occasionally taking walks around the block. Several times she stirred restlessly. Once she opened her eyes and looked at me. I read her some poems by Yeats that she used to like: "The Wild Swans at Coole," "The Second Coming," the Crazy Jane poems. Then I recited "Death."

Mom didn't react. I looked closely.

Flipping through her dog-eared anthology, I ran across a curious, apocalyptic four-line poem called "There," and read it out loud. When all the dragons bite their tails, becoming whirling gyres, the planets will crash into the sun.

Mostly I graded exams.

I spoke with Wendy again. She told me she'd brought her cello along a few times and played for my mother, mostly Bach's suites, but also once Elgar's concerto, to a cd with the cello part left out. Until a week ago, my mother had responded. She'd applauded the concerto.

David, Wendy told me, had read her passages from the Torah and the Book of Job. He had tried to get her to recite the Shema, without success.

I left early the next morning. I kissed my mother for the last time, knocking into the glucose drip holder.

145

❧

My flight wasn't until noon, and I stopped by the tar pits again. I sat down on the same bench. Suddenly, I remembered how much my mother had liked Helene. "She's such a nice girl, Jon," my mother said. "You're a good match." At seventeen, this was not what I wanted to hear.

Then I recalled waking up late at night, after one of my parents' dinner parties. I must have been around ten, and the drunken goodbyes had roused me from sleep. Mom sat with me in the breakfast room while I had a left-over schaum torte from the party. My mother smelled slightly of Chanel No. 5 and Grand Marnier, and the kitchen was still fragrant with the odors of the dinner, beef bourguignon and ratatouille. I started complaining about my brothers.

"You need to be patient with them," Mom said. "They may not show it, but they look up to you. Remember that, and set a good example for them, no matter how they act. One day, when you're older, you'll all be friends."

I gave her a skeptical look.

My dad came into the kitchen. "Let's hope we both live long enough to see *that* day," he said.

My mother whirled around. "Len!" she said, and then turned back to me and smiled. "Trust me, Jon."

❧

At LAX I called Cheryl. I told her about my mother's condition, and how she had asked for my cousin to be her nurse.

Cheryl said she would have liked to oblige, only she was in the hospital now, as a patient.

"It's not good, Jon," she said when I asked what was wrong. Cheryl had pancreatic cancer.

"You're kidding!"

"No, unfortunately. It's not as bad as it could be. T1, N1, M0. You can look it up online."

146

"God, Cheryl. What an awful coincidence."

"Well it's not the first time for me. Remember, I had breast cancer ten years ago."

"So what's the treatment?"

The doctors believed it was curable, Cheryl explained, and she was going to have the Whipple procedure in ten days. "It's not an easy operation," she said. "Then I'll probably get some adjuvant chemo."

"I'm so sorry, Cheryl. I want to see you before your surgery."

"I'd like to see you, too," she said.

I told her I'd get back in touch when I'd booked a flight.

"You sound OK. Hang in there, sweetheart." The words echoed hollowly as I looked around the Southwest terminal. But what can you say to news like Cheryl's that doesn't sound trite or foolish?

Things had not gone well for my cousin over the past decade. There was the cancer, and some ovarian cysts. Either from the chemo or for some other reason, she'd had bone problems. She'd had an elbow and hip replaced. Cheryl was in a lot of pain before and after the surgeries, but had bounced back and returned to work. Her son Chuck was a lighting tech and had worked for a couple of long-running Vegas shows. But he'd gotten into drugs, and spent stints in rehab. Hailey was a sous-chef at a high end restaurant on the Strip and seemed to be doing well. But Cheryl and Steve had gotten divorced. Cheryl didn't go into details, but apparently things had fallen apart after the kids left home.

CHAPTER 18

The day after I returned, Joyce phoned. The principals were in town, and there was some rumbling on the part of Sarastro, she said. Would I have lunch with the malcontent?

Civic Opera of Tampa Bay could not afford top-flight European and American singers. The stars are booked five seasons ahead and paid at least $25,000. The figure would be higher, but the major opera houses collaborate to fix fees. So COTB relies mostly on obscure Eastern Europeans. Few in the audience will have heard of the Romanian soprano Nina Dinescu, but she was singing the Queen's two arias for half the cost of Diana Damrau, and would do a creditable job.

Kurt Zimmerman, our pudgy Sarastro, was hired along with the Slavs, Bulgarians and Romanians, and he needed some persuading about the brown uniform and black boots. At least he wasn't a Mason.

Over a salad and vegetables at the Vinoy bistro—Kurt was a vegan—we discussed the Tampa Bay *Zauberflöte*.

Schikanender's libretto tells the story of a prince, Tamino, and his sidekick, the bird-catcher Papageno. The prince—"dressed in a Japanese hunting costume," for some reason—has entered the realm of the Queen of the Night. He's being chased by a serpent and unheroically faints. Luckily, the Queen's three Ladies have been watching, and kill the monster merely by willing it dead, though some productions have one of them stab it.

The Ladies fall in love with the handsome prince and quarrel over who will stay with him while the others tell the Queen. He remains unconscious through their six-minute trio.

Tamino revives as soon as they leave and spots Papageno, who introduces himself–"*Der Volgelfänger bin ich, ja*"–and claims to have killed the serpent with his bare hands. The Ladies return, chastise the bird-catcher, put a padlock on his lips, and give the prince a miniature portrait of the Queen's daughter. He falls in love with the image, and vows to save the girl, who is apparently a captive. Thunder and lightning herald the arrival of the Queen, whom Papageno has never seen, though he dutifully catches birds for her every day. She explains that her daughter has been kidnapped by a wicked scoundrel, and describes the abduction in dramatic detail. She commands the "innocent, wise, and pious" prince to rescue Pamina, and promises to give her to him in marriage if he does.

Papageno is assigned to accompany the prince. He is not happy about this, but the Ladies give the pair magical instruments, a flute for Tamino, bells for the bird-catcher, and tell them three wise Boys will guide them and assist them.

Tamino unchivalrously gives the medallion with Pamina's portrait to Papageno while he searches for the Boys. Unassisted, the bird-catcher sneaks into Sarastro's palace and encounters the unhappy girl. She is about to be raped by the wicked Moor employed by Sarastro to guard her. The villain is frightened off by the specter of a man dressed as a bird. Papageno is simultaneously terrified by the black man.

The bird-catcher returns, carefully identifies the princess from the portrait, and tells her that a prince has so impressed her mother that she ordered him to free her. When he saw her picture, the prince fell in love with her and instantly agreed, he tells her. Pamina is delighted, and in turn falls in love with the prince on this slender basis, though she's a little peeved he hasn't come in person. Pam and Pa sing the lovely duet "*Weib und Mann.*"

Meanwhile, after being given some good advice by the three Boys, Tamino unsuccessfully tries the front entrance to the Temple of Wisdom. He's impressed by the facade. A priest emerges and berates him for believing the word of a woman, but he won't tell the distraught prince if Pamina is dead or alive. Unseen voices oblige, however, and, learning that she is alive, a delighted Tamino plays his flute, which charms various animals in the vicinity and lures Pamina and Papageno. They are intercepted by Monostratos, but the bird-catcher plays his bells. The tune captivates the villain, who goes prancing off with his slaves.

Sarastro returns from hunting and is hailed by his subjects. Pamina falls on her knees and begs his forgiveness for having tried to escape. There were extenuating circumstances, she explains: the Moor tried to rape her. Monostratos returns with Tamino, whom he has captured. The flute is apparently not as effective as the bells in diverting the villain. Tam and Pam are delighted to see each other at last. Instead of the reward he expects, the Moor is condemned to receive seventy-seven lashes. His subjects again hail Sarastro, Tamino and Papageno are led off to begin their trials, and the first act ends.

When a couple of priests express reservations about the prince, Sarastro reassures them. And if Tamino should die during his initiation ordeal, well, he'll just join Isis and Osiris before the rest of them. The prince proclaims that he is willing to die for friendship and love. Papageno requires more persuading. He's told he'll get to see the young and pretty *mädchen* he's already pined for several times.

The first trial is not particularly demanding. The pair has to remain silent. The three Ladies appear, telling them that they're doomed. The frightened bird-catcher speaks with them, but Tamino doesn't respond to their dire warnings, though he breaks his vow by repeatedly shushing Papageno. Given the fact that the

Ladies saved his life at the beginning of Act I, this is a little ungracious on the prince's part. Already affected by the misogyny of the initiates, Tamino dismisses the Queen as a mere woman, with a woman's mind. The prince is congratulated by the priests, after they expel the Ladies.

Monostratos is back on the scene, and tries once again to rape the captive Pamina, asleep on a sofa. This time it's the Queen who interrupts him. Pamina, who has slept through Monostratos's aria, now wakes up, and is delighted to see her mother. But the Queen, when she learns the young man she sent to rescue her daughter has joined the initiates, tells Pamina that she can't protect her, they can't escape together, and her only option is to kill Sarastro. The Queen doesn't explain why she can't do this herself. Anticipating that Tamino would let her down, she's brought a dagger along, and gives it to the reluctant Pamina. The Queen tells her that Sarastro's power comes from something called the sevenfold circle of the sun that he wears on his chest. Her late husband gave it to Sarastro, his lieutenant, not trusting a woman. Pamina must return the circle to her and, in her brilliant aria *"Der Hölle Rasche,"* threatens to disown her daughter if she doesn't oblige.

Monostratos has overheard the dialogue and tries to blackmail Pamina, so to speak, but is foiled yet again, this time by Sarastro himself. The ruler interrupts the Moor, and tells his servant that his soul is as black as his face. However, the recidivist's only punishment is to be sent off to the wings. Sarastro won't punish the Queen either, he assures Pamina, because the brotherhood doesn't believe in vengeance.

A second trial of silence follows, during which Papageno meets his intended, disguised as an old woman. The boys descend with some refreshments and also return to the pair the magic flute and bells, which apparently Sarastro had confiscated. While Papageno gorges himself, Tamino plays the flute. This draws Pamina, who is distressed when the prince won't speak with her. Papageno, who might have explained, is stuffing his face.

Sarastro congratulates Tamino, Pamina is summoned and the two would-be lovers are told to bid each other farewell. Sarastro and the prince assure the princess that he shares her love for him, and that they will be reunited.

After singing his delightful aria, "*Ein Mädchen oder Weibchen*," the bird-catcher gets to see Papagena without her disguise. But he's told he is not worthy of her yet, and she's chased off.

Pamina, who has apparently forgotten the reassurances of Sarastro and Tamino, now tries to kill herself, but is thwarted by the three Boys. They perform the same service for a despondent Papageno, who has forgotten his magic bells.

Before this happens, Tamino passes his final trial, this time accompanied by Pamina. They walk through fire and water, while Tamino plays his flute.

After Papageno and Papagena are reunited, the Queen and her Ladies attempt to storm the temple, led by the indefatigable Monostratos. The Moor has been promised Pamina's hand. But the quintet is vanquished by a flash of lightning. Sarastro proclaims that the rays of the sun have expelled the night, and that the power of the hypocrites has been destroyed. The chorus thanks Isis and Osiris and the opera ends.

The action is interrupted from time to time to allow the singers to turn to the audience and impart a moral or two derived from the preceding scene.

∽

It doesn't take a Carl Marcus to poke a few holes in the plot, and I tried to convince Kurt that Sarastro is not exactly the omniscient and beneficent ruler he's made out to be. In the first place, he was evidently once second-in-command to the King of the Night, a fact a little problematic for the opera's sun-moon symbolism—unless the Queen inherited her throne after her husband's death. Sarastro seems himself to have been smitten by the daughter of his sovereign. He tells Pamina at the end of Act I that he

153

sees that "she loves another." If it was necessary to kidnap the girl, Sarastro might have explained to her his reasons, and given his own feelings for her, was it really just because he didn't want to see her raised by a proud and hypocritical woman? In any case, why consign her to the care of the lustful Moor? This doesn't seem to show much forethought. Was Monostratos possibly an affirmative action hire? Not likely, given Sarastro's feelings about blacks. Why does Sarastro keep a troop of African slaves, anyway? That's not particularly enlightened of him. But it's his attitude toward women that is apt to annoy even a non-feminist today. A man must lead you, Sarastro tells Pamina. No woman is competent to act without one. And the first duty of the brotherhood, the priests gravely inform Tamino, is to beware of the treachery of women. They ensnare men and lead them to death and damnation.

"But you know," said Kurt, "Sarastro was modeled on an admirable chap, Ignaz von Born. He was a geologist, an engineer, the director of the natural history museum, the director of the mint, like Isaac Newton. The director of the government's mines. There's a mineral named after him. And Born, you know, was a ferocious anti-cleric, as only an ex-Jesuit can be." Kurt popped a portobelo slice into his mouth. "He hated monks."

I told Kurt I was familiar with Born, but he went on. "The chap wrote a rather scholarly work on the mysteries of the Egyptians. One of the books Shickenader cribbed from. Born says the goal of the priesthood was to lift the veil of Nature."

"OK, but then why the esoteric initiation rites? Why the secrecy? That's not how scientists operate today."

"Well, you know, scientists were Romantics then. There were no men in white jackets and goggles, with test tubes and zentrifuges."

"But the initiates in the *Weisheitstempel* have no curiosity about the natural world. They're the priests of Isis and Osiris."

Kurt switched tack. "This is such a German opera. I think perhaps a non-German might not appreciate it." He took a sip of his Perrier. "Mozart's great Italian operas, the collaborations with da Ponte, they are all so cynical. They are about sexual predators and manipulators, about lust and deceit. *Die Zauberflöte* is...uplifting. It speaks about truth and wisdom. That's why it's magical."

I ran through the p.c. critique of the *Eingeweiten*: the racism, the misogyny, the torture, the kidnapping.

"But look," said Kurt, picking at his polenta, "you have to cut Sarastro some slack about the kidnapping. He knows that the gods have destined Pamina and Tamino for each other. He's serving the will of the gods."

"But who are these gods?" I asked. "Isis and Osiris. Why should we like and respect their devotees? Tamino thinks it's possible that Pamina has been sacrificed to them. Why don't the priests say, 'Goodness, no! We don't believe in human sacrifice'?"

"Ah, but there's something noble in Tamino's quest, don't you think? 'What do you seek?' the Speaker asks him. '*Freundschaft und Liebe*,' he says. Friendship and love. And the Speaker asks, 'are you prepared to risk your life for these,' and Tamino says '*ja*.'" Kurt smiled. "Aren't you a little stirred by that?"

"Not really," I said. "Think of how many idealistic young men have joined dreadful causes." I hesitated for a second, then plunged ahead. "It was the idealists in Germany in the '30s who signed up for the S.S." Kurt's handsome face clouded over.

I suddenly remembered a conversation with an elderly woman at a cafeteria in Munich years earlier, when I was in college. I'd sat down at her table and after some small talk, she told me how Hitler had been given a bad rap. He did some wonderful things for Germany. He built our highways. And he made us proud again to be Germans. The woman glanced around nervously, but no one was nearby. Of course he was crazy in the end. He should never have gone to war. He should have made peace with England in 1940. But, she repeated slowly, looking at me intently, "*Hitler war nicht so schlimm für Deutschland*." Hitler was not so bad for Germany. I didn't say anything for a moment and then, my German failing me, all I could think to say in reply *auf Deutsch* was, "But look around this room, please. There are no men your age." Ach, she said, he was crazy later on. She squeezed my hand. But remember what I said.

Now Kurt replied, "Well, you are with Papageno then."

"Yes, at least he has a little curiosity about the trials he's supposed to undergo. He doesn't take things on faith."

"'*Ja nun*,' said Kurt, "'*es gibt noch mehr Leute meinesgleichen!*'" "Right. And there are more people like me." This is Papageno's reply when the Speaker tells him that, because he's only interested in food and drink and sex, he'll never be able to experience the heavenly pleasures of the initiates, the enlightened ones. Papageno is supposed to gesture at the audience as he says his line, and this usually gets a laugh.

Getting a little too much into the spirit of the libretto, Kurt motioned to a passing waiter and ordered another glass of wine for me. Papageno's next line is that all he wants at the moment is a good glass of wine. This he receives at once. It's often handed up to him from a trap door in the floor. In our case, the guy said, "I'll let your waiter know."

"I just don't want to lose the magic in *The Magic Flute*," Kurt said.

"We won't" I told him. "We're not trying for some Brechtian *Verfremdungseffekt*. We're not flouting any theatrical conventions. We're not propagandizing the audience." I sipped my water. "We just want people to rethink the happy ending. They seldom happen in real life."

"All the more reason for them to happen on stage," said Kurt. The wine arrived.

"Look, you haven't convinced me," he said. "But I'll give you your Sarastro." We clinked our glasses and said "*Prosit!*"

∞

156

The Bulgarians, Romanians, and Slavs apparently had no objections to our *Zauberflöte*.

I went to the afternoon rehearsal and returned the next evening.

I hadn't been around performers much since my own high school acting days, but it's usually amusing to see how members of the cast interact in real life. Inevitably, Tamino and Pamina, both Bulgarians, didn't seem to care much for each other. The prince, a tenor called Petar Vlachov and a little too old for the part, was married to the youngest and prettiest of the Ladies, and may have resented that his wife hadn't been offered the role of Pamina. The oldest and most Lady-like of the Ladies–the most flirtatious–was a buxom Slovene diva who had studied with Lucia Popp as a girl.

Papageno was Papagenish off stage, joking with the other singers and teasing the giggly sopranos who played the Three Boys. Joyce had dressed them in paramedics' uniforms. The bird-catcher's *mädchen*, however, was very intense and wore glasses backstage. Seductive and high-spirited on the boards, Papagena sat in the wings during rehearsals poring over *The Saragosa Manuscript*.

Things did not always go swimmingly between Joyce and the young conductor, Milan Jovanović. She wanted Pamina to take her aria "*Ach, ich fühl's*" more slowly. He wanted her to speed up. "I feel the bliss of love has disappeared forever," sings Pamina. "That time of ecstasy will never return," she tells the prince. "These tears flow, beloved, for you alone. If you no longer feel love's longing, I'll find peace in death."

CHAPTER 19

The day after I had lunch with Sarastro, I played tennis with the Queen of the Night.

Nina Dinescu had been complaining loudly about not having anyone to hit balls with. She'd brought her racquet and had looked forward to getting on the court in the Florida sunshine. But she had apparently intimidated the Tampa cast members and crew by letting everyone know what a superb player she was. She'd taken lessons from Virginia Ruzici as a girl and had dreamt of turning pro, she claimed, before she was discovered by Nelly Miricioiu.

Nina hadn't made herself popular on the set. No doubt there are Queens who are warm, gracious, and maternal, and stitch loose buttons on the blouses of chorus members and tuck stray wisps of hair into their bonnets. But Nina was old school. She believed a prima donna should act like a prima donna.

When Nina mentioned that she wasn't able to serve and just wanted to hit the ball, I took her up. "I fuck up my elbow," she said. "I get no extension."

She had good ground strokes, and took malicious pleasure in sending me back and forth along the baseline. I believed the story about Ruzici.

Nina was an attractive woman in her early forties, Hungarian looking, with high cheekbones, slanting green eyes, and wavy auburn hair. Her small, pouty lips gave her a slightly spoiled look.

After we hit the ball for an hour, I suggested we get something cold to drink at Moon Under Water, facing Bayfront Park. We sat outside, under a silver Cinzano umbrella.

"So I have to ask," I said, "how come you're reading Casanova?" Papagena wasn't the only bookworm in the cast. Nina, I'd noticed, had been lugging around a thick French edition of selections from the *Memoirs*.

"In fall I am Donna Elvira in Cincin," she explained.

"Cincinnati?"

"Yes." She sipped her ice tea. "Da Ponte, you know, he is friends with Casanove. Casanove is model for Don Giovanni."

"I'd heard. So what have you learned about Casanova that will be useful?"

"He is just man, but only more honest."

"You mean all men would act like him if they weren't hypocrites?"

Nina nodded vigorously.

"Well, I guess I disagree. That's like saying all whaling captains would be like Ahab if they weren't hypocrites."

"Do you not think about having screw with every attractive woman you meet?"

Nina adjusted her polo shirt, lifted her sunglasses, and waited.

"Well, yes, it sometimes crosses my mind. But I don't act on the impulse."

"Only sometimes?"

I didn't reply.

"You know Ilya Natase?"

"Of course. That is, I know of him."

"I am one of the two thousand girls who screws with that awful man."

"We should mention that in the program notes," I said. Nina didn't smile.

"Every man would do like Ilya, if he had same chance."

160

"Well, lots of guys, sure, in Western Europe and the U.S. after the 1960s. And maybe in Venice in the 18th century. But hardly in all times and places."

I changed the subject before Nina could resume her cross-examination. "You've sung in the U.S. before, right?"

"Oh yes. Four years ago I am Elettra in House-ton."

"You seem to specialize in Mozart."

"No no," said Nina. "I am Lady Macbeth last year in Liège. And next spring I am Desdemone in Birmingham *Otello*. I am not always crazy lady with dagger." She flashed another flirtatious grin. "But if I am real Desdemone, I kick Moor in balls."

"So tell me about Nelly Miricioiu," I said quickly. "Didn't she leave Romania when you were just a little girl?"

"She discovers me in Paris. Then I go to London and am discovered by Ileana Cortubas. My uncle is diplomat, and I live with him and auntie for two years. "

"And your parents?"

"My father is doctor. My mother is chemist."

I asked what life was like for her family under Ceaucesçu.

"Don't start me on him please. We be here all evening. Is very hard for people in West to know what things is like in Romanie before 1990. Is unbelievable. We have so little food. Stores have only cans and jars of disgusting pickled things. You always go out with bags, in case you spot line at store. We have no heat. Power keeps going off. This is Europe in 1980s. Is unbelievable." Nina looked out at the bay behind me, then shut her eyes for a moment. "Is not easy for doctor. People who need x-ray, they must buy x-ray film on black market and bring to hospital. Same with some medicine. Because of power going out, Papa very nervous to do surgery. Hospital has only two little e-meergency generators. My uncle sends them from Brazil. Is crazy." She took a sip of tea. "This is country that is so rich, so cultured before 1940s. My father tells me what is like. Wonderful restaurants in Bucharest, street vendors, you are smelling delicious food all the time."

161

Nina rotated her glass, then squeezed the lemon wedge into her tea.

"You know we are Dacians and Romans. We are not Slavs. Romanian language is like Italian. We have marble temples and forums and baths and aqueducts when Germans and Slavs and Magyars wear smelly animal skins and sleep in tents. They have no farms, no towns. They live by stealing. Is still in their blood." Nina's eyes narrowed. "World War is terrible for Romanie. You do not want to live between Germany and Russia in 20th century. And things is almost as bad with Communism. Ceaucesçu goes to North Korea in 1971. Is inspiration. He destroy villages, makes peasants live in giant apartment buildings. They have no gardens, no chickens and rabbits. In Bucharest, he destroy neighborhoods to make biggest building in world, for Party and government. Is hideous. He destroy one quarter of Bucharest. He is crazy man with bulldozer." She looked at me intently. "We have no underground, no samizdat in Romanie. Spies is everywhere. Every typewriter and copy machine is registered with government. You see why I say unbelievable."

We sipped our drinks in silence for a moment.

"I tell you something." Nina picked up her knife. "When I sing about Sarastro, I think of Ceacesçu."

"Well, that may be going a little overboard," I said.

I asked her about 1989.

"Now we be here all night. Is worst of both worlds in Romanie. We have a thousand peoples killed. No one dies in Prague or Berlin. And they get revolution. We get coup."

Nina pulled up her sunglasses and again gazed out over the bay. "You know," she said. "I do not think Kurt is vegan. How can you be fat vegan? He is hypocrite, like Sarastro. And his clothes. Bright yellow Hawaiian shirt. Florida is not Hawaii. Too tight shorts. Sandals with yellow wool socks. Barbarous. I want to put sunglasses on when I look at him."

162

"Well, maybe you're being a little unfair to Kurt and Sarastro," I said, "but I'm glad you're into the spirit of the production."

Nina put her hand on my arm. "When I die, audience will weep."

⁂

That evening I got the call I'd been expecting. "Mother passed away at 3:52 p.m.," David said. The funeral was Friday.

"Did Mom want a funeral?" I asked.

"Jonathan, don't be contentious."

"Did she want a funeral?"

"It's not something we discussed. Are you coming out or not?"

"Of course I'm coming," I said.

He told me it would be at Pierce Brothers in Westwood, with the rabbi from his temple presiding.

"I can tell you, David, Mom would have wanted a simple memorial service, where people got a chance to stand up and talk about her. Just like we did with Dad."

"Don't be difficult."

"She would never have wanted a rabbi. This guy doesn't know her from Adam."

David didn't reply.

I asked if he'd gotten in touch with Carl. He said no and I told him I'd try.

My youngest brother was at his farm outside Aix. He took my call. "Well, David was always the black sheep of the family," Carl said.

"I would have said Danny."

"Why would I fly nine hours to listen to a rabbi? Besides, I've got a reservation at *Auberge du Pont de Collonges* on Saturday."

"You could come for the reception afterward."

"Do you have any idea how long you have to wait to get a Saturday night reservation at Bocuse's?"

I didn't.

"Look, I saw Mom. I said goodbye. I don't need to shoot the breeze with the schmucks."

I canceled my flight to Vegas and arranged to fly there from LA on Monday morning instead. Thank God for Southwest. And thank God for spring break, which would start that day.

CHAPTER 20

Amy flew down for the funeral and I met her at LAX. She had an exam the next morning and had to fly back the same day. Angela begged off. It had been many years since she'd been out to LA, and she had to give a presentation Friday to the President's Council about the College of Arts and Science's remote learning programs.

The service was worse than I expected. The text for the sermon was the hoary line from Proverbs 31:10, "A wife of noble character who can find? She is worth far more than rubies," and the reb filled in the few blanks with information David had given him about Mom's education and career and the names and occupations of her husband and sons.

Vera showed up and gave me a warm hug. Karen was also there, sitting beside Gordon. She turned her back on Amy and me as we approached.

After the service, I walked Vera back to her car. It was a bright, crisp day.

"I guess Mom would be happy that the sun's shining," I said.

"Yes, she hate rain. And it remind us her soul is viz God."

When we reached her car, Vera turned to me. "Your mozzer is sometimes deefeecult, but is good person here," she said, thumping her left breast. Then she hugged me tightly. I felt her silver crucifix against my chest.

Danny and David had decided to dispense with a reception at Mom's house. This was probably fine with most of the mourners.

After expressing their condolences and chatting briefly with us at the back of the chapel—several times I was told how much I looked like my dad—my mother's old friends doddered out into the small memorial park and paid their respects to Marilyn Monroe, Natalie Wood, Donna Reed, Dean Martin, Jack Lemmon, Burt Lancaster, and the other stars interred there. Mom suffered the posthumous indignity not only of having Kadish recited over her, but of being eulogized next to the final resting place of so many of the Hollywood idols she loathed.

I took a detour myself through the park on the way back from Vera's car. The sitcoms I'd adored as a kid were well represented. Stars from *Green Acres*, *Gilligan's Island*, *Bewitched*, and *The Andy Griffith Show* lay six feet under. After I passed a trio of graves, Roy Orbison, Frank Zappa, and Oscar Levant, I noticed, under a large, gnarled oak, tablets for Will and Ariel Durant. The champions of civilization slumbered among the glitterati.

I found Wendy by the door inside the chapel. She was chatting gamely with my former pediatrician, Harold Bergman, who was nearly deaf. Dr. Hal could hum a vast repertoire of opera arias, and was encouraging my sister-in-law to give him some tough challenges. "*Come scoglio immoto resta*" Wendy shouted into his left ear—Fiordiligi's moving pledge to remain firm as rock in her devotion to her lover in *Cosi fan Tutte*.

"Too easy," Hal shouted back, and launched into a falsetto rendition.

When Wendy had extricated herself, I told her I was taking Amy to LAX in a few minutes and was stopping by the crematorium on my way back. They'd agreed to keep Mom in the freezer until today, and I'd made an appointment before I left for the service. When we stepped outside the chapel, Wendy whispered, "Danny and David got your mother to amend the trust. You need to talk to them when you get back to the house."

I went back inside the chapel. There was a table on the podium with photos of my mother and two vases of white orchids. Amy

166

was sitting by herself on the carpeted steps below the table. She was poring over a textbook called *Behavioral Genetics*.

∽

Heading back from LAX on the Santa Monica freeway, it felt odd passing by Fairfax and exiting at La Brea. It felt odder still to be driving toward downtown along Sixth Street. I couldn't remember the last time I'd gone east of La Brea, except to take my mother to the Music Center. As I passed through the Hancock Park district, Margaret van Vlack's old stomping ground, I thought about the president, who'd died three or four years earlier. Dame Margaret wouldn't have been caught dead in the proximity of Marilyn Monroe.

I slowed down as I approached my junior high school, John Muir. Here the scions of LA's patrician families once rubbed shoulders with Jewish kids from Beverly-Fairfax and with a few middle-class blacks from south of Wilshire. Some of the guys with Roman numerals after their names and the girls called Buffy, Cuffy, and Muffy were whisked off to Marlborough, Harvard, and Westlake after the 7th grade. Most stuck around. Muir's sterling academic reputation was matched by its reputation as a bastion of high standards in dress and morals, when LA's other public schools were going to hell in a handbasket. Every day you could see girls on their knees outside Miss Rutherford's office–their skirts had to touch the ground–and hear the thwacks coming from Mr. McKinzie's office, where swats were liberally administered for infractions of the code of ethics we signed each semester. Danny was a frequent customer.

At the crematorium, I was greeted by a bouncy, middle-aged blond woman in a dark purple pants suit, not quite the Dickensian character I'd expected. "You spend as much time in there as you want, honey," she told me.

The room was small and bare, with pale green walls and harsh fluorescent lights overhead. There were two rows of metal folding

167

chairs. Whatever the saleswoman's sentiments, the management apparently didn't want to encourage prolonged leave-takings. My mother lay at the front of the room, on a long wooden table. She was wrapped in a sheet. Beneath the table was the black plastic box in which she would be carried to the oven.

Mom's eyes were shut, and except for her bluish skin tone, she looked as if she were asleep, as the dead are supposed to. If her funeral wasn't what or where she'd have wanted, at least she'd been spared the posthumous ministrations of a cosmetologist.

I tried to imagine what other people did in the viewing room. Presumably they prayed. Did they thank God that the deceased was no longer suffering? Did they ask God to admit him or her to His presence? Did they ask His help in dealing with the loss He'd inflicted on them?

My mother hadn't left all instructions in matters theological and ethical to Shalom School. I suddenly recalled a visit by a neighbor when I was about six or seven. Mr. Shuster was in tears over his wife's death. I'd never seen a man cry before. "She was only fifty," he kept repeating. That seemed like a ripe old age to me. When he left, I asked my mother about what happens when people die. She told me it was like being asleep, except without dreams.

"Do you ever wake up?" I asked.

She shook her head.

"You don't go to heaven?"

My mother shook her head again. "You live on in the memories of people who loved you. And in their dreams." After a moment she added, "That's why you want to be a good person, so lots of people will have nice memories of you."

"Well what happens when *they* die?"

"Maybe they've told other people about you. Their children."

She could see from my expression that this was not a very satisfying answer.

"Jonathan, everything has to end." She reconsidered. "If you create something beautiful or useful, if you write a poem or a

168

novel, or paint a picture, or compose a symphony, or design a building, well, that lives on after you die. That's the only immortality we get."

This was no more consoling.

She checked her watch. "Jon, look. You have your whole life in front of you. Don't worry about what happens after you die. Just try to enjoy life."

I thought about this for a moment. "Should I enjoy life or be a good person?"

"Both," my mother said quickly. "You'll enjoy life more if you're a good person. There's a lot of pleasure in helping other people."

"Can I do all three?"

"All three?"

"Enjoy life, be a good person, and create something beautiful."

My mother's face clouded over for a second, but she said, "Sure. Of course you can."

I was still frowning.

"You're such a little skeptic. Why don't you believe me?"

I tried conjuring up some good memories. What surfaced were scenes from a couple of family vacations to Yosemite that Mel had talked my dad into.

I remembered stepping out of the car at a motel in Modesto just before dusk. The horizon in the west was a pale lavender. Sprinklers were shooting water over an intensely green lawn, and clicking as they rotated. The drops sparkled in the dying light. In front of the lobby was a long bed of gold poppies. Our guide book had called the motel "charming." "Looks like the Triple A is right for once," said my mother. I was glad to get out of the car after three hours, I liked staying in motels, but I was happy because my mother seemed to be.

Then, on a second trip, we were sitting in a Basque restaurant in Fresno. A big deal had been made about this restaurant and its "family style" service, where bowls and platters were brought out and everyone helped himself. I liked going to restaurants even more than staying in motels. We seldom ate out as a family because of the scenes my brothers and I created. My parents praised the tangy lamb stew, the garlicky chicken, the spicy meatballs. Dishes clattered, steam rose from the food, an accordion and clarinet played a Basque rhumba, the cheery waitress hovered with fresh bowls. We seemed like a normal family, and my mother beamed.

Then, in Yosemite Valley, my mother and I were walking in El Capitan Meadow, west of the first road that cuts across the valley floor. It was very early in the morning. The lupine were up to my waist. We paused under a grove of black oak and ponderosa. I examined the pine next to me and ran my fingers over the thick black grooves between the plates of bark. Mom was staring back at El Capitan. "Look, Jon, can you see the climber?" I could just make out the tiny figure in red working his way up the massive granite face. "It's so lovely here, isn't it?" my mother said. "No one's here but us." I started humming "Climb Every Mountain," and she rewarded me with light, silvery laugh.

Then Carl and I were walking on the valley floor, east of the Ahwahnee. I had one of Mel's flower books. I identified the dog-wood, and then, as we crossed into a meadow, Indian paint brush and white shooting stars. I hadn't been paying attention to the clouds. Suddenly it got dark and started to pour. I took Carl by the hand and we raced back to the hotel. Dripping wet, we careened through the Great Lounge, with its stone fireplaces, Navaho rugs, and wagon-wheel chandeliers, and ran up the stairs. I'd expected my mother to be angry, but she laughed when we burst into the room. "You're soaked," she said, put down her scotch and soda, and made us some Swiss Miss hot chocolate.

⁂

Though she loathed LA, Mom seemed to like the rest of California. But she resented being whisked off to the Golden

State by her bankrupt father. Inspired by a teacher called Miss O'Reilly, my mother had been looking forward to attending Hunter College High School and Barnard College, then living in the Village, drinking espresso in the morning and chianti at night, wearing a black beret, and having love affairs and doing other exciting things that she would turn into poems. Her writing had already won prizes. One was for a couplet called "Monarch": "On the grass, Not under glass."

Kids at John Muir made fun of my mother's New York accent. She'd skipped a grade, and was now placed in classes with students two years older than she. Mom had already had a couple of years of Latin and French, and had read all the books the class was doing in English.

Why didn't she go back to New York after she graduated from high school, or after Berkeley? I'd never asked, and now I'd never know. And why did she wait so long before she got married?

I shut my eyes and suddenly I was in Grand Central Station. I was walking with Laura across the lobby. We were early for her train and stopped to admire the ceiling. We stood beneath the Gemini. The twins are arm in arm. Below them is Taurus, horns pointed upward, and above, Cancer, the sidereal killer. The crab is as big as the bull. Laura turned to me, pulled me toward her, and recklessly we kissed, a passionate two-minute affair, with lots of groping and tongue-thrusting.

∽

I opened my eyes and looked at my watch. Then I pulled out my phone and took a couple of pictures of Mom. It seemed a little weird, and I glanced back before I raised the phone. After I checked the pictures, I went into the office of the blond woman, thanked her and left.

Passing by Muir on the way back, I recalled the motto engraved on the proscenium arch at the front of the auditorium: "You Shall Know the Truth and the Truth Shall Make You Free."

171

For making fun of this maxim in gym one day in 7th grade–
"you shall drink the juice and the juice shall make you pee"–I got
sent to Mr. McKinzie's office. Mr. Higgs wrote on the citation
that I was disrupting class. It was the only time I got a swat.

&

"So how was Mom?" Danny asked, after I got back to the
house.

"Dead," I said.

My brothers hadn't been interested in looking at the body.
"Not my thing," said Danny. "Morbid," said David.

I put some water on for coffee. "I want to hear about the new
trusts," I said.

"Sure, let's go over them in the breakfast room."

Wendy, David, Danny, and I sat once again around the white
formica table. Danny distributed copies of the agreement in shiny
black binders. The two trusts that had been created at my father's
death became four successor trusts, as planned. Each of the brothers was to have been sole trustee of his own trust. Now Danny
and David were co-trustees of all four.

"I figured you guys might do something like this," I said, and
pulled out of my briefcase the notarized statement my mother
had signed. "No judge is going to recognize it."

Danny looked at the statement. "Sorry, bro. Check the date on
the amendment to the trust."

It was the day before Mom had signed the form I'd faxed Vera.

"You shit," I said.

"Don't get bent out of shape. Your daughter's still the beneficiary of yours, and when you die, it's all hers."

"Her name's Amy. You guys have no right to take over the
trusts."

"Since when have did you become the Wall Street maven?"

"I wouldn't necessarily have invested in stocks. But my experience is irrelevant. It's unethical to replace me and Carl."

"It's done," Danny said. "You and Carlo don't need the money, and you don't have the time and interest to manage investments. The house is part of the trust. David and I are going to be the ones who'll sell it. You planning to come out for a month and help us?"

Wendy shook her head. "Danny, I'm sorry. This is really unconscionable."

"Keep out of this, Wen," Danny said.

"Who did you get to do it?" Wendy asked.

I slid my binder over to her so she could see. "I'm calling Neil on Monday," she said, after she'd taken a look.

Danny shrugged. "Call him." He turned to me. "And you're welcome to call Rosenblatt."

❧

The meeting adjourned. "I want to show Jon your mother's stuff," Wendy told Danny, and we headed off to her bedroom.

The curtains and windows were open, the bottles of pills, the plastic cups, the needles, the latex gloves, and all the other sickroom paraphernalia were gone, and on a couple of white towels on the black and red Peruvian spread was most of my mother's jewelry.

Wendy handed me a manila folder with several sheets of paper inside. "It's not a complete inventory," she said, "but it may be helpful. Personal effects, clothes, jewelry, art, furniture, flatware, silverware, etcetera, none of that's in the trust. Your mom's will says the four of you are supposed to divide it as you see fit. Of course Danny and David have laid claim to a lot of things."

"Of course."

"I told your mom several times she ought to stipulate in the will who should get what, and have some of the jewelry and art work appraised. But she didn't want to talk about it. So you guys need to negotiate over what you want. Anything you'd like shipped, I can take care of that next week."

173

I thanked Wendy and gave her a hug. I told her Angie didn't want anything, and that I'd just like a couple of pieces of jewelry for Amy and some of the memorabilia, photos, letters, and journals Mom had hung on to.

The ethnic chatchkas were lined up on the low walnut table at the foot of the bed, looking particularly demonic in the late afternoon sunlight. Most of the jewelry was also Third Worldly, amber and turquoise beads and silver bangles from Central America, horn, ebony, and brass necklaces and earrings from Africa. I felt sentimental tugs over a couple of the objects, a bracelet with stylized silver hands dangling from it, a star in each palm, that had fascinated me as a kid, and a necklace with a flat grey stone pendant on which a dog, outlined in white, was baying at a mother-of-pearl moon. I put both of these on one side, along with my mother's wedding ring. "They don't want it," Wendy told me. Vera had slipped it off after my mother's hands began to swell, put it on a chain, and had her wear it around her neck. The bi-metal ring had two raised ridges around the rims, and two smaller stippled ridges on either side of the band of silver at its center.

"So where are the diamonds and pearls?" I asked. These necklaces and earrings were gifts from my mother's Aunt Selena. Angela and Amy had no interest in them, but I couldn't imagine that Karen did either, and Wendy would never have taken any jewelry without discussing it with me. "I thought we'd include them in the auction, or sell them separately."

"Yes, that would make sense," Wendy said, "but David wanted both rings and both necklaces for Karen."

"Karen doesn't wear pearls and diamonds."

"She said she wanted something to remember your mother by."

I rolled my eyes but didn't say anything.

"David needs to get those appraised," Wendy muttered, and made a note on the manila folder. "He should reimburse the rest of you."

"I'm not holding my breath."

Among the pieces left behind was a brooch with a lustrous taupe moonstone in a marcasite setting. It looked like something Amy might like, and I added it, and a necklace with tiny jade beads, to the bracelet, pendant, and ring.

Wendy began pulling Harry and David boxes out of my dad's closet. They were filled with old papers and memorabilia. I'd moved them from cabinets in the garage after Dad died, thinking Mom might want to look over the stuff. Though she got rid of my father's shoes and clothes the day after his memorial service, the boxes just sat there.

I spent a couple of hours sifting through them. There were sundry diplomas, certificates, awards, pins, and badges, and some essays and poems that had garnered a few of the prizes. There was a sheaf of brittle yellowed articles she'd written for the *Daily Californian* at Berkeley, and some college papers exploring ambiguities in James, color symbolism in Melville, garden imagery in Austen, etc.

I was more interested in a couple of short stories my mother had written. She had never mentioned them. The first was called "Dragon." A young high school English teacher at a small town in California is attracted to one of her students. He seems older and wiser than his peers. He has a dry sense of humor. But as a result of some conflict with his brutish father, the boy drops out of school, enlists in the army, and is shipped off to Korea. Some time later, he sends the teacher a small cloisonné vase. On a deep blue background are hundreds of tiny white blossoms. A long, sinuous dragon flies through the air on the upper part of the vase. It has a light brown back, a white belly, gold claws, and pale coral wings. Each scale is carefully rendered. In the dragon's mouth is a moon, or perhaps an egg. A week later the teacher gets a letter from a friend of the student, telling her that the boy was killed in the retreat from Chosin Reservoir. The story ends with the friend, perhaps familiar with Joyce's "The Dead," describing flakes of snow falling on the boy's face in the moonlight.

175

I knew the vase. It sat on the little desk in the corner of the den that my mother used for writing letters and paying bills. I'd asked Mom about it once and she'd said a friend had sent it to her when she was teaching in Bakersfield. I retrieved the vase and added it to my collection.

The second story was called "The Waterfall." A co-ed is visiting her half-brothers in upstate New York over the summer and falls in love with the younger brother, Jack. He has long brown hair, and is pale, poetic, and impractical, unlike his older brother and father, who are lawyers. The girl and Jack go for a long walk to a waterfall. Here they possibly make love, though it's not quite clear. Locked in an embrace, they wind up rolling down a hill, into a gully. Some time later, back in California, the girl gets a letter from the older brother telling her that Jack has killed himself with his father's pistol.

My mother was thirty-six when I was born, and carefully pre-served my earliest finger-paintings and my first attempts to write letters, and most of what followed. I'd taken a quick look at my oeuvre when I'd moved the boxes from the garage, but now I noticed a carton I hadn't opened. On top were some sunsets I'd painted in the fourth grade. They were washes. Beautiful Miss White, smelling of vanilla, had bent over us and showed us how to wet the paper and then slowly stroke the pinks and purples and oranges onto the damp surface. When the bands of color dried, you could paint little black birds in front of the clouds. It gave the sunset a pleasingly ominous touch, and I sometimes went overboard with the ravens.

Willie Clump would get my own analyses of *Moby Dick*, *The Turn of the Screw*, and *Sister Carrie* and my appreciations of Voltaire, Tom Paine, and Abe Lincoln, but I lay the sunsets next to the vase on my mother's bed.

Two little prints joined the pile. These were reproductions of "Stars" and "The Knave" by Maxfield Parrish, exactly the sort of kitsch my mother scorned. How had she come by these and why had she hung on to them?

In "The Knave," an illustration from *The Knave of Hearts*, one of Parrish's androgynous young men sits on a grassy hill covered with small flowers, leaning on his right arm, his left leg extended, his right bent under it. The light is behind him, catching the top of his thick chestnut hair and the edge of his profile. He wears a short tunic with puffy white sleeves and long soft brown boots. Behind him, in the bright sunlight, is a waterfall. A stone bridge spans the river, and trees angle across the canyon from the bank on which he sits.

In "Stars," a nude with blond hair sits in profile on a rock above a calm sea. It's just after dusk, and her skin is bathed in moonlight. The horizon is white, the upper sky deep blue, with a few stars. She leans back, holding her ankles, balancing on her buttocks and heels, her head angled up. She has a somber, contemplative expression. Is she looking at the moon or at Venus or at a constellation, or is she just thinking deep thoughts?

My freshman year at Reed I'd had a poster of another, more famous girl on a rock. The model for "Ecstacy" stands on a sloping outcrop of porous red stone and greets the sunrise. Her head is titled back and her hands are behind her head, elbows up, the underside of her arms and her face catching the sun. The wind swirls her Grecian dress around her, and whips back her thick dark-blond hair. Parrish culumli billow behind her in a cerulean blue sky. In the distance are pale blue hills and a blue lake, ultramarine where in shadow. Though happy to be stretching in the early morning light, the girl is not ecstatic.

"Ecstacy" provided a little sunshine in bleak and rainy Portland. I thought I knew Mom's feelings about Parrish, and I never mentioned the print to her, any more than I did the Polaroids of a naked Julie I kept in an envelope at the bottom of my trunk.

Under my mother's two prints was a single playing card, the Jack of Hearts. But it was not the stylized double silhouette of a Bicycle pack. The Jack was kissing a young woman. Her head was tilted back to receive his kiss and she was baring her breasts. The couple was rendered naturalistically, in a dreamy, chocolate-box style. The card looked as if it were French, from the '20s or '30s. The Jack was as pretty as his girlfriend. They both had heavy-lidded eyes and sensual red lips. In the obverse image, the pair was standing chastely side-by-side, the woman holding a pink rose.

I slipped the card under "Stars" on my mother's bed.

CHAPTER 21

Danny was flying to Sacramento Sunday afternoon, and Wendy agreed to meet me in Venice.

We still had to work around her kids, now in their mid-twenties. Neither Sam nor Ashley left home for long. Sam had boomeranged back from Santa Cruz and Ashley, an ex-Scientologist, was again installed in her old room, and studying art history at Northridge.

I chose a little boutique hotel five minutes from the beach. "It's been way too long," I said as I helped Wendy undress, after a bone-jarring embrace and a long kiss.

I'd asked myself, of course, how long would have been not long enough.

I saw Laura and Wendy about twice a year. I was grateful to be in equilibrium with my wife's melodramatic little sister. We both looked forward weeks ahead to our rendezvous, but she rarely pressed me to come up more often. Like her dad, Laura was afraid of flying, and had never suggested coming down to Florida when Angela was out of town. Laura, I would frequently remind myself, was ideologically opposed to marriage.

I would ask my sister-in-law from time to time, in an avuncular way, if she was seeing anyone. Part of me–most of me–hoped that now that she had a lover, she'd acquire a boyfriend. This didn't happen.

I knew that if Laura and I lived in the same city, there would be difficulties within a month. If we lived under the same roof, within a day. But with Wendy, I found myself wondering from time to time if she would cease being my lover if she were to become my wife.

✍

After we made love, I fell asleep holding Wendy, pressed against her back. I dreamed I was walking with my mother in the Ahwahnee. We were in a crowd of well-dressed men and women in the Great Lounge. A pianist was playing "Moonlight Sonata." My mother was wearing a sheet. I knew I ought to tell her that she was dead, but was embarrassed. I suggested we go into the Mural Room, with its oak paneling and William Morrisy tableau of peaceable animals in a forest. There was no one in the room.

"Turn on the light, Jon," my mother said. When I flicked the switch by the big French doors, the sun went out and it became night. Panicked, I flicked the switch again, and it was daylight. People are going to be very irritated, I thought. I turned back, but my mother was now a small block of ice and rapidly melting. I flicked the switch three more times, thinking it might restore my mother. In the moonlight, the puddle of water on the floor was the color of blood. I woke up.

I told Wendy the dream. Angie, like most people, was instantly bored by accounts of dreams, but my sister-in-law the analysand always seemed to be curious.

"It's good," she said. "You're letting go."

"You think so? I'm not so sure," I said.

We started to get dressed. "I should have asked my mother more questions," I said as I pulled on my pants. "I might have been a better son if I'd known her better."

"Don't, Jon. Our parents tell us what they want to tell us." Wendy shook her head and started brushing her long black hair. She looked at me in the mirror.

"Still," I said, "I wish I'd been more curious."

"Believe me, most secrets get taken to the grave, and it's for the best."

"Really? I thought you were a believer in *lux fiat*. You've been in analysis for years."

"That's about recovering your own unconscious. But whether or not your repressed memories correspond to some objective reality is irrelevant."

"I'm sorry. I'm an historian. I don't believe that."

"Jon, sometimes I wonder where you've been for the last couple of decades."

"Not reading Foucault and Derrida."

When we were seated at Joe's on Abbot Kinney, I attempted to resume the discussion. "If we don't try to understand our parents, we can't break the cycle, don't you think? We perpetuate their crimes and misdemeanors."

Wendy laughed. "It's a little late to help our kids at this point."

"OK. But maybe we can help ourselves. If we can forgive our parents, a burden gets lifted. The owl of Minerva may fly at dusk, but there's still the whole evening ahead of us."

"Jon, you're such a Californian. You think you're not, but you are."

When the starters arrived, Wendy became lawyerly.

"You still have a good shot at overturning the new trust," she said. "Hang on to that notarized statement your mom signed." Wendy took a bite of her smoked salmon. "What's particularly egregious is the treatment of Carl. He doesn't have kids. He may not have any. The terms of the original trust were very liberal. You could spend down 10% a year on virtually anything. Carl may be a multi-millionaire, but he has a right to make decisions

181

about disbursements. I think a judge or mediator is likely to find for him." Wendy sipped her chardonnay. "You need to have Mark send a registered letter requesting a copy of all the nurses' notes from the week before your mom signed the new trust. Show it to Vera and Craig and have them verify it, and then ask them to give you their best recollections of your mother's mental state day by day. Record it, have it transcribed, and ask them to sign the transcript." Wendy took another bite of her salmon. "You also want to have Mark write another letter to Danny requesting monthly–no, bi-weekly–reports on every investment in the trust. Danny needs to explain and justify each decision he makes. He'll hire someone, of course, but it'll cost him, and he's going to have to forward a lot of material. Your mom's portfolio is very diversified. Maybe he'll have some second thoughts."

"You're so crafty, Wendy." I reached across the table and took her hands. "I love you."

She squeezed my hands. "Jon, I'd be telling you this even if we weren't lovers. Even if we weren't friends."

"That's why I love you."

We had just resumed eating when I saw someone waving and heading for our table. It was Donna Salvucci.

"Jesus, Donna, you're everywhere," I said, and stood up and gave her a hug. "Great to see you. How're you doing?"

"Fine," she said. "But listen, I'm so sorry about your mom. Angie told me. I really liked her. She was a sweet lady."

"Thanks. Donna, you remember my sister-in-law Wendy. Wendy, you remember Donna, Angela's sister." They'd met at our wedding reception, and one or two times since, when Donna had been out in LA during one of my summer trips.

"So what are you doing here?" I asked.

"Oh, we're out for LA Fashion Week. This is Carolyn Bulgari and Francesca Dorfman."

"Good to meet you," I said. We chatted for another few minutes.

182

As they walked off to their table, I heard Carolyn ask, "Why does he keep calling you Donna?"

⁊

Wendy and I started talking about Venice, and how much it had changed since we'd been coming out there. Money had poured into the tawdry beach town. Even after property values headed south, homeowners still seemed to be renovating and landscaping furiously along the canals and on the walk streets west of Lincoln, where the pavement between the homes is only about two yards wide, and no cars or motorbikes are permitted.

Wendy and I had done the walk streets after we'd made love. The neighborhood oozes charm. The homes are small. Many are boxy, painted in bright primary colors or cool pastels, with big redwood decks and floor-to-ceiling windows, but there are some traditional bungalows and arts-and-crafts cottages with stained-glass windows. The gardens overflow with flowers. Wendy took botany at Berkeley, and pointed out the purple heliotropes, the scarlet begonias and violet bachelor's buttons, the phlox and fuchsia and zinnia. A carpet of white and pink mums spread below the porch of one bungalow. Bird of paradise was everywhere. We saw Japanese gongs, Buddhas, nymphs and satyrs, and in one yard, a copy of Rodin's *Thinker*. With a few exceptions, the fences were low. The homes and gardens were on display. Giant ferns hung over the sidewalk, and queen palms converged above us.

After dinner we walked along the canals. The houses fronting the water are mostly on a grander scale. They're not up against the canal, like the palazzos, and there's nothing Venetian about them. But the path was almost deserted, and the moonlight glistened on the dark water.

Then we headed over to the boardwalk. Even at 9:00 it was still a circus. We passed a slim, bronzed fire-eater and, further on, a girl in a gold lamé belly-dancer costume, handling a python. Some of the usual characters were there, the seventy-year-old muscle-bound guy in his speedo, strutting back and forth, and other body builders, one with a parrot on his shoulder. He offered to pose for $5. There were Haitians aggressively hawking their cds, and guys offering "medical marijuana." A pack of bikinied girls on roller blades swept by. A circle of drummers was beating a monotonous tattoo, and a scruffy guitarist was playing "Puff, the Magic Dragon." You got a blast of weed from time to time. And there were groups of tourists like us, gawking and stuffing their faces with pizza and corn dogs.

A guy was selling postcards of Venice when it looked a little more like Venice, and I picked up several of St. Mark's Square. This was at the intersection of Windward and Ocean Park, and featured a passable imitation palazzo, the Hotel St. Mark, with tiers of gothic arches and winged lions on its cornices. But further on, the Ocean Park Bathhouse looked like an Arabian fortress. The rest of the entertainment was out on the pier, a roller coaster, rides, including a tunnel of love and "Hades," a ship restaurant with strings of lights in its rigging, a ballroom and bandstand, and a Japanese pavilion. The visitors strolling under the St. Mark's colonnades and out on the pier were dressed to the nines. Everyone had a hat, the men wore ties, the women full length dresses. And everyone covered up on the beach. No bare limbs until the '20. What would they have thought of the current lot?

There must have been beach bums, even then. Mel Kravitz surprised me once by saying how much he admired guys who lived in the rough, outdoors all day long, picking fruit, riding on top of freight trains. Then they would retire to beach towns like Venice. They never saw a doctor or dentist, but they were in great shape, until their livers started to pickle. The tanned and tattered flotsam of the pre-'60s decades might have been a little happier with today's revelers in their mini-bikinis and speedos, letting it all hang out.

Then we encountered a drunk Goth girl with purple hair and a chalk-white face. Without the dye and mascara, the nose rings and tattoos, she'd have looked a lot like Laura. The girl was wearing a black t-shirt with silver script: "We're all in the gutter, but some of us are looking at the stars." She stared at me truculently. Wendy and I moved apart to let her pass.

I walked Wendy back to her car. "Thank you so much," I said, and hugged her tightly.

"My pleasure," she said.

"Some time we'll have to spend the night together."

Wendy nodded, but didn't say anything.

CHAPTER 22

Late Monday morning I flew up to Vegas. I got a good deal online on a room at the Venetian. Of course it wasn't anything like the suite Angela and I had stayed in when Nino and Donna had hosted us. It turned out to be one of the handicapped rooms they release at the last minute, with a low toilet and a cushioned seat, and nothing blocking off the shower.

I threw my bag down and headed out to the Nevada Cancer Institute in Summerlin. I'd forgotten my sunglasses and squinted into the glare off the rear windows of the cars ahead of me as I drove west.

Cheryl looked terrible. Her face was puffy and her eyes swollen partly shut. Her skin was yellowish. When she extended her hand, her arm looked skeletal. She had an I.V. in the other arm.

My face must have betrayed my reaction. "I know I look awful," she said.

"No, no. You don't look bad. It's just been awhile." I'd last seen my cousin at my dad's memorial service five years earlier.

"Jon, those are old lady flowers," Cheryl said, spotting the pot of gardenias I'd picked up in the lobby. "I may look like shit, but I'm not seventy."

I laughed and apologized.

Cheryl asked where I was staying and then how I liked the Venetian.

"Well, it's a lot more Vegas than Venice. I'm not a big fan of kitsch, but there's something appealing about it."

"I never made it to Venice," Cheryl said. "The real Venice. We never got to Europe. Steve hated traveling."

"Cheryl, you'll beat this. You'll have a chance to go."

She didn't reply, but told me again how sorry she was about my mother and how much she'd liked her. Then she said, "There's something I never told you about your mom." I pulled up a chair and sat down. "She used to work as an extra in high school. She had small speaking roles, too."

"I know."

Cheryl exhaled. "Well, one evening she got raped by one of the stars in his trailer."

"You're kidding."

"It really traumatized her. You know your mom. She was so upset at herself for trusting him. He told her she looked like Donna Reed and he promised her a good role in his next film. He said he wanted to hear her read a script. That's about the oldest line in the book." Cheryl told me the actor's name. "She was bitter that nothing happened to the guy. She went all the way to Schenk. He told her to get over it."

"Jesus," I said.

"She only mentioned it to me because I was working as an extra at Universal one summer."

I told Cheryl about Danny and David, and the fights over my mom's care and the trust. "What shits they are," she said. She took a sip of water. "But you know, in the end everyone's their own worst enemy."

I asked her about Julie.

"Case in point," she said, and told me about how Julie's fourth marriage had broken up. This time the guy had money. He was a landscape architect, and they had a nice home in the hills that he'd designed. But he drank, like the others. "So she's married an Italian drunk, a French-Canadian drunk, a Hispanic drunk, and an Irish drunk. What's she got left? A Russian? That shouldn't be too hard to find."

I asked about Jayson. He seemed to be doing OK. He hadn't been in any trouble recently, and was living with his girlfriend.

Then Cheryl's face clouded over. She winced.

"Are you OK?" I asked. "You want me to get the nurse."

"No, no. Shut the door, Jon."

When I returned, Cheryl was in tears. "I have to tell you this, Jon. Promise me won't tell anyone."

"I promise."

"You know why Steve left?"

I shook my head.

"He caught me in bed with Jayson."

"What?"

"Yes," she wailed. Tears were streaming down her cheeks. "Yes." She cried silently for several minutes, shaking her head.

"It was so stupid. I'm so ashamed. But I was drinking. I was so unhappy. He started coming over and, well, we wound up in bed. Then, maybe the fourth or fifth time, Steve came home during the day. He'd been fired."

"So he was already in a good mood."

Cheryl smiled for a second, then started weeping again. "I begged him not to tell the kids. But of course he did." She shut her eyes for several seconds. "Jon, I'm so ashamed. Do you forgive me?"

"Of course. But you haven't hurt me. I'm sure Jayson enjoyed it."

Cheryl gasped. "I did too. But it's so sick."

She started crying again. Her whole body was heaving. I hugged her.

"Now you know," she said.

"What about Julie? Does Julie know?"

The tears started flowing again. Cheryl nodded.

"Jayson still doesn't know I'm his dad, right?"

"No, but he's curious about you."

"You didn't tell him we were lovers."

"Of course not," she said.

"Steve never found out, right?"

"I never told him." She shut her eyes for a moment. "If something can bite you, it will," she said.

Then tears started sliding down Cheryl's cheeks again.

"I'm such a bad person. I deserve to die."

"You're not. You're not, Cheryl. Please don't say that. You're a good person."

She closed her eyes and shook her head.

"Listen," I said, "you just have to concentrate on beating this."

She continued to shake her head. When she opened her eyes, she gave me a look of utter despair.

I bent over and kissed her. "I love you," I said.

My cousin didn't reply.

I knelt down beside the bed and took her hand. "Cheryl, when you get better, we'll go to Venice together. I promise. Just the two of us."

Cheryl looked at me a long time, then gave me a half-smile and a wink. "It's a deal," she whispered.

I returned to the hotel, and walked past the sugar cake palazzo, in reality a mall, with its inflected arches and its second-floor columns topped by the Venetian quatrefoil, the disk pierced by four lobes. In the turquoise water below were the black gondolas, beside the barbershop poles. Everything was far too pristine in the bright Nevada sun. I passed through the sumptuous hotel lobby, with the gold pseudo-armillary sphere at its center. The orb is supported by four armless, topless nymphs, and is circled by a broad, titled band with the signs of the zodiac. I gazed up at the imitation Veronese, then headed down the wide hallway, its vaulted ceiling decorated with Michelangelesque panels, to the Grand Canal. You walk from the Sistine Chapel into fake *plein air*. Overhead are fleecy clouds in a preternaturally blue sky. It's always just before dusk in the Venetian, the magic hour, the hour to get a drink.

I sat in a cantina beside the canal and had a couple of beers.

Cheryl *is* a good person, I thought. She'd become a nurse, and I was sure she was an excellent one. She'd trained to do neurosurgical nursing. She'd cared for severely disabled patients. Cheryl had described in emails some of the grisly routine procedures and some of the more dramatic code blues she'd been involved in. Later, she'd worked in the psychiatric ward, and had regaled me with more horror stories.

Why should she get pancreatic cancer?

I walked into St. Mark's Square. It was still nearly dusk, and I had another beer. I watched a group of musicians in *commedia del arte* costumes play the first movement of "Winter" from Vivaldi's *Four Seasons*, then the last movement of "Summer." A juggler performed, then a tumbler. A red-haired soprano in a black, rhinestone-speckled Venetian mask and a black cape sang "That's Amore." I had another beer. After a white-painted Dantesque-looking mime took the stage and froze, I left the Square and resumed walking down the Grand Canal.

Venice ends abruptly in Vegas. A couple of hundred feet after the Rialto Bridge, the canal widens. Here the gondolas turn around and take on and let off passengers. There are more shops, and then a double flight of stairs. Walk down them and you're in the Palazzo Hotel, standing beside a large pool. At its center, alabaster nymphs preen against marble columns. Overhead are crenellated burgundy and amber balloons, with tassels dangling.

I sat down beside the pool. My eyes filled with tears. I hadn't cried for my mother, my father, or anyone else except Julie since Grandma Marike died. Only my cousins could make me cry.

I shut my eyes. Ward and June Cleaver hovered in front of me, arm in arm. I thought about how I'd wanted to be just like Ward when I grew up. It seemed so easy. The couple shimmered and faded.

191

I opened my eyes and saw a little boy staring at me. His parents were behind him, and they called him away from me. "Jason, get over here."

I rose, trudged up the stairs, and returned to my room.

CHAPTER 23

When I got back to Tampa, I looked for my half-uncles on line, hoping they had kept my grandfather's name. It didn't take long to google an obituary notice for a guy who may have been one of the brothers, Michael Stern. The obit was from a funeral home in Utica, New York. I emailed them and was told that if I wrote a letter, they would forward it to a family member. My mother had never mentioned any children of her half-brothers, so I wrote to "Dear Sir or Madam," explained who I was, and asked for any information the relative might be willing to give me about Stern and his brother.

Among the emails waiting for me was one from Jerry Bender suggesting we get together for a late lunch on Friday at the Bombay Palace on Fraser. I said fine.

I'd never told anyone about my affairs with Julie and Cheryl, or with Wendy and Laura. If I were to confide in someone, it would be Jerry. He was my closest friend. And he was a guy. As Henry Higgins says, "a man will buck you up whenever you are glum." In college and after, I'd listened to friends' sad stories about heartless vixen who'd lied to them and cheated on them. But I'd also heard tales in which the girlfriend or wife was clearly the victim. I'd extended my sympathies to the guys in both cases. *Tout comprehende, c'est tout pardoner.* That's what friends are for.

Jerry and I didn't talk a lot about personal things. We usually exchanged stories about recent absurdities at WFU and USP and talked some history.

Jerry was a specialist in the *Aufklarung*, the German Enlightenment, but he was as fascinated by Venice as I was, and we'd occasionally discuss the *Serenissima*.

Once the wealthiest and most powerful city in Europe, its days of glory were ended by the Ottoman Turks advancing through the eastern Mediterranean and by the kingdoms of western Europe coalescing into nations, with large armies and vast tax bases. Dutch and English shipbuilders, captains, and merchants delivered the coup de grace.

But at least one of the new kingdoms admired the Republic enormously. Thanks to that great moat the English Channel, warriors had become gentlemen, and after Europeans got tired of murdering each other over the meaning of the Eucharist, English aristocrats flocked to Venice as part of the Grand Tour. They were the first cultural pilgrims.

The English were intrigued by the city's success as a republic. The other medieval city states of Italy had been wracked by violent conflicts between families and between classes, and were soon taken over by unscrupulous *condottori*. But there were no successful revolts or coups in Venice. Its governing councils, with their elaborate systems of voting and the rapid rotation of members—no one served for more than eighteen months—maintained peace and stability. Power was diffused among two thousand families. The doge became a figurehead, the office ceremonial. The aristocracy closed its ranks to outsiders at the end of the thirteenth century, but maintained a rough equality among members by the strictest sumptuary laws in Catholic Europe. Justice was cheap, fair, and accessible, and the economy was mostly booming, despite setbacks, as conquests expanded trade. The hammers and saws of the Arsenale, where the fleet was constructed, were rarely idle.

Discontent was rechanneled. There was *Carnivale*, where masks were donned and roles were reversed. There were the *scuole*, the fraternities, part guild, part lodge. Workers were loyal to their *scuola* and loyal to their *sestiere*, their neighborhood. The fraternities all had roles in the great annual festival of the *Sensa*, which celebrated the marriage of Venice to the sea. The doge was rowed out into the Adriatic in his glittering barge, the *Bucintoro*, and threw a gold ring into the water.

What was the secret to the city's stability, the English wanted to know. A humming economy? Civic pride? Rites and rituals binding citizens to the republic? A clever foreign policy that played off Rome against Constantinople, Milan against Florence, Bourbon against Hapsburg?

The nineteenth century took a darker view. Venice was a police state. *I Dieci*, the Council of Ten, Grand Inquisitors answerable to no one, terrorized the population. Spies were everywhere, and suspected dissidents were sent to the sweltering *piombi*, the prison under the lead roof of the ducal palace, or the fetid *pozzi*, beside the canal, and then sometimes strangled in their cells—or hung from the campanile, or suspended between the columns topped by the city's patron saints, Mark and Theodore.

Nineteenth century liberals also had a less benign take on Venetian imperialism. Rival Dalmatian ports were subjugated, their walls leveled, Cyprus, Crete, and coastal Greece were seized and exploited and Byzantium reduced to a dependency, then in turn raped and looted—with the help of gullible French and Flemish knights, duped by the wily Venetians. The rulers of the republic were shrewd and ruthless—"crafty and malignant foxes." Finally, at the beginning of the sixteenth century, all of Europe united against them.

But eighteenth century English writers had had a different view. What government before their own day was not despotic? They decided that the key to Venice's success was a balanced government with powerful checks on the ambitions of individuals and cliques. Could a constitutional monarchy emulate these? How about a nation that was planning to be a republic? Venice, with perhaps 120,000 residents in the Middle Ages, was the largest city in Europe. But what if you were designing the government of a country with two and a half million, stretching along the entire Atlantic coast of North America, and perhaps one day to the Pacific?

Could a careful division of power insure stability, Americans asked themselves in 1789. Or did a nation wishing to be a republic have to depend on the virtue of its citizens? If they had to be selfless, abstemious, and civic-minded, how would you instill these qualities? Maybe they came naturally to small independent farmers, but what about the riff-raff in the cities?

∽

Most of the English tourists didn't come to study the Venetian constitution. By 1700, the city had nearly twenty theaters and seven opera houses, including the first in Europe. From Monteverdi through Vivaldi, Venetians dominated the new art form that so brilliantly combined music, drama, and painting with spectacular effects achieved by artist-engineers. When Carlo Goldini began scripting the improvisations of *commedia del arte* troupes, audiences applauded the first modern plays in Europe not based on classical models.

The city was also home to the first public casino on the continent, the *Ridotto*. There were nearly one hundred fifty private casinos by the end of the 18th century, where tourists and natives lost money at *spigolo* (poker), *biribisso* (roulette), and *faro* (bacarrat).

Venice introduced Europeans to the café–the coffee house. By 1700 over 200 cafés in the *Serenissma* served the addictive brew, more popular even than now.

There were other diversions. The city was famous for its courtesans, reportedly the most attractive and sophisticated in Europe. The flourishing trade in vice didn't preserve the reputations of aristocratic wives. Still another Venetian invention was the *cicisbeo*, a gentleman attendant who helped his mistress in and out of gondolas, ordered her meals, fed her, if she wished, and, if she also wished, helped her achieve orgasms. Any hour of the day you could see large black gondolas, curtains drawn, rocking vigorously in their moorings. The *cicisbeo* was the ultimate fashion accessory. Well before Casanova's memoirs appeared, Venetian women of all classes were reputed to have the laxest morals in Italy. Three convents, a French tourist wrote in 1739, were vying for the honor of providing a mistress for the new papal nuncio.

Venice, for nearly two hundred years, was the Vegas of Europe.

∽

When rebellious colonists in North America announced that the pursuit of happiness was a natural right, they didn't have in mind what went on in the *Serenissima*. But when everyone becomes middle class, middle class values disappear. Eventually, citizens of the new Republic would comport themselves much like the hated aristocrats of the Founders' day—except without their good taste and polished manners.

∽

Jerry was a big Mozart *afficionado*. "Whoever your favorite 'B' is," he'd said, "he's a distant second." His own number two was Haydn. Jerry didn't approve of my plans for staging *Die Zauberflöte*, and was bemused that they'd come to fruition. But he promised he'd interview Joyce Creighton for the WFU alumni magazine and write a dispassionate review of the performance.

Over the muligatwny soup and samosas, I asked Jerry about Mozart's relations with his sisters-in-law. Before he married Constanze Weber, the young prodigy had been hopelessly in love with her older sister Aloysia. Had they slept together?

Mozart was reputed to be a philanderer–he and Constanze lived together before they got married–but Jerry considered this highly unlikely. What about Josepha Weber?

Aloysia was a brilliant coloratura, but the oldest sister may have been the best singer in the family. Mozart wrote the score of the Queen of the Night for Josepha. Constanze was taking the waters at Baden while *Die Zauberflöte* was being rehearsed in Vienna, and there were rumors later that Mozart was having affairs with both Pamina, Anna Gottlieb, and Papagena, Barbara Gerl. Was he sleeping with the Queen as well?

Impossible, said Jerry.

Then how about his cousin Maria Anna Thekla, called "the Bäsle"? Bingo. Jerry thought this was likely, judging by several letters from Mozart filled with sexual innuendos among the scatological outpourings. ("Ah, muck! Sweet word! Chuck! That too is fine. Muck, chuck!–muck!–suck–*o charmante*! Muck suck! That's what I like! Muck, chuck and suck! Chuck muck and suck muck!") The Bäsle may have hoped to marry Wolfgang, but the composer's tyrannical and ambitious father made sure that didn't come to pass. The girl into whose purse he deposited his gold, and whose behind he promised to smack, and to wash her front and back, and to shoot off his gun in her rear, never married, though she had an illegitimate daughter with a priest of perhaps similar tastes.

I was on the point of bringing up my own cousin Julie when the entrees arrived. But after we helped ourselves to the tandoori chicken and lamb korma, Jerry, it emerged, had a confession of his own he wanted to share.

Jerry and his wife Maureen had two daughters. Abby, the oldest, was a bright kid. She'd taken ten A P exams and had gotten a five on each, had a 4.1 grade point average, and SATs over 1500. But she hadn't been accepted by Harvard, Yale, or Princeton. Jerry had been bitter. "It shows you where their priorities are," he said. They take way too many legacies, athletes, and minorities. They admit a lot of little Al Gores and George Bushes. "Any really bright student," Jerry proclaimed, "any student with intellectual curiosity, should go to Hopkins, Chicago, MIT, or Cal Tech."

Abby went off to Hopkins. At the end of her freshman year she announced she was a lesbian. Jerry and Maureen were devastated.

Now he had bad news about his younger daughter Erin. Surfing porn sites, he was mortified to discover a video of her masturbating with a cucumber. "Of course I can't talk to her about it," he said. "But I'm worried like crazy about who she's hanging out with." He wondered what I thought he ought to do.

"It could just be an ex-boyfriend taking revenge," I said.

Jerry was doubtful.

"Kids do some pretty dopey things for each other. Tattoos."

"Don't tell me about tattoos. Erin has one on her ankle, one on her wrist, another on her shoulder, and a tramp stamp."

"A tramp stamp?"

"A butterfly just above her butt."

I suggested that he quiz her about boyfriends and see if she'd broken up with one recently.

"That's Maureen's department," Jerry said. Of course he couldn't tell his wife about what he'd seen.

"Say a friend sent you a link," I suggested.

"She'd never believe me."

And so we talked more about the wayward Erin, and what Jerry's options were. Once more I gave a silent prayer that Amy was so ethical, even puritanical, and self-disciplined.

The moment to bring up my own messy relationships passed.

I'd wanted to tell Jerry about Wendy. For the tens of thousands of dollars she was spending on her therapist, my sister-in-law didn't seem to be getting much good advice about Danny. But then if she left him, she might not need to see her shrink every week. And if Wendy divorced my brother, she and I would have to make some decisions.

I'd wanted to talk about Laura. When Angie and I had made love in a hotel room, it was a subdued coupling. There were gasps,

199

but no cries or groans. Laura, however, gave no thought to the neighbors, nor to the guests on the rest of the floor. Or the floor above or the floor below.

I wanted to tell Jerry that on those rare occasions when I made love to my wife, it was Laura I imagined I held, Laura I kissed, Laura I penetrated, and Laura I exploded inside of.

I didn't expect he'd give his blessing, but maybe he'd nod sympathetically and absolve me. "Jon," he might say, "you're living in a fucking Faulkner novel." Then he might tell me, "You need to get to work on a new version of *Don Giovanni*. In the last scene, the statue of the Commendatore pulls Giovanni up to heaven."

CHAPTER 24

The day after I had lunch with Jerry, a letter arrived with a postmark from Utica, New York.

Dear Jonathan,

I'm afraid I am an old-fashioned person and do not use the internet. Therefore, I cannot send you an email. I am typing this on my IBM Selectric.

Please accept my condolences on the death of your mother.

I will try to answer your questions.

My father, Michael Stern, was an attorney in Utica. He had a general practice, but specialized in bankruptcy and divorce cases. My father graduated from Hamilton College and Syracuse Law School and served in the 322nd Bombardment Group in the Eighth Air Force during World War II. He was a member of Temple Beth El, a Rotarian, and a 32nd degree Mason.

My father was a decent, caring individual and was liked and respected by everyone who knew him. He called himself an old country lawyer, but he was an avid reader and a supporter of the Utica symphony orchestra. He died six years ago of congestive heart failure.

His mother, some years after she and your grandfather were divorced, married an older man, George Kochav, the proprietor of a small hotel in the Adirondacks. They did not have any children. Mr. Kochav adopted my father and his brother, but I don't think they were particularly fond of their step-father and they continued to use their original name.

My father said very little about your grandfather. He was devoted to his mother, who died before I was born, and I know that he was bitter about the divorce. He did not blame your grandmother, who he said was only eighteen when his father abandoned his family for her.

He once told me that he and his brother had visited their father one day at his factory a year or so after the divorce. His father pretended not to know them and told them to go around to the delivery entrance. He met them there and said that they should never come to the factory again. He was very angry.

My father mentioned your mother and her sister a few times. He had the impression that they were well off. He said your mother visited once when she was in college, and that she was pretty and vivacious. But they didn't stay in touch.

You ask about my Uncle Paul. I have very few memories of him. He died by his own hand when I was five. According to my father, he was a brilliant and promising young man. He went to Columbia College, where he studied English literature. I believe he began, but did not complete, a Ph.D. at Harvard. He had a nervous breakdown and was in an institution for a year or two. Later he taught at a preparatory school in Massachusetts.

I suppose I have followed in his footsteps in a way, as I taught Latin for forty-one years at Sacred Heart Academy. I have recently retired.

I'm sorry I cannot give you more information, but I hope this has been of some help. I am having pictures of my father and Uncle Paul reproduced and will send them to you.

Yours sincerely,

Evelyn Stern

P.S. There is a Latin motto, "Non obiit, abiit." It means that a dead person has not perished, but has only gone away. When someone we have loved dies, we still carry them with us in our hearts. I hope you have lots of good memories of your mother to console you in this time of sorrow.

CHAPTER 25

The Sister-in-Law Problem
from Henry VIII to Today

Jonathan Marcus
University of St. Petersburg
New England Association of British Studies
Boston, Massachusetts

In 1502, the older brother of the future Henry VIII died. The sickly Arthur had been married to Catherine of Aragon. This was an excellent match. Arthur's and Henry's father, King Henry VII, was, unfortunately, a usurper. His grandfather, Owen Tudor, had been an ambitious Welsh soldier. Henry had royal blood on his mother's side, but only because Edward III's younger son had gotten his mistress pregnant.

Catherine was the daughter of Ferdinand and Isabella of Spain, the wealthiest and most powerful rulers in Europe. She also had a better claim to the English throne than her father-in-law. Catherine was too good a catch to let go, and so Henry arranged for his second son to marry the young widow. Catherine testified that she and Arthur had never consummated the marriage, and the pope gave his blessing.

When Henry fell in love with Anne Boleyn fifteen years later and believed Catherine no longer capable of bearing him a son, he decided that his marriage had been illegal. Whether or not Art and Cathy had had sex, she'd been his brother's wife. As two of Shakespeare's characters put it, "'It seems this marriage with his brother's wife has crept too near his conscience.' 'No, his conscience has crept too near another lady.'"

Thomas Cramner, the chaplain of the Boleyn family, was appointed Archbishop of Canterbury on the death of the incumbent. He happened to agree with His Majesty, but to resolve "the King's Great Matter," Henry was ultimately obliged to break with Rome. Now, as head of the Church of England, he was free to plunder the country's rich monasteries and convents, as well as marry the canny Miss Boleyn, who had refused to sleep with him until they were legally wed.

In Henry's day, you made your case by citing passages from the Old and New Testaments. Catherine's supporters pointed to Deuteronomy 25:5, which commanded a man to marry his brother's widow if the brother had been living with him and had no son. The passage even stipulates that he must have sex with her. Henry's theologians invoked Leviticus 18:18, which says you should not screw your wife's sister, or even "uncover her nakedness," tempting as that might be. Henry's case was not strong. Catherine was not, after all, the sister of Henry's wife. In any event, the prohibition is in force only if the wife is still alive.

God, it seemed, or at least the writers He inspired, wanted you to wed and bed your brother's wife if he should die, but stay away from your wife's sister. The brother's children, however, might take a different view, cf. Hamlet, Prince of Denmark.

It makes sense that the OT would be worried about an unmarried woman in the household getting pregnant. On the other hand, if you knocked up your brother's wife while the poor bugger was still alive, though it might chill relations with him were he to find out (or worse, cf. Giovanni Malatesta), the baby would be legitimate and mother and child provided for.

But the authors of the Bible were not pragmatists. What was no doubt more important for them was that the wife's sister was within the prohibited degree of kinship. She was considered a blood relation, while the wife of a brother was not.

⁂

All cultures forbid incest, but, as anthropologists since the late 19th century have been tickled to point out, different societies define it differently.

Malinowski, studying the Trobriands of New Guinea, concluded that while "in the Oedipus complex there is the repressed desire to kill the father and marry the mother, in the matrilineal society of the Trobriands, the wish is to marry the sister and to kill the maternal uncle."

But both fans of Freud and many critics, like Malinowski, agree that the urge to have sex with family members is powerful and dangerous, and needs to be curbed for the family to survive.

A different take comes from Levi-Strauss and others, who focus on the importance of exogeny. It's not so much that sex within families would result in painful scenes in the cave or hut, but that the tribe that didn't form alliances with other tribes would perish. Women were chattel and it was to your advantage to trade them skillfully. Margaret Mead reports an answer she kept getting from the Arapesh of New Guinea: "What, you would like to marry your sister! What is the matter with you anyway? Don't you want a brother-in-law? Don't you realize that if you marry another man's sister and another man marries your sister, you will have at least two brothers-in-law, while if you marry your own sister you will have none? With whom will you hunt, with whom will you garden, whom will you go to visit?"

But still another school of theorists downplays the taboo. For Westermarck and his followers, proximity in childhood leads to sexual repulsion, rather than attraction. There is no craving to sleep with family members, at least not your sister or brother. This has been confirmed in some studies of children raised on Kibbutzim. Many brothers and sisters would second the idea. The incest taboo is almost unnecessary.

∽

Though extended families had not lived together under the same roof for centuries in England, unmarried women in the nineteenth century still often lived with a married sister.

In 1835, when Lord Lyndhurst's Marriage Act was passed, the country was not yet Victorian. The future Queen was just sixteen and still a prisoner in Kensington Palace. It was not prudishness, but the itch to reform and regularize the law, so strong in this decade, that induced Parliament to legislate on the subject.

From the time of Henry VIII, marriages by widowers to their wife's sister were sometimes considered legitimate and sometimes not. When the kids of the first wife took the cases to court, the verdicts were not consistent. And if there was no lawsuit, there was no problem.

The new law arbitrarily decreed that all marriages to ex-sisters-in-law that had taken place before the legislation was passed were legal, while in the future such marriages would be illegal. This did not please logical members of the House of Commons, but the Lords passed the bill.

Middle-class and upper-class men wishing to regularize relations with their former sisters-in-law could go abroad and get married. This wasn't so easy for the lower classes.

The case against the bill was made on pragmatic grounds. It was not that a man's longing for his wife's pretty little sister ought to be gratified, but that it was in the interest of the children that the relationship should be regularized. They needed a new mother, another angel in the house, not a maiden aunt. Dozens of men interviewed by a Royal Commission testified about how wonderfully well their sister-in-law would fill that role. The kids were already so fond of her.

Supporters of the 1835 law, on the other hand, argued that if the law were overturned, brothers- and sisters-in-law would be regarding each other in an unwholesome, more lascivious light—especially when the wife was sick. The possibility of a future marriage might kindle lust. Would the husband and sister-in-law even be tempted to experiment while the wife was still alive?

Supporters of the Deceased Wife's Sister's Bill may have been hidebound reactionaries, but they were on to something. Lithe, winsome, playful, the little sister could be a standing temptation, the devil the house, the subject of engrossing fantasies.

Mr. Knightley may have had something to say about this, if we could have overheard his thoughts. Emma Woodhouse was not his sister-in-law, but her older sister had married his younger brother. They were family. They'd been in close contact for years. Familiarity may breed contempt—or be a sexual turn-off—between siblings, if Westermarck is right—but certainly not between in-laws, who encounter each other later in life.

At the end of Chapter 38, Emma provokes her admirer into asking her to dance. "Indeed I will," she replies. "You have shown that you can dance, and you know we are not really so much brother and sister as to make it at all improper."

"Brother and sister! no, indeed," Mr. Knightley declares. This exchange is a turning point in the novel. We see the sparks flying.

Sigmund Freud might also have had something to say about the attractiveness of in-laws.

Minna Bernays was sharper, livelier, and apparently sexier than her older sister Martha, whom Freud had married. It's not clear when their affair began, but we know that in August of 1898, the forty-two-year old Freud took a two-week vacation with his thirty-three-year-old sister-in-law in the Swiss Alps. He signed the guest registry at the Schweizerhaus in Maloja *Dr. Sigmund Freud und frau*" and the couple shared a bedroom. Freud sent postcards to his wife describing the magnificent scenery he was seeing.

This was not just a summer fling. Minna had an abortion a couple of years later.

Carl Jung knew Minna Bernays, and it was his testimony, until the discovery of the hotel register, that provided the best evidence of the affair, which he said Bernays admitted to him. But Jung was Freud's rival, and the Master's initiates dismissed the information as the malicious slander of a jealous competitor. "In one respect Freud was undeniably superior to Jung," proclaimed the director of the Sigmund Freud Archives, who had recently ordered the interviews with Jung sealed for sixty years. "His sexual record was lily white."

Readers will not fail to have noticed that the sister-in-law question was almost always discussed from the standpoint of the male. Luckily, one of my wife's sisters, a prolific blogger, will be joining me in Boston and can perhaps open up new vistas on the question from a woman's perspective. The scenery should be spectacular.

CHAPTER 26

After lunch with Jerry, I gave Amy a call. We hadn't spoken in several days. "I'm fine, Daddy," she told me. "I've just been very busy." She asked me what I wanted for my birthday. It was coming up April 1st. No one had an excuse to forget. Amy didn't mention Jayson, and I didn't ask.

The next day I got an email from Laura. I'd seen her in New York three weeks earlier, when I was ostensibly attending a conference of the Victorian Studies Society of North America. There was no message, only a link to a youtube video of Ray Peterson singing "Tell Laura I Love Her."

I clicked on the link and listened to the song. In order to buy his girlfriend a wedding ring, Tommy enters a stock car race. Though "no one knows what happened," he crashes. The song's title is his dying words as he's pulled from the wreck.

"Tell Laura I Love Her" was recorded in 1960, when teenagers in America got killed trying to buy a ring or going back to retrieve one from a car. Their "reputation was shot" if they stayed out too late at a movie, and, if their parents told them to, they gave up boyfriends and girlfriends who came from the wrong side of the tracks, though it was the end of the world when they said good-bye. Kids were intent on getting married. Insults to girlfriends were avenged. Adulterers committed suicide. There was such a thing as guilt. There was such a thing as renunciation. I could almost remember that world.

Five days after the email, in the middle of a driving rainstorm, the dogs started barking. Fifteen seconds later my phone rang. "Jonny," Laura said, "I'm in your driveway. I've only got one twenty. You need to come out and pay the driver."

I did and brought my sister-in-law and her small suitcase back inside. The dogs greeted her enthusiastically. "What in the world are you doing here, Laura?" I asked.

"Aren't you glad to see me?"

"Of course," I said, giving her a hug. "It's just a total surprise. You never fly."

"I have a special birthday present for you, and I had to deliver it in person."

I swallowed hard. Thank God Angela was teaching an evening class and wouldn't be home for at least an hour.

"So what's the present?"

"Me." Laura beamed at me. "And…"

She put her bag down, rummaged inside, then pulled out a plastic baggie, opened it and brandished a small stick in front of my face. She waved it back and forth.

"What's that?"

"Jonny, look. Two lines. I'm pregnant."

I shut my eyes.

"Don't look so crestfallen, love. Everything'll be fine. We're flying to Albuquerque tomorrow morning. I already bought the tickets. We'll rent a car and go house-hunting in Santa Fe."

"Let's sit down for a minute, Laura."

Incredibly, part of me was as elated as my sister-in-law. Angela hadn't wanted to have a kid after Amy. We'd discussed it, then argued about it, for several years. Amy was a delight and a full-time job at home, but I'd always wanted more children.

Most of me, however, was in agony.

"Sit down," I urged Laura again.

I rummaged in the cabinet and found some unopened Tension Tamer herbal tea, my sister-in-law's favorite. She had sent a couple of boxes for Christmas. I boiled water and made us each a cup.

"Let's not rush into anything, Laur," I said. "I'm going to cancel the reservations and tomorrow morning I'll make a doctor's appointment. We'll see what he has to say."

"Or she," said Laura brightly. "But, Jon, there're doctors in Santa Fe."

"I know. But let's just take this one step at a time."

"It's so exciting to be here!"

"Yeah, I'll give you a tour and show you Amy's room. That's where you'll stay." I took a gulp of the tea. "Now listen, sweetheart, Angie's teaching an evening class. She'll be back before ten. Let's not say anything to her right now, OK? Promise me."

Laura grinned. "I do solemnly swear."

"We'll say this was just a spur of the moment thing. You got laid off from work and wanted to escape for a few days."

"It's true," Laura said. "I was fired."

"How come?"

"Carol said I was spending too much time on the internet."

"Were you?"

Laura smiled broadly. "Guilty as charged."

I glanced at her hand. "Laur, let's take that wedding band off, OK?"

Laura moved it to the ring finger of her right hand. "For now," she said, and winked.

Angela returned early. She spotted her sister at the table as soon as she came in the door from the garage, and was not pleased.

"Laura! What are you doing here?"

Laura stood up. "Hi, Angie. Guess what? I'm pregnant. Jonny's the father. We're moving to Santa Fe tomorrow."

Angela put down her book bag and briefcase and looked at me.

"No one's going to Santa Fe," I said. "And we don't know Laura's pregnant."

"But she could be? By you?"

"Would you like a cup of Tension Tamer tea?" I asked.

"Jon!"

"Yes, it's possible."

"I didn't think even you were capable of doing something so stupid."

I stood up. "I'm getting some sheets for Amy's bed."

"Don't bother," said Angela. "I'm going over to Sara's. My sister can sleep with you in our bed."

"That's very generous of you," said Laura. "But it's not necessary. I can sleep in Amy's room tonight."

"Ange, I can explain," I said.

"Goodbye, Jonathan." Angela turned and went out the back door.

"She didn't even get her toothbrush," Laura observed, after the door slammed. "So where do you keep your glasses?"

I pointed to the cabinet. She grabbed two wine glasses, unzipped her suitcase, and pulled out a bottle of Korbel Brut.

"Of course it's not cold any more," she said. Laura tore off the foil and popped the cork. The champagne exploded all over the table. She filled the two glasses and offered me one. "To us!" she proclaimed, smiling beatifically.

A better man would not have had the champagne. A better man would not have made love with his sister-in-law on the queen bed he'd shared with his wife for most of their twenty-five years together. But a better man would have walked back into the rain after that feverish kiss from Laura in Providence on moving day.

✧

The next morning Laura was a little more subdued. I was able to get an appointment for the early afternoon with a gynecologist

214

in New Tampa, someone Angie didn't see. Laura hadn't wanted me to call and didn't want to go. "The test is a hundred percent accurate," she said.

"Well it still makes sense to go to the doctor and confirm it. She may recommend some changes in your diet, or some supplements. Or she may see some problems."

In the car, Laura put the ring back on her left hand. Her eyes were shut and I could see her lips moving. She held my hand tightly in the waiting room, still praying silently.

I accompanied Laura back when she was called and sat in a big leather chair outside the examining room. The door opened and the doctor invited me in. Laura looked away when I entered. "I'm afraid your wife isn't pregnant," Dr. Hart said. She put her hand on my shoulder. "I'm sorry." Then she smiled. "The two of you will just have to go back to work. I've given Laura a thermometer and some instructions. Good luck!"

Laura took my hand as we walked out to the car.

"I guess the test isn't a hundred percent accurate after all," I said.

There was a long silence on the ride back.

But once we were home, she was kittenish again. "I have a confession to make."

"Yes?"

"I had a friend of Melissa's take the test for me. She's pregnant."

"So you knew you weren't?"

"Well, that's what the test said, but I just had this gut feeling I was. My period still hasn't come."

"Laura. Jesus."

"I really thought I might be, Jon." She looked up at me pleadingly, "Do you forgive me?"

"Laura, did you switch medications or something."

"Well I seemed to be doing fine on the Paxil, so I cut back on the Eskalith."

"Did a doctor tell you to do that?"

215

"Well, not my doctor, but Shari's doctor."

"Did you see Shari's doctor?"

Laura smiled. "No, dummy. But Shari and I are like twins. Sometimes our periods come at the exact same time."

☙

I made a reservation for Laura on a flight back to Providence for late Sunday afternoon. That morning she insisted on a tarot reading. She'd brought the twenty-three Major Arcana cards in the Rider-Waite deck. Like Angela, Laura couldn't shuffle, so I did the honors. Following her instructions, I drew three cards and lined them up on the table face-down without looking at them. Laura sat behind me, her arms around my chest, her head on my shoulder.

"OK," she said, "the left is the past, the middle is the present, and the right is the future."

I turned up the cards. The Fool. The Hanged Man. Death. "That doesn't look too good," I said.

Laura stood up. "No, no. Death doesn't mean literal death. And it's facing away from you. But it could mean the end of a relationship." She grinned mischievously and elbowed me in the ribs.

Death, a skeleton in black armor, rides a white horse and holds a black banner with a stylized white rose. The horse steps over a prone king, and his crown and scepter. A woman and child grieve and a bishop prays, while between two towers on the horizon, a sun rises or sets.

The Fool holds a white rose, and carries a staff with a sack. The effeminate young man, his head tilted back, his eyes closed, is about to step off a rocky cliff. A little white dog prances at his side.

The Hanged Man dangles by his right ankle from a cross-shaped tree. Foliage hangs from either end of the two branches. The young man, blond like the Fool, doesn't look uncomfortable.

216

His arms are behind his back, his left leg is crossed behind the right, and a sun or halo blazes from behind his head.

Laura came up with benign interpretations of the boy on the rock and the boy suspended from the tree. They apparently represented renunciation leading to enlightenment and inner harmony. I had not been a fool. I was not choking on my own blood.

"Your turn," I said, and reshuffled the deck.

Laura drew The Star, The Moon, and Lovers. When she turned over the last card, her eyes filled with tears and she hugged me tightly. She didn't say a word.

∽

Before we headed to the airport, we went walking in Wildwood, the nature reserve off Brewster. As we headed down one of the little trails, past palms and palmettos, loblolly pines and live oaks, I explained why I was not going to go to Santa Fe and why she shouldn't either.

"I have a wife, and a home, and job here," I said.

"Had a wife," said Laura.

"You don't know anyone in New Mexico. You've never been there in your life. You have no job there. All your family and friends are in Providence."

"I need to escape. You need to escape. This is America. You can start over."

"We're not starting over. You're going back to Rhode Island. I'm staying here."

We sat down on a bench. Two bicyclists whizzed past.

"Where there's love, there's a way," said Laura.

I didn't say anything.

Quietly, Laura began singing "The Wedding Song." Her voice was thin and high, but clear and tuneful.

Laura hugged me and looked up at me with her big saucer eyes, and for a moment the Santa Fe adventure seemed plausible.

The moment passed. I stood up, took her hand, and we walked back to the car.

At the airport, Laura appeared to be reconciled to returning. I'd made appointments Friday with her doctor and with a counselor she'd once liked. Nothing was ruled out, no bridges were burned. We'd email each other every day, and talk frequently. I'd let her know what was happening with Angela.

But I had a bad feeling at TPA, and hung around the Airside C shuttle stop. Laura's plane had left the gate and was heading toward the runway when she had a panic attack. She undid her seatbelt and began crying inconsolably, her head thrashing back and forth, as I would be told multiple times. The plane returned to the gate. There were reports to be filed by the airline, the airport authorities, and TSA. We didn't leave the airport for three hours.

Late Monday afternoon I drove Laura to the Amtrak station on Nebraska, and she boarded the Silver Star for the thirty-hour trip to Providence. There were no messages from Angela when I returned home.

I gunned the ball to Lucy and Nick, and watched Lucy make her usual acrobatic leaps to snag it. Did she take half as much pleasure in her performance as I did? Then I sat down with a snifter of brandy and watched the sunset. A broad line of white cirrus turned a fiery orange, then pink, like a gash opening up. Then the clouds darkened to a dull purple, and became a long bruise.

Could things get any worse? They could. Until Death tramples you, they always can.

CHAPTER 27

Later that evening I reread the story we were going to be discussing the next day in Modern European History.

"Death in Venice" describes the moral disintegration of the celebrated German writer Gustav von Aschenbach. The author of a biography of Frederick the Great, among other works, Aschenbach has taken Frederick's motto as his own: "stand fast." "'Aschenbach has always lived like this,'" a friend says, making a fist, "'never like this'"–opening his hand. The lesson his books teach is that anyone who achieves greatness does so "in defiance of affliction and pain, poverty, destitution, bodily weakness, vice, passion..." His heroes resemble St. Sebastian, stoical under torture, sublime in their suffering. Aschenbach is the spokesman for all who spurn "the flabby humanitarianism" of "a psychology-ridden age."

Yet art is debilitating, a favorite theme of Mann's. Like other of his protagonists, Aschenbach on his father's side descends from a long line of boring Silesian officials. But his Bohemian mother, the daughter of a musician, has introduced the fatal artistic gene. Aschenbach knows that while art heightens life and "gives a more deeper joy, she consumes more swiftly." Under his dignified exterior, a "nervous fever" rages, "such as a career of extravagant passions and pleasures can hardly produce."

One day, outside a Byzantine chapel, Aschenbach sees a figure who will recur in the story: a snub-nosed, red-haired individual with milky, freckled skin, a prominent Adam's apple, and glistening buck teeth, who stares at him aggressively. The distinguished writer suddenly wants to travel, though the destination that first comes to mind is a steamy primeval wilderness. Instead he goes to an Austrian resort on the Adriatic. But there are too many Austrians, and Aschenbach decides, abruptly, to head to Venice.

On the boat over, he observes a group of rowdy young clerks. Looking at them more closely, he sees that the loudest and most rakish is in fact a repulsive old man with a dyed moustache, rouged cheeks, and a wig. "Keep me in mind," the reveler tells Aschenbach when they disembark.

Gus then has another unpleasant experience. He hires a gondola to take him to the vaporetto stop for the Lido, where he's staying. But the gondolier, one of that pale, snub-nosed breed, reminds him that the vaps don't take luggage, and insists on rowing Aschenbach out to the island. Gus makes only perfunctory protests, and reclines in the lacquered, coffin-black gondola.

Aschenbach likes the international clientele at the Hôtel des Bains. Announcements are made in English. The staff knows that the English and American guests don't speak other languages. *Plus ça change.*

Gus is immediately attracted to a gorgeous Polish boy, Tadzio, with honey-colored ringlets and marble skin. In contrast to his nun-like sisters, he's indulged by his mother, an aristocratic woman always draped in pearls.

The rest of the story tells simply of Aschenbach's growing infatuation with Tadzio. The idea pleases him that the boy is delicate and sickly, and probably will not live long.

Venice oppresses Gus and he decides to leave. He's at once seized with regret about abandoning Tadzio and is immensely grateful that his luggage has been sent to the wrong destination, giving him an excuse to return. He resumes watching the boy, consoling himself with the thought that the contemplation of higher things begins with the contemplation of corporeal beauty.

We ascend to the spiritual through our senses. Then he thinks: the lover is nearer the divine than the beloved.

Aschenbach soon becomes aware that though the season is at its height, the number of guests is declining. He smells carbolic acid in Venice and sees ominous signs warning about swimming in the canals and eating shellfish. He's told repeatedly that it's just a precaution because of the sirocco. But the German papers mention cholera. Then the papers disappear from the hotel lobby. Aschenbach finds himself secretly approving of the cover-up. He doesn't want Tadzio's family to leave.

Gus learns the truth about the plague from a tweed-clad Englishman at Cook's. The English are no better liars than they are linguists. Aschenbach thinks about warning Tadzio's mother, but is unable to do so.

His attentions have been noticed. Tadzio is called away from his vicinity. Aschenbach's "pride revolted at the affront, even while conscience told him it was deserved." He permits the hotel barber to dye his hair, rouge his cheeks, and color his lips. "Now the signore can fall in love as soon as he likes," he's told. Gus has a dream where, though summoned by an Appolian flute, a shrieking horde of Dionysian revelers dance around a phallus—"the obscene symbol of the godhead." They laugh, they howl, they gesture lewdly. Aschenbach joins them.

Finally, pursuing the Polish family, Aschenbach stops to eat some over-ripe strawberries. He dies the next day in his beach chair, watching his beloved.

∽

When Aschenbach arrives in Venice, there is a short paean to "this most improbable of cities." But for Mann, the voluptuous South—the sun, the sand, the sea, the wine—is a snare for hard-working, conscientious Northerners. And Venice, entrepôt of the Orient, is more dangerous still. Aschenbach is repulsed by the sultriness of the narrow streets, the odors assailing him, the beggars waylaying him, and "the predatory commercial spirit of the fallen queen of the seas."

Because there's almost no dialogue–Gus does not of course confide in anyone–students get bored with the story. And a couple of other stories in the collection are more germane for European history—"Disorder and Early Sorrow" about the *Inflationzeit*, the hyper-inflation of 1923 and '24, and "Mario and the Magician," about the hypnotic power of sadistic Leaders. But I still assign "Death." Some students, after all, have discovered how deranging love is, and can relate to Gus's desperate longing.

The novella was written in 1911. No one–at least no character in a published story–would have considered acting on an obsession like Aschenbach's. People were not encouraged to live the fantasy.

❧

The consensus about Venice was already a couple of centuries old when Mann wrote. "I know what is good and what is bad for young people," Leopold Mozart told his wife, and Venice, he said, is "the most dangerous place in all of Italy." Wolfgang was enjoying getting his bottom smacked–the "*attacco*"–but his dad whisked him away.

Venice may have meant immorality, and immorality death, in 1911, but within a dozen years Berlin and Hamburg had over-taken the *Serenissima* as sin cities. That can happen when you lose a war–or even when you win one. After the '20s came the '60s. It was America's turn.

There was resistance. When I gave my girlfriend Helene the Rolling Stones' album *Between the Buttons*, her mom scratched out the first track, "Let's Spend the Night Together," though a decade had passed since the album's release. Mrs. Fein had read my mind. But she and her ilk were like King Canute. The FDA had approved Enovid for contraceptive use in June 1960. The tide rolled in, and within a dozen years, songs celebrating sex without love were as common as seaweed.

By the '80s, to switch metaphors, all the strawberries on two continents were over-ripe.

∞

As soon as I entered Cocke Hall the next day, Richard Head motioned to me to come into his office. He looked grim. "Did you hear the news?" he asked.

"What news?"

"Ed Shultz's son Troy killed himself last night."

Troy's girlfriend had broken up with him and he'd taken his dad's Ruger and shot himself in the temple.

I asked if anyone had spoken to Ed. Richard said no. Ed had called the econ secretary and told her the news less than an hour ago.

I phoned Ed from my office. "I'm so sorry," I said.

"Holly's taking it very badly."

"Of course," I said, and asked if he'd like me to come over. He did. It would be good for Holly to have more company. Relatives were on their way, but none lived close by.

After my last class, I turned off onto 375 and headed for the Schultzs' Snell Isle home.

Some friends and neighbors were there, and after giving Holly a hug and telling her how sorry I was, I went out into the back yard and spoke with Ed. He looked worse than I expected, as if he'd aged ten years. He kept jabbing the nosepiece of his black plastic glasses with his index finger.

"Troy was such a level-headed kid," he said. "I don't understand how he couldn't get past this thing. It was so impulsive. So thoughtless."

Troy had come back late at night and shot himself in the garage, in the front seat of his car. Ed, Holly, and Wayne had been asleep. Ed had rushed out when he'd heard the shot. "What I saw is something no one should have to see," he said.

I asked if there was anything I could get them, anything they needed.

Ed shook his head.

Holly wanted to talk about other things. She asked about my mother and I told her about the quarrel over her care and the trust. I even gave her a highly edited version of Laura's escapade. Holly had been offered a pharmacopeia of sedatives, but had turned her doctor down. Tonight, though, she'd probably need one, she said, and God knows how many nights after.

I spoke with a friend of the family who I knew slightly. He was a prominent psychologist who'd served with Ed on the board of the Pinellas County Red Cross. "Boys can feel things so intensely. We forget," he said. "We know they take risks. We sometimes don't appreciate how vulnerable they are."

I asked the psychologist what was going to happen to Troy's car. He told me some guys from a car washing and detailing place would come out the next morning and take it away. Then it would go directly to a dealer. No one would have to look at it again.

Something possessed me to go into the garage. The sickeningly sweet, slightly metallic smell of blood hit me when I opened the side door, but I didn't see much blood inside Troy's blue Honda. However, there was a lot of what must have been brain and skull spattered on the driver's side window and on the upholstery. The window was open a couple of inches, but if anything had gotten onto Holly's Explorer someone had wiped it off. Then I saw a little piece of bloody cartilage on a white paint can on a shelf along the wall beside the SUV. I went back into the house, got a couple of paper towels, and wiped it up. I looked around carefully, but didn't see anything else. After I stuffed the towels inside a Hefty sack in the garbage can, I left by the side door and sat down for a moment on the grass next to the big AC unit. I thought about tall, friendly, cheerful Troy. Though he hadn't seen her for years, he always asked about Amy, and told me to say hi to her.

There was a message on the answering machine when I got back. It was from Hailey Lloyd, Cheryl's daughter. "Mom passed away early this morning," she said.

I'd spoken with Cheryl three or four days earlier. She'd had the Whipple procedure. There had been some complications. She'd had internal bleeding and had some trouble breathing. But the doctors were optimistic and she expected to be home in less than two weeks.

When I called back, Hailey told me that a blood clot had traveled to Cheryl's brain. She'd had a stroke and never recovered. Her mom wanted to be cremated. There would be a small service just for the family.

I poured myself a big snifter of brandy and went out onto the lanai. How could this have happened to my cute little cousin? Cheryl was so buoyant, so upbeat, so helpful. And how could someone I'd made love to be dead? How could a warm body I'd held and kissed be nothing but ashes? I knelt on the deck. The dogs bounded up to me, and I hugged each. Lucy rolled over to get a belly rub and I obliged.

This evening the clouds formed massive, billowy columns. The northern edge was bright, illuminated by the sun. As I watched, the white turned pink. The columns became puce, then grey. Then only the clouds just above the horizon were on fire, delicate lines of cirrus that looked like waves.

I finished the brandy and went back inside. I called Angie's cell and left a message about Cheryl and Troy. I hadn't heard from her since she'd left. She'd come back to the house while I was at USP and had taken some clothes and things from the bathroom. The two earlier times Ange had left the house, she'd returned after a few days. But that had been over the dogs.

I poured myself another drink and tried Julie. It had been years since we'd talked. I'd called her on her birthday a few times, but she didn't seem to be too thrilled, and recently I'd just sent her e-cards. She didn't pick up, and I left a message.

225

I realized when I'd been out at Wildwood with Laura that I hadn't taken the goldens there in weeks. I had no meetings on Friday, and after breakfast I held open the door to the garage and the dogs raced over to the car, whimpering with pleasure, then muscled into the back seat when I swung open the car door.

On the trail, Lucy, as usual, lunged at armadillos and squirrels, and strained at the leash when we walked. Old Nick was meanwhile intent on sniffing the base of every palmetto. After half an hour, Molly sat down and refused to budge. It was not a successful outing.

I started thinking about the shelter dogs that would be killed on Monday. I'd seen euthanasia once. I'd gone down early on a Friday to pull a golden, and then found out that the guy who was taking him down to Naples had gotten a late start from Ocala, and couldn't meet me until noon. I asked if I could watch while they put the animals down. No one minded.

Cats and kittens were killed first. The great cat massacre takes place each weekday morning in every open shelter around the country. About eighty percent of cats coming into shelters go out in garbage bags. The cats got an intraperitoneal injection of sodium pentobarbital. The tech doing the killing that day, a guy I didn't know well named Dave Martinez, picked up the animals in their cages and gave them the shot in the abdomen. They looked OK for a moment, then seemed to get drowsy. It took about ten to fifteen minutes for their hearts to stop, Terry told me.

All the animal care techs are supposed to take their turns in the rotation, but it was just guys that morning, and I suspected most mornings. Shorty, a heavy-set middle-aged tech, led the dogs one by one into the bright little room and hoisted them on to a table. Terry held them and comforted them and then Dave gave them an intravenous shot in the left leg. The dogs immediately keeled over and died.

The sodium pentobarbital is light blue and has a sickly sweetish odor. I could smell it on the dogs after they went down.

Death has to be verified by an intracardiac stick. Dave plunged a syringe into each dog's heart, and we all watched to see that it wasn't vibrating. Then the dogs went into their garbage bags and the animals were dragged off to the big horizontal freezer by the back entrance.

It was weird to see the dogs come in, frightened but obedient, and die so suddenly. One was pretty sick, an old shepherd mix with mange, and another, a beagle, had been hit by a car. Most of the rest were pit mixes. None was huggable, but no one was vicious. A lot of bad dogs wind up in shelters, but they're still a small minority. The only dog that got to me was a sable hound mix. He stared at me balefully when he came into the room, as if he knew what was going to happen and hoped I might help him.

So Saturday afternoon I went back out to the shelter and took some of the condemned for a last romp. As I was taking off my clothes on the lanai, I thought I heard the door to the garage open, but it must have been one of the dogs thumping against it. No messages from Angela. It was just me, Lucy, Molly, and Nick, and the hum of the refrigerator and the roar of the AC.

⸎

Late in the afternoon I got a call from Wendy. "I've got some interesting news," she said. Danny and David were getting the house ready to be sold and had a guy come out to inspect the basement. They were told that the heating pipes were insulated with asbestos, and that some of it was crumbling. A team in hazmat suits came out two days later and removed it. That evening, David went down and took a look, and reported that the pipes were made of thin, cheap aluminum. He saw some fissures along the seams and small gaps at the joints, where they'd pulled apart. Wendy started to talk about the trust, but I wasn't listening.

A brandy aperitif seemed to be in order. I paused as I reached up to open the liquor cabinet above the oven, and studied the ropes of light, reflected off the pool, dancing on the kitchen ceiling. I took the drink out on to the lanai and thought about our heating vents. They were wrought iron, like the front gate, with an intricate pattern of interlocking hearts and ovals. At the center was what looked like a butterfly, with its wings spread. In winter, Danny and I would turn on the heat, pushing a button that made a deep, resonating bang. Then we'd kneel in front of the warm air and pretend we were Roman soldiers sitting around a camp fire, or knights at the mouth of a dragon's cave.

That evening the sunset looked as if a dying animal had smeared itself against the horizon. The reds were so intense they seemed to throb. Then two anhingas winged their way south below the clouds.

When I finally went back inside, the house was dark. Angie used to lie on the couch in the living room during the evening with the lights out, working on her laptop. I missed the white glow of the bitten apple.

CHAPTER 28

It was Sunday, the following weekend, that I got the call from Amy.

"Daddy, sit down," she said. "I've got some wonderful news."

"What, hon?" I hadn't told Aim about Angela, and apparently Ange hadn't mentioned anything either.

"I've been seeing Jayson. He's been driving in on his off-days. He gets them in the middle of the week."

"That's nice," I said guardedly.

"I'm so in love. We're both so in love. We're getting married."

"What!"

"We're getting married."

"Amy, you can't."

"Of course I can. Cousins can marry in California."

I didn't say anything.

"And Daddy, we really have to. I'm pregnant."

"You can't be!"

"I am. Why aren't you happy for me?"

I sat down at the dining room table and took a couple of deep breaths.

"Amy, there's something important I have to tell you. You can't marry Jayson. You can't have his baby. He's your brother. Your half-brother. I'm his father."

"You *can't* be. How can you be? "

"Aim, before I met Mom I had an affair with Julie."

229

Amy didn't reply.

"When Julie married Giovanni she was already pregnant with Jayson."

"Daddy," Amy said, "why are you so desperate that I not be happy for once in my life?"

"I want you to be happy, Aim."

"That's so incredibly mean. I can't believe you're doing this to me."

"Amy, I wish I were making this up, but I'm not."

"I can't believe you're that desperate. I thought you'd be so happy for me."

"Call Julie. Ask her."

"I'm marrying Jayson. I'm not getting an abortion," Amy said, and hung up.

I called her back and she didn't pick up. I texted her: "Please call, sweetheart. I love you."

It was only 11:00 in the morning, but I poured myself a brandy, emptying the bottle. I had no doubt Jayson knew exactly what he was doing.

I called Julie, got her voice mail, and told her she needed to call me back right away.

～

The phone rang an hour later, but it was neither Amy nor Julie.

"Jon, I have something important to tell you," Angela said.

"Ange, hi, how are you?"

"Jon, I'm moving in with Sara. We're going to be living together."

"What?"

"Yes. Permanently."

I didn't say anything.

"I've hired some guys to move my books and things. I need to make arrangements with you about when they can come over."

"You're seriously moving in with Sara?"

"Jon, we've been lovers for three years."

Again I sat down at the dining room table. "You're kidding," I said.

"I'm not kidding. I can't tell you how wonderful it is to be with someone who cares about me. And who I care about. And someone who is very sexy."

"OK," I said. "OK."

There was a long silence. For a second I considered telling Angela about Amy. But then I would have to tell her about Jayson. She knew nothing about Julie and me. I kept putting off mentioning it to her, and at some point it seemed too late. Instead I said, "Ed Schultz's son Troy killed himself a few days ago."

"Do I know him?"

"Sure, you've met. Tall guy with glasses, teaches econ."

"Well, give him my condolences."

Then we arranged a time when Angela could come over with the movers. She wouldn't be taking much, she told me. She wanted to start over with Sara. Her lawyer would be getting in touch.

I sat at the dining room table for a long time, looking out at the pool, the pond, and the line of trees.

Angie and I had been so happy when we moved into our home. We hadn't owned a house before. With its cathedral ceiling, double sliding glass doors, pool and lanai, it seemed the quintessential Floridian dream home. We were on a conservation. Across the pond there were only oaks and pines and foliage. No neighbors. Six-foot high cypress fences ran down to the pond on either side of the property. We felt like we were at a resort.

The first night we had a bottle of Mumm's with our Chinese take-out. We went swimming under a full moon and made love afterwards. Then we went back in the pool.

We felt so lucky. We both had good jobs. We were living in a semi-tropical paradise where it would be in the 70s most of the winter. We had Amy, the perfect baby. And we had each other.

∽

I didn't sleep much Saturday night, and the next afternoon I decided to go out to the shelter again. The sky was clouding over in the west as I pulled out of the garage.

"Can't stay away, huh," said Terry, when he swung open the big metal door to Building C.

"Well, I thought everybody could use another walk."

The wind started picking up. The flag behind me flapped loudly. "Better hurry," Terry said.

I tried to remember where the dogs were who were going to get the blue poison on Monday, but had to go down each row again in the three blocks of cages. I shoved in my earbuds, flipped on my MP3, and selected Mozart's *Requiem*.

First were a couple of frightened black puppies that were labeled lab mixes. I took them out together. All the other dogs, I remembered, were housebroken, and relieved to relieve themselves outside.

Next I took out a dog listed as a pomeranian mix, but who looked like a little red fox. She was limping. Her left rear leg had been injured. I carried her out on to the grass and let her sniff around. The Kyrie boomed in my ears. I skipped a pit with battle scars who was listed as aggressive, and took out an old, deaf rottie with a skin condition. I turned up the volume on the Dies Irae. A sweet white cattle dog with doleful eyes was next. Lightning flashed high overhead as we walked along the line of oaks at the edge of the field. The crash of thunder followed after a couple of seconds. Then it started raining.

I took out a high-strung, intelligent-looking Aussie mix who pranced beside me, looking for something to herd. We both got soaked. I passed on a white and brown boxer cowering at the back of her cage, and slipped a leash on an owner release, a mutt called "Beauty." She was anything but. Beauty was black, with a pointed snout and whip-like tail, long floppy ears and short bow legs. Her ribs showed, her nails were long and curved, and she was filthy. She was happy to go out. It was pouring now.

232

The storm was right overhead. We started for the oaks when a bolt of lightning hit the cell tower just beyond the end of the field. As we turned back, I slipped on the wet grass, tripped over Beauty, and fell to my knees. She went sprawling, but got up quickly and began licking my face. I hugged her. We were both covered with mud. She rolled on her back to have her belly scratched. I saw another flash. Thunder boomed a second later. The *Requiem* was cycling through again, and the choir was singing the Lacrimosa.

I heard Terry yelling from the back door. "What the fuck are you doing? Are you crazy? Get back in here."

We walked back to the roofed area where the animal control officers parked and I hosed Beauty off. "That's it, Jon. Go home. What am I supposed to tell Mike if you and a dog get zapped?"

Then I did something really stupid. I borrowed a pen from Terry and wrote on the side of Beauty's cage card "Hold: GRRWF," and put a line through the "EU." I did the same for the cattle-dog, the Aussie, and, after a moment's hesitation, the lame fox. GRRWF was Golden Retriever Rescue of Western Florida, and of course they would take none of these dogs. I'd have to board them and call the local all-breed rescues and see if any of them would take them off my hands. If not, I'd have to try other rescues in the Southeast. If no one wanted them, they were mine.

"Congratulations," said Terry, after I slipped Beauty's card back in its slot. "You picked the ugliest dog in the shelter."

Julie had phoned the land line while I was gone and this time she picked up when I called her back.

"I'm so sorry about Cheryl," I said.

"I know, I know. I am too." She started crying. "Jon, I can't believe it. I just can't believe it."

"I can't either. She was very special." My voice got husky. "I loved her."

"I know." There was a long pause. "Listen, I'm really sorry about your mom. Cheryl told me. I should have called. She was a nice lady. She tried to help. I always liked her. I always wished she was my mom."

"Thanks. That seems like a long time ago now. Listen, Julie, have you been in touch with Jayson recently?"

"No. Why?"

I filled her in.

"God, I'm so sorry. I can't believe he'd do that." She paused. "Yes I can."

"Can you give me his number? I've got to talk to him."

"I'll give it to you, but it's not going to do any good talking to him. He's the most headstrong person I know."

She gave me the number.

"I don't suppose it would help if you tried to talk to him too," I said.

"Me? Are you kidding?"

☙

Jayson didn't pick up when I called, but phoned while I was preparing dinner.

"Howdy, 'Dad,'" he said. "You rang?" The "Dad" dripped with sarcasm.

"Yeah, we need to talk."

"So you want to have a heart-to-heart after all these years? I'm touched."

"Jayson, I did what your mom wanted," I said.

"Yeah, well that wasn't necessarily what I wanted."

"You were a baby."

"I didn't stay a baby."

"Jayson, what you're doing is not only immoral, it's illegal."

"Like father, like son."

"I did nothing illegal. I did not intentionally hurt anyone."

"Just unintentionally."

234

"I told you. Julie did not want you to know. I had no idea that you knew until today." I sat down on the sofa next to Molly. "Please listen to me. What you're doing is incredibly vindictive and destructive."

"What goes around, comes around, 'Dad,'" Jayson said. "And it just so happens I love Amy and she loves me."

"If you loved her you wouldn't be doing this to her."

"You mean to you."

"She's your sister, Jayson. Does that mean anything to you?"

There was a pause, and then Jayson said, "This conversation's getting a little boring, Dad. Toodle-oo." He hung up.

I called back, but of course he didn't pick up.

I phoned Julie and asked where Jayson was working.

"I think he's at the Gold Nugget," she said. "At least that's where he was the last time we talked. But he moves around."

I called Jayson again and left a message: "You need to call me back. If I don't hear from you later today, I'm talking to the management of the Gold Nugget tomorrow."

Fifteen minutes later I got a text message: "Long gone from GN, Daddy-O. Youll never catch us. There r casinos all over the U S of A. Honest injun. Good luck." A couple of minutes later I got another text: "maybe u want to take out ads on tv or put r faces on milk cartons."

❦

That night I dreamed the world ended. I was walking with Cheryl, holding her hand, above what looked like a Roman forum. It was intact, the white marble gleamed, and there was a crowd of people milling around below. We were up on top of one of the temples, by ourselves. A choir was singing Sarastro's aria "*In diesen heil'gen Hallen*"–In These Sacred Halls. The sun started flickering, then sprayed geysers of fire from its sides. And then it went out.

It didn't get totally dark, more like twilight. Then I saw a full moon overhead.

"It's the end of the world," Cheryl said matter-of-factly.

"We still have the moon," I said.

Cheryl shook her head. Tears glittered in her eyes.

It was all very vivid. I woke up with a start.

I called Amy from school on Monday and left another message. I told her to please not do anything she'd regret later. I said that Angie and I had separated, and that I loved her and wanted to talk to her. Then I booked a flight to San Jose for Friday morning.

I skipped a meeting and got to the Packer shelter in time to pull Beauty. All Creatures could take two of the dogs, and I asked for a full exam and a bath and delousing. I prayed that neither she nor the three others would be heartworm positive. That would mean a $400 treatment and no exercise for a month. Before getting involved with Laura, I'd always paid my balances in full. Now I was maxed out on two of my five cards.

Early the next morning I pulled the cattle dog and found a vet who could board the Aussie and the pseudo-pom. I got them the following day.

CHAPTER 29

On the flight out to San Jose I thought: I'm Jason's second cousin as well as his father. If he and Cheryl had had a baby, the kid would have been not only my grandson, but both my second and third cousin. If Cheryl had conceived during our affair, Jayson and Cheryl's child, my grandson, would also have been the little half-brother or sister of my son or daughter.

If Jayson and Amy went ahead with their plans, I would be both the father and father-in-law of each, and the only grandfather of their kid. I imagined some future in which incest was warmly approved of by the *bien pensants*, and the government distributed a pamphlet in the public schools called "Heather Has One Grandpa."

I thought about my mother. Did incest run in the family?

Going through airport security, I'd noticed that the Thomas Mann paperback was still in my briefcase. I pulled it out and flipped to a story in the collection I hadn't looked at in years, "The Blood of the Walsüngs." The title refers to Wagner's Ring Cycle. The Walsüngs, Siegmund and Sieglinde, are the illegitimate twin children of Wotan or Wälse. Sieglinde is abducted as a girl and forced into marriage. Her wounded brother arrives at her home, she nurses him, and they make love. Things end badly for the siblings, of course.

In the Mann story, the twins Siegmund and Sieglinde are the two youngest children of a wealthy assimilated Jewish family in Munich. Not much happens. The four siblings are each unattractive in his or her own way, the older brother in the hussars, the free-thinking law-student sister, and the two snooty little aesthetes, S and S. All four despise their parents. Sieglinde is engaged to a groveling non-entity, von Beckerath. Everyone has dinner, S and S go out to see *Die Walkürie*, which tells the grim story of the original Wälsungs, then they come back and make love. Mann was preaching against the Religion of Art, but his animus toward assimilated Jews almost overshadows the Aschenbachean parable.

∽

I drove directly to Amy's apartment from the airport. She wasn't there and a neighbor told me he hadn't seen her in several days. I called her department. The Genetics office manager wanted to see me in person before she would talk, so I drove over to the Stanford Medical School. After she'd examined my driver's license, the woman told me that Aim had withdrawn from the program three days ago. She'd requested a leave of absence and had asked to be given incompletes in all her classes. She hoped to return in the fall, she'd said.

I asked the office manager if she could give me the names and numbers of Amy's closest friends. She said she would check with a few classmates who my daughter hung out with, and if they agreed, she'd pass their numbers along.

None of the four friends I called had any clue as to where Amy might be. One didn't even know she'd withdrawn from school. I guessed that Jayson had taken Aim back to Vegas. I'd left messages for her every day since we'd spoken, and now I told her I'd arrived in Palo Alto, that I was very worried about her, and that she should get in touch with me asap.

I called Julie. She had no idea where Jayson was living. She said

238

she felt terrible about what was happening, and asked if I'd like to come up to Sonoma.

∽

Julie lived in the hills west of the town, close to the crest, in a stunning home designed by her ex-husband Kevin. It looked something like a ski lodge, with a high peaked roof and an enormous redwood deck overlooking Sonoma. There was a hot tub on a lower deck to the right. Immediately below was a garden, with a bed of purple hydrangeas and white azaleas, and another of lavender and begonia. Two baskets of stargazer lilies hung from poles.

The last time I had seen Julie was the day I'd met Jayson and Giovanni and we had said goodbye. She'd aged well, as petite women often do. I gave her a big hug, and we chatted about other things.

I told her how happy it had made me feel to go over the Golden Gate Bridge again. The sun was sparkling on the water, and Mt. Tam and the Marin hills were carpeted in dark green. Memories of other crossings had rushed back–en route to Muir Woods with friends, to the Russian River, to Sausalito with a girlfriend. I'd turned off the radio and started singing "California Here I Come."

Talking with Julie about Jayson and Amy, the situation didn't seem as hopeless as it had a few hours earlier. Amy would get back in touch, she would get an abortion, Jayson would return to Vegas.

We talked about Cheryl and my mother, and shared some memories.

Like her sister, Julie was a good cook, and she made a spicy ragout with homemade noodles and a gingery, garlicky carrot soufflé. We had an excellent cabernet. After the crème caramel, she brought out some old photo albums and we looked at pictures of Cheryl, and then of Julie and me. We were always arm in arm or holding hands.

239

We were arm in arm again on the big leather couch in front of the fireplace. Then we exchanged a familiar look. "One eye," I said. We kissed, and the years dissolved. There was the nineteen-year-old Julie, with her elfin half-smile, cradled in my arms. We walked into her bedroom and made love.

"Just like old times," Julie said afterward.

"Amazing," I said.

"Do you ever think how different our lives would have been if we'd gotten married?" Julie asked.

"I used to."

Suddenly Julie was serious. "Jonny, you're the only person I've ever loved."

Suddenly there were tears in my eyes. "I love you so much, Julie."

"I love you. I love you. I love you," Julie said, and we gripped each other tightly.

Then we rolled over on to our backs and watched the blades of the ceiling fan circle slowly above.

"Of course we would have gotten divorced," I said after a couple of minutes.

"Of course."

"But then maybe we would have remarried."

"And divorced again," said Julie, laughing now.

We started reminiscing about Phyllis the Kangaroo and Samuel the Alligator and our other characters, the fortune-bearing ice cubes and the enchanted butterflies. Once again, Julie and I were in a universe that included just the two of us, twins in a thick and warm cocoon.

∽

It was weird to be vacationing in Sonoma when my life was unraveling, but there was no reason to stay in a motel in Palo Alto waiting for Amy to call. I phoned USP and left a message saying I needed to cancel classes through Wednesday. Then I called

Richard Head and told him I was in California looking for Amy, who was involved with some guy from Vegas and had withdrawn from Stanford.

I phoned the vet on Monday and sent emails to a dozen rescue groups. Only the Aussie was heartworm positive, but a collie rescue was willing to take him. No one was interested in the other three. I corrected exams and thought about how I'd have to restructure my courses. We weren't going to make it past World War II in Modern Europe. I like happy endings, and always tried to get to 1989.

I called Amy several times a day. I called back three of her friends and asked if there were other friends who might know where Aim was. They said they couldn't think of any.

I gave Laura a call. She seemed to be doing OK. She was interviewing for a job as a secretary with the zoning board in Cranston. She sounded chipper.

The rest of the time Julie and I walked in the hills above Sonoma, and around the big plaza downtown. We sat on a bench in the shade and shared a wedge of aged Monterrey Jack and a fresh baguette. When I finished my lemonade, I reached into the cup and fished out an ice cube. I held it up to Julie. "What's going to happen?" I asked.

Julie studied the cube for a moment. "I don't think it works for grown-ups," she said.

Wild deer roamed the Sonoma hills, and we saw several on our walks. Once, as we approached the crest of the hill, a swarm of Monarch butterflies fluttered in front of us. They'd disappeared when we reached the top.

Back in the house, over coffee, Julie told me how she had deliberately stopped taking the pill during our last summer together. "I had this crazy fantasy that if we had a baby together, everything would be OK. But then, when I realized I was pregnant, I knew that was nuts. I panicked. I started hanging out at bars and went home with Giovanni."

"I would have married you, Julie. I swear I would have."

Tears came to her eyes again, and then to mine.

∽

Later, I asked about her other husbands. Julie shook her head. More mistakes.

Why hadn't she had other children? She sighed and shut her eyes. She'd gotten pregnant by Raoul. They were married, but he didn't want to have kids. They'd argued bitterly, but in the end she went ahead and had an abortion. She'd waited a long time, hoping he'd change his mind. Julie wasn't sure exactly what went wrong, but somehow she was never able to conceive after that. She'd gotten an infection, but had taken antibiotics. There was no perforation of the uterus. Kevin had had kids from an earlier marriage, and had wanted children nearly as much as she did, but she couldn't get pregnant. They'd gone to fertility clinics. Nothing worked.

Could I marry Julie and live with her in her House Beautiful above Sonoma? The thought occurred to me more than once. Maybe I could teach at one of the community colleges in Santa Rosa or Solano.

But leaving the magic mountain to pick up some groceries in a convenience store outside town, the reality of what life would be like here hit me.

Then there was the issue of our kids.

Julie tried a couple of Jayson's friends in Vegas, but they were no more helpful than Amy's. She called Hailey, but her niece said she hadn't been in touch with Jayson recently. We just had to wait.

On Wednesday morning I finally heard from Amy. It was a text: "At Stanford Hosp. Please come. I love you."

∽ ∽ ∽

CHAPTER 30

I was by Amy's side in two hours. She'd had some bleeding and had been hospitalized as a precaution.

Amy told me she had been staying with some of Jayson's old friends in Santa Cruz. She was sorry she hadn't answered my calls and texts. Jayson had convinced her that I would force her to get an abortion. She'd told him what I'd said about him, but he had hotly denied that I was his father. His mother had sworn to him that she and I had stopped sleeping together before she met Giovanni and got pregnant.

I asked why Santa Cruz. She said she didn't want to be too far from Palo Alto, but of course it was Jay who had suggested the town. I wondered if he was still living with someone in Vegas, but didn't mention this to Aim.

"The important thing is that you're OK, sweetheart," I said. I asked her what she'd heard from Stanford, and she said the department was supportive. She could get incompletes and retake her classes. She hadn't officially withdrawn from school yet, so there'd be no problem with Aetna. Then I told her I wasn't going to force her to do anything she didn't want to do, she was over twenty-one, but that I'd told her the truth, and that she should give Julie a call.

Then Amy said, "Daddy, I've been talking to Mommy. Did you really sleep with Aunt Laura?"

I took a deep breath. "Yes, I really did," I said.

"How could you?"

"It's a long story. I'm sorry I hurt your mom. But we haven't been a real couple for a long time, sweetheart."

"But Daddy, Aunt Laura?"

"I know."

"She's such a Kookalootz. I mean if it were Aunt Wendy, maybe I could understand."

"Laura's like Mommy in some ways."

Amy wasn't buying this.

"Physically." This was not where I wanted the conversation to go, so I asked what she'd heard from Jayson.

She said she'd told him about the bleeding yesterday, and he was coming out to see her. She didn't know when he'd get to Palo Alto, but she thought early evening.

So Jayson was laying his cards down and I would meet him at last. I expected that he would want to be well compensated for agreeing to an abortion for Amy. And for eighteen years of child support, with compound interest. I wondered how much he'd ask for.

Amy looked sleepy and I said I'd check back into the motel and let her rest. I wrote down Julie's number, and again urged her to please give my cousin a call.

☙

I came back before dinner and we ate together. Amy hadn't heard from Jayson. She hadn't spoken with Julie either. "Call her at some point, Aim. You need to know the truth."

She nodded. Then she said, "Daddy, I love Jay so much."

"I know, honey. But love blinds us." Amy gave a snort. "I know, I speak from experience."

About half an hour later, Amy's cell went off. It was Hailey Lloyd. I couldn't hear what she said, but Amy frowned. Then her face crumpled. She let out a short harrowing scream. She

244

screamed again, and then a third time. The phone fell to the floor.

Amy couldn't speak for a couple of minutes. She was sobbing and shaking. I knelt next to the bed and hugged her. Finally, she told me between gasps that Jay had been in an accident. He'd been hit by a fuel tanker on I5 outside Bakersfield, his truck had caught fire and he'd burned to death. "Aim, I'm so sorry," I said, and tightened my grip. When I looked up, there were nurses and technicians behind me, standing beside emergency equipment.

I stood up and explained what had happened. A nurse took Amy's vitals and gave her a sedative.

Later, when my daughter had drifted off to sleep I took her phone to the lobby and called Hailey. She picked up and I got a few more details about the crash. Then I said, "Hailey, I have to ask you something. Have you slept with Jayson?"

She was quiet for a moment and then said, "Of course."

"Recently?"

"He did love Amy, if that's what you're asking."

I called Julie. Hailey had phoned her right after she'd spoken with Amy. Julie was inconsolable. "He's the only thing I had in this world," she kept saying.

At the nurses' station, they told me Amy would probably be out another four or five hours. I grabbed a sandwich and headed up to Sonoma. I left a note for Amy telling her I'd driven up to see Julie, and that she should text me as soon as she was up, and I'd come back to the hospital.

Julie had lots of friends in town and the house was full of people. I met some of the other stylists at her salon, and girlfriends and neighbors. I heard how smart and handsome and promising Jayson was, but how impatient and reckless. "The kid was driven by some demon," an older neighbor said.

245

I got a chance to talk with Julie alone on the lower deck. She seemed to be doing a little better and asked about Amy. Then I said, "Julie, I'm curious about something. Did you ever tell Jay I was his father? Or was it Cheryl?"

Julie looked down at the deck. I raised her head with my hand and we stared at each other. "I'm not a good liar," she said. "As you know." She turned toward the rail and gazed down the hillside. I moved next to her and put my arm around her. "Somehow he got the idea in his head. I wasn't from Cheryl. It must have been something I said about you. Anyway, he got obsessed with it. He kept grilling me." She sighed. "Jon, believe me, for the longest time I denied it. Then one day after Kevin left, he just kept after me. I was exhausted and unhappy and I admitted it." Julie was crying now, quietly.

I said, "It's OK, Julie. It doesn't matter." We looked down at the dim lights of Sonoma below.

"Jon," she said after several minutes. "Would you like to see some of his stuff, his artwork, his poems?"

"I'd like to very much," I said.

We went into Jayson's old room, sat down on his bed, and looked at pictures of him. There weren't a lot. Some Sears baby portraits, Jay in a Little League uniform, at a Y camp, at his senior prom, graduating from high school. There were some shots of him in Golden Gate Park and at his easel on the Santa Cruz wharf. He was a good-looking kid, short, with sharp features, sandy hair, intense blue eyes, and a mocking smile. I didn't see much of a resemblance.

Julie pulled down folders of his drawings and poems, and left the room. Jayson was a good draftsman. Al Weiss had been an avid watercolorist, and Jay had inherited his grandfather's talent. There were some detailed studies of flowers and butterflies, but mostly he had drawn portraits.

Then I did a double-take. There was one of a girl who looked uncannily like Amy. I checked the date and saw it was done two years before Jay had friended my daughter on Facebook.

The poems were short and morose and, like the portraits, mostly about girls. They were full of cynicism and *weltschmerz*. But there was one called "Dad."

Oh Father who art in Heaven,
You are everywhere and nowhere.
An eagle whispered to me in a dream
I must kill you if I want to fly.
For years I've been sharpening my dagger.
But I can never see you,
Never feel you.
Though we're cuffed together
With links of lead.

I shuddered. Then, finally, I felt a stab of grief for the son I would never know.

I left Sonoma after a couple of hours, telling Julie I'd call the next day. There was no message from my daughter, and I got back to the hotel at 1:00 a.m.

⨯⨯

Amy had a miscarriage early in the morning. She looked wretched when I arrived at 7:00. There were dark circles under her eyes. Her hair was damp and matted. She was deathly pale.

I spent the day with her. I tried to tell her that things would get better. Amy wasn't buying it. She looked so stricken. No one should have to go out to the garage and see his son slumped in the front seat of his car, with his brains splattered on the window and dashboard. But no one should have to see his daughter after her lover has been killed and she's had a miscarriage.

I tried to persuade Amy to come back with me to Tampa. "The dogs miss you," I told her. But she wasn't interested.

By evening she was talking about trying to finish the semester. This seemed like a good idea. If she could start going to classes in a couple of days, she would have missed less than two weeks. I was sure the faculty would cut her a break. It would be tough, though. Six days in her biology and genetics classes meant hundreds of pages of material, a dozen lectures, and several labs. But this would be by far the best therapy.

Amy talked a lot about Jayson. "Daddy, I know you would have liked him if you'd gotten to know him. He was like you in so many ways."

I had a sandwich in Amy's room again, and left around 9:00. I wanted to get to bed early.

Back in the motel, my phone rang. It was Wendy. She had more interesting news. She and Danny had finally split up. He was moving to Sacramento to live with Deleece. I told her about Angie and me, and Wendy laughed. "I guess we were both way overdue," she said.

Then I told her what had happened to Amy, without going into details about Jayson. She commiserated. I said I was still in Palo Alto, and would like to come down and see her in a few days.

"Sure," she said.

I'd already canceled classes for the week, and now booked yet another flight.

There was a memorial service for Jayson at a funeral home in Sonoma the next afternoon, and I drove up with Amy. A Unitarian minister who knew Julie spoke for awhile, and then a couple of Jayson's high school friends.

Amy and Julie hit it off. Julie gave her a big, tearful hug when we got out of the car at her house. We'd agreed to drive to the service together. They went into the kitchen and talked about Jayson. Afterward, Amy said to me, "I didn't expect her to be so pretty. And so kind."

The day Amy returned to her classes, I flew to LA.

CHAPTER 31

On the flight down, I tried on the idea of marrying Wendy. I liked it.

I would end the relationship with Laura. Wendy and I would have a commuting marriage, of course. It would be tough finding teaching in LA. But Wendy had a successful practice and I would never ask her to take the Florida bar and relocate. Maybe eventually something would come through at one of the community colleges in Southern California, and if not I could teach high school. But for awhile we'd just see each other during breaks and over the summer.

Wendy was decent, humane, and reasonable. I respected her. I wasn't passionately in love with her, but then I wasn't eighteen. I didn't feel the physical addiction I felt with Laura, but it was very nice making love with her. And I could talk to her afterwards.

If the moment seemed right, I would ask her to marry me.

Wendy wanted me to meet her at Holmby Park on Comstock after work. Sam and Ashley were both home. I stopped by Gelson's and picked up a chilled bottle of Mumm's and some plastic glasses and waited for my sister-in-law at a table by the rose garden at the north end of the park.

Wendy arrived looking lawyerly in a navy tailored suit and pumps, her hair in a tightly coiled chignon. We hugged and exchanged muted congratulations. Then, as we sipped the champagne, I told her Amy's story in a little more detail, still not disclosing Jayson's identity.

"What a horrendous experience. And what an awful week for you," she said.

"It gets worse." I told her about Cheryl and about Troy Schultz.

Wendy asked me the question I'd dreaded, "What was the last straw with Angela?"

I said that Ange decided to make a clean break, leave the closet, and move in with her girlfriend. Another time I would tell Wendy about Laura, just as I would one day tell her about Jayson.

There was no last straw with Danny, either, according to Wendy, though there may have been one between him and Unique. He'd been bouncing between her and Deleece for years. In any case, Wendy felt hugely relieved. A crushing weight had been lifted.

Then Wendy started grilling me about my pending divorce. Had I gotten a lawyer yet? She didn't know anyone in Florida doing divorce, but would get me some names. Even in an uncontested divorce, it was important to have someone good. She didn't recommend *pro se*. It was too much work.

She asked more questions. Angela and I didn't have assets in common, except the house. Just as we had our own checking accounts, we had our own portfolios and made independent investment decisions. As for the house, I didn't think Angie would ask me to sell it and return her share. It was not something I'd even considered before Wendy asked. I'd assumed I would pay the taxes and insurance in full now, and of course it would eventually go to Amy.

Wendy didn't want a second glass of champagne, so we stashed the bottle in her car, she put on some running shoes, and we walked around the park. Wendy wanted to know what was going on with my mother's house since the asbestos removal. I said I had no idea, and she clicked her tongue. "Jon, you need to keep on top of them."

250

I asked about her plans, but she was vague. She said she wanted to take some vacation time and travel.

We returned to our table, and I gave her a hug. Wendy seemed so level-headed, so *sympathique*, so wifely. "Where would you like to have dinner?" I asked.

She looked down and swallowed hard. Then she stared at me sadly for several seconds. "Jon, we're not going out to dinner. This is it."

"It?"

"I need a break. You and Danny are so connected in my life. I have to cut loose. Completely. I care about you. I enjoy being with you. You're a kind person. But we can't see each other any more."

"I...I don't see why not," I said.

Wendy sighed. "You have to trust me."

"This isn't something your shrink threw out, is it?"

Wendy shook her head. "It's a gut feeling I've had for a long, long time."

"But Wen, I don't understand. I wasn't using you to get at Danny, for God's sake, and you weren't using me to get at him, right? Our relationship has nothing to do with him."

Wendy smiled ruefully. "Believe me, I've given this a great deal of thought. I'd like to stay friends with you. But we can't be lovers any more."

I tried again. "Wen, I understand how you'd want some time off. But why foreclose on the relationship. Let's see how you feel in a couple of weeks."

"I know how I'll feel."

I picked at a splinter on the side of the table. "Well, we can still have dinner. As friends."

Wendy shook her head. "I need to say goodbye now."

She gave me a quick hug and told me she'd get back in touch with the names of some lawyers.

I sat down and watched my sister-in-law walk over to her car. She didn't look back.

I'd booked a room at our boutique hotel in Venice and a return for the next day. I might as well stay there, I figured. If I tried to fly out this evening, I'd lose the deposit and probably wind up spending the night on a bench in the Kansas City airport.

∽

I didn't go right back to the hotel. I headed for Sunset. But instead of going straight up Beverly Glen, I drove down to Wilshire, over to Santa Monica Boulevard, and then all the way east to Fairfax. I wanted to take the ride I'd taken each day my senior year in high school.

As I drove north on Fairfax, I thought about how, between my brothers and I and my two cousins, we were a perfect 0 for 9 in marriages. With Grandpa Mort, it was an even dozen divorces. I wondered if Jayson, unbeknownst to Julie, and made it a lucky thirteen.

I turned onto Sunset. I was seventeen again, cruising along the sinuous boulevard at sixty miles an hour in my yellow Mustang. The top was down and the sun was shining. "Good Vibrations" was blasting on the stereo. I was on my way to UCLA, where I would sprawl on the lawn before Intro to Philosophy. After a lecture on the mind-body problem, I would head out to the Valley and make love to my gorgeous cousin Julie. I had no worries in the world. The future was as bright as the late summer sun hanging over the Pacific.

I parked in a metered space on campus and walked to the lawn below the Powell Library. It was 7:00. There were few students around. I was suddenly exhausted. I lay down on the grass and closed my eyes.

I had a vivid dream. I was in Building C at the Packer County Shelter, but it was brightly illuminated. An organ was playing Bach's "*Wachet Auf,*" "Sleepers Awake." Suddenly all the cage doors swung open in unison. A blinding light came from inside each cage. Then the dogs emerged. They were all clean and

252

healthy. They walked slowly toward the back of the building, past the freezer, under the corrugated iron roof. I followed. When we got outside we were somewhere else, facing rolling hills covered with white poppies. The music swelled. We were walking up a hill, under a bright full moon, when I woke up.

CHAPTER 32

The Magic Flute was performed the weekend after I returned. I was pleased with the production, but I was in the minority. The reviews were, as they say, mixed. The critics either hated it or were puzzled by it. On the strength of the novelty of the production and Marge's network of contacts, a couple of reviewers flew down from New York. They were among the haters.

I emailed Joyce: "Let's have dinner and commiserate. We might as well have done Monostratos in blackface."

Joyce wrote back that she was proud of the production, and that it would be appreciated one day. A couple of dozen people had already asked for copies of the DVD. She suggested a late lunch on Saturday in Sarasota, after a conference she would be attending.

I put in Bach's cantata *Ach Wie Fluchtig* as I turned onto I75, and began thinking about how deluded I'd been in LA. Wendy and I weren't suited for each other. What could I have been thinking? All the effervescence had come from adultery. The secrecy, the risk-taking, the clandestine sex–that's what was attractive. And, of course, the fact that the cuckolded husband was my sibling rival. After a couple of weeks of marriage with that uptight lawyer, I'd be bored to death.

I ejected the CD and inserted *Cosi fan Tutte*.

∽

Joyce and I met in front of the Crab and Fin. "I'm sorry about you and Angela," she said after we sat down.

"Well, it happens," I muttered. No one had commiserated with me so far. I would have to come up with a more intelligent response.

Over our salads, Joyce mentioned that she was thinking of staging *Cosi* in two or three years.

"That's so weird," I said. "I was listening to highlights in the car on the way down."

"Wow," Joyce said. She took a sip of her chardonnay. "It's such exquisite music. But what can we do with that silly libretto?"

I told her I felt the same way about the opera. The lyrics are sometimes clever and charming, but, apart from the maid Despina, the characters are puppets, the plot absurd, the moral rebarbative.

The soldier-lovers of two sisters wager with a cynical "old philosopher," Don Alfonso, that their betrothed will remain faithful despite temptations, unlike other women. Directed by Alfonso, the soldiers pretend to leave for the front, then reappear disguised as Albanians. Each lays siege to the other's fiancée, with some help from Alfonso and Despina, until, by evening, each girl has agreed to marry the man betrothed to her sister. Having proven *"cosi fan tutte"*—all women are like that—the wayward sisters are restored to their former beaus.

"It's always bothered me that the original couples are reunited at the end, sadder but wiser," I said. "Nothing changes for them."

"Of course in most productions today, the girls are depicted as discovering their sexuality," Joyce pointed out. "They're liberated by the masquerade."

"I know, but I'm not sure that's really in the libretto. The girls aren't seduced. All the faux-Albanians do is bombard them with fulsome compliments and threaten to kill themselves. Think about it. All that sublime singing, and yet only one duet between each suitor and his victim."

"Yes, but what wonderful duets," said Joyce. "'*Il core vi dono,*' I give you this heart. '*È il mio coricino, Che più non è meco. Ei venne a star teco, Ei batte batte batte cosi,*' they tell each other." Joyce sang the lines, her hand fluttering over her heart. "'My heart is no longer mine, that's why it's beating, beating, beating so.' Singers who are good actors can infuse a lot of passion into the seductions. And lot of drama into the girls' dilemma. And the guys'."

"I don't know, I still think it's pretty contrived. And unsatisfying. Why *don't* the girls marry the guys they fell for?"

"Well, Ferrando and Guglielmo are playing roles. It's a charade."

"Yes, but with a better libretto, they'd be revealing something important about who they really are." I snapped a breadstick in half. "We like to think the nineteenth century didn't like the libretto because they were prudes. But the nineteenth century discovered history and psychology. They didn't like it because it has no depth."

I started revising the story. "How about a version in which Ferrando and Guglielmo are brothers? The two sisters, Fiordiligi and Dorabella, are their cousins. But the couples are mismatched. Ferrando is serious and scholarly, like Fiordiligi. He writes poetry. But he's engaged to the frivolous Dorabella, while her sensitive, soulful sister is the fiancée of foppish, foolish Guglielmo." I took a sip of my beer. "Or maybe Dorabella and Guglielmo are ambitious, calculating proto-yuppies. He's a commodities trader. She's a lawyer or a dean." I liked the idea. "So there are no disguises. Don Alfonso just points out the obvious, and he and Despina incite the lovers to switch partners."

"I don't know," said Joyce. "That's pretty radical. You'd be rewriting the whole libretto. Is your Italian good enough?"

"God, no. I'd have to do it in English."

Joyce made a face. "There's a reason there are no great operas in English," she said. She took another sip of wine. "Anyway, I'm not so sure I like the idea of their all being siblings and cousins."

I looked into Joyce's large azure eyes. "You could be right," I said.

∽

After lunch we strolled around St. Armand's Circle. There are a few high end jewelry, clothing, and shoe stores, and a couple of galleries and a bookstore, but St. Armand's isn't exactly Rodeo Drive, Palm Springs, or Carmel. There are shops selling beachwear and outrageous Floridian chachkas, funky fashion jewelry, weird pet paraphernalia, sundry gourmet products, and ice cream and gelato. Lots of restaurants and realtors.

"So who was St. Armand anyway?" Joyce asked as we walked into Le Macaron.

"The patron saint of boutiques," I said. I bought her a Belgian chocolate macaroon. Then I checked my watch. "Too bad it's a little late to head out to the Ringling."

Joyce said she'd never been there.

"You're kidding? We've got to go some time," I said. "The miniature circus diorama is cool, even if you're not into circuses. The art museum is excellent. And you must see Cà d' Zan."

John and Mabel Ringling had been enchanted by Venice and built an imitation palazzo on Sarasota Bay. The stucco and terracotta mansion has gothic arches over the windows and along the balconies. Above the marble terrace fronting the bay, below the crenellated roof, are the ducal quatrefoils within circles. The building is a creamy white, the tiles decorating the second floor and the Belvedere tower a warm brown, and the exterior is studded with striking blue glazed ceramic circles, and floral and animal figures. In front of the entrance is a handsome mosaic. At the center of an eight-pointed star, against a pale blue background, is a gold sun, its rays extending in all directions. In dark red ovals on a band circling the sun are the signs of the zodiac.

Joyce said she'd been meaning to stop by the Ringling, but always wound up heading straight back to Tampa after meetings or conferences at WFU-Sarasota.

"Have you been to Venice, Florida?" she asked.

I hadn't.

"It's not very Venetian, I'm afraid, but worth a look. There's a wonderful restaurant you'd enjoy. I owe you lunch. We ought to go some time."

❧

We walked over to Lido Key and headed south down the beach. It was low tide, and acres of fine white sand were exposed. Joyce kept stopping to pick up shells. Brown pelicans swooped down to catch fish, and terns dived straight into the shallow water. Black-legged egrets strutted back and forth. The gulls had arrayed themselves in two long lines, faces into the breeze.

A distinguished-looking old man with slicked-back silver hair was sitting in a beach chair on the damp sand. He was staring intently at the horizon, but turned around as we walked past, and smiled.

I learned a little more about Joyce. I knew she was a dog fan. Now she told me about her five dogs. There was Roddy, a chocolate lab, Mimi, a little blond golden retriever, two King Charles spaniels, Figgie and Susie, and an old silver-tip German shepherd she'd rescued, Leporello.

I told her about Beauty and how that sad, abused dog had tried to comfort me when I fell. A rescue had taken the cattle dog, but Beauty and the little fox dog, now called Martha, were still at the vet's. I was going to try them one at a time with Lucy and see if they hit it off. Joyce offered to take either dog or both if things didn't work out.

I found out Joyce liked to hike. Each summer she took Rod and Mimi to a stretch of the Appalachian Trail in North Carolina. She'd gone to the Rockies with her parents every year when she was growing up. Joyce had been to Yosemite, but never to the Eastern Sierra. I started telling her about Mammoth, and got on to Mel. I described Lake Ediza and she said she'd love to go there some time.

Joyce had mentioned at one point that she was an only child. Now I learned that both of her parents had been only children as well.

"So you have no relatives?" I asked.

"Well, my dad had an older cousin, but I never met him. He moved to Australia before I was born. Or New Zealand."

"New Zealand," I said under my breath.

"We used to get Christmas cards when I was little. I don't imagine he's still alive."

We'd reached the end of the peninsula. Across the water was Siesta Key. To our left was a tide pool and a small park with loblolly pines and sea grapes.

"There's no one else?" I asked. "No other relatives?"

"Nope."

"Oh, Joyce!" I said, and put my arms around her. She turned her face up to mine. We kissed.

After a couple of minutes we disengaged and began walking back hand in hand. "Would you like to get a room at the Lido Beach Resort?" I asked.

She nodded.

"Joyce," I said again and hugged her tightly. There were tears in my eyes.

www.ingramcontent.com/pod-product-compliance
Lightning Source LLC
Chambersburg PA
CBHW020744250626
47155CB00003B/908